T0356907

ADIRONDACK GHOST STORIES

ADIRONDACK GHOST STORIES

Edited by

DENNIS WEBSTER

BOOKS
NORTH COUNTRY BOOKS

North Country Books
An imprint of The Globe Pequot Publishing Group, Inc.
64 South Main Street
Essex, CT 06426
www.globepequot.com

Distributed by NATIONAL BOOK NETWORK

Copyright © 2025 by Dennis Webster

All rights reserved. No part of this book may be reproduced in any form or by any electronic or mechanical means, including information storage and retrieval systems, without written permission from the publisher, except by a reviewer who may quote passages in a review.

British Library Cataloguing in Publication Information Available

Library of Congress Cataloging-in-Publication Data

Names: Webster, Dennis, 1966– editor.
Title: Adirondack ghost stories / edited by Dennis Webster.
Description: Essex, CT : North Country Books, 2025. | Summary: "Adirondack
  Ghost Stories features tales of hauntings, apparitions, and the hidden
  lives of spirits that lurk within the towns and mountains of the
  Adirondacks"—Provided by publisher.
Identifiers: LCCN 2024059147 (print) | LCCN 2024059148 (ebook) | ISBN
  9781493088348 (paperback) | ISBN 9781493088355 (epub)
Subjects: LCSH: Ghost stories, American—New York (State)—Adirondack
  Mountains Region. | Haunted places—New York (State)—Adirondack
  Mountains Region. | Tales—New York (State)—Adirondack Mountains
  Region. | Adirondack Mountains (N.Y.)—Folklore. | LCGFT: Ghost stories.
Classification: LCC GR110.A2 A36 2025 (print) | LCC GR110.A2 (ebook) |
  DDC 133.09747/5—dc23/eng/20250120
LC record available at https://lccn.loc.gov/2024059147
LC ebook record available at https://lccn.loc.gov/2024059148

∞™ The paper used in this publication meets the minimum requirements of American National Standard for Information Sciences—Permanence of Paper for Printed Library Materials, ANSI/ NISO Z39.48-1992.

The authors dedicate these stories to those who embrace the otherworldly spirits, believe in the ghosts of the afterlife, and delve into stories that herald their existence.

Contents

CHAPTER I

Ready or Not, Here I Come

Holly Aust

". . . 28 . . . 29 . . . 30 . . . ready or not, here I come."

Tommy opened his eyes and pushed himself away from the old oak tree. He was on a mission. He might have only been nine years old, but he knew these woods like the back of his hand. He paused for a moment to listen and tilted his head to the left. With his luck, Tommy spotted a blue sweatshirt shaking under a log. Jason. The little detective slowly inched forward, avoiding the newly fallen leaves. When he reached the log, he slithered his hand down the side and tapped the blue-coated, red-capped boy.

"Gotcha," said Tommy.

"Aww, man, why do you always get me first?"

"Come on, Jay, don't be such a baby."

The boys continued walking through the woods. Tommy quizzed Jay to see if he knew where the others were, while Jason kept complaining about always being the first to be found. It was when they turned left after passing the weeping willow tree that they knew they were in Lily's territory. They could feel Cheshire Cat eyes following them and a Cheshire smile giggling at them. They could hear the echoes all around:

"Over here, Tommy."

"Come on, Jay, you're so close."

Then one of the boys would swat at a tree or leaf, and the air would fall silent. Their eyes would search for her, but they still couldn't see her. And then she would start again:

"On your left."
"Oh, come on, don't you want to find me?"
"You should really try harder."
The girl's voice started to get to Tommy.
"You look over there, Jay. I've got this side."

The boys split up. Tommy was running through tall grass in the swampy area, the sound of sticks breaking and sludge coming apart from the ground increased.

While Tommy was on a goose chase, Jay wandered onto the train tracks, and it was quiet. Too quiet. Everything was still, no sign of life. But every time the kids played hide and seek, Sarah hid around the train tracks. She was one of the oldest of the five and the most quiet, but even her presence brought life to the space. Even she would have brought some kind of noise to this old train station. Jay kept searching. He was running from the ticket booth to the old carts to the trees surrounding the tracks, but there was nothing. Absolutely nothing. This would be fine if your friends didn't hide in the same spot every single time you played hide and seek, but Sarah wasn't like this. She always hid at the train tracks. Her not being here was just peculiar.

Tommy finally got out of the sludgy marsh and could hear Lily's giggle echoing through the trees. Tommy decided that if he could get high enough, maybe he could find her. He grasped a few lower branches and set his feet on the side of the trunk. He started to climb, grabbing one branch and then another, pulling his body up. When he got to a good, sturdy branch, he leaned his body on it and wrapped his legs around the tree. He looked around, scouting like an eagle. By narrowing his eyes, he spotted Lily. The rambunctious eight-year-old with blonde pigtails and leaves in her hair was swinging upside down from an old maple tree.

Tommy got down from the tree as quickly and quietly as possible. When he reached the grass, he remembered what the tree looked like and went around it from the back. When he got there, there was a note that said, "Nice try." It was signed by Lily.

She may have been a crazy eight-year-old, but she had shorter legs than he did, so he concluded that she couldn't be far. Instead of sprinting down the woods, he simply lifted his head and looked up. He tagged her foot.

"Found you."

"Not by much. I let you win."

Lily was a fiery little eight-year-old and never admitted to anyone else being right. And Lily was right—she could have won, but she let Tommy have it.

"So, who's left, Tommy?"

"Well, if Jay hasn't found anybody, then it's Gabe and Sarah."

The two of them walked through the dark green forest, waiting to see any signs of Gabe or Sarah. As they walked, they heard the crunch of red and orange leaves. And that's when something grabbed the back of the two kids' shoulders. Both Tommy and Lily let out a shriek and fell to the ground. It was just Jason.

"Hey, guys," snickered Jay, unable to wipe the smile from his face.

"Hey, Jay, have you found Gabe or Sarah?" asked Tommy.

"No, but I see you found Lily."

"He didn't find me; I just let him."

"Okay, Lily, we get it. Anyway, did you check for Sarah at the tracks?"

"Yeah, actually I did, but she wasn't there."

"She wasn't there?"

"No, I just said that!"

"Well, we've still got to find Gabe. Let's look around."

Forty minutes passed, and the trio had not found Gabe or Sarah. The three of them decided to go back to the tracks. That's when they saw Sarah and Gabe hiding behind a bush.

Jay was dumbfounded, his eyes wide open. "When did you guys get here? You weren't here earlier."

"Shhh, stop talking," snapped Sarah.

Lily, Tommy, and Jay stood there bewildered until they realized that the quiet girl and curly-haired boy weren't hiding from them; they were watching another little boy. This little kid looked all alone. His eyes were a fountain of tears, and his nose had snot oozing down his face. The little kid in front of the train tracks was lost in his own head, a place where none of these kids wanted to go.

"He's been sitting there for twenty minutes," whispered Sarah.

Gabe, the curly-haired boy, couldn't keep his eyes off the kid. He looked familiar. He felt like he knew him, and he felt bad because he couldn't remember from where.

"I know that kid. I'm gonna go talk to him."

Gabe walked up behind him. "Hey kid. . . . Yo, kid, can you hear me? I'm right here." He walked around and started waving his hand in front of the kid's face. But it was no use; the kid couldn't see him between all the tears and snot on his face. His sobs just kept getting louder. He spread his hands over his face and started yelling, "NO! NO! NO! Why?!" The cries grew longer. Gabe tried again. "Hey, kid. Stop. What's wrong?" He tapped the little boy's shoulder. Nothing. Gabe thought the kid was ignoring him. He started throwing rocks at him. Pebble after pebble. "Hey, kid, can you see me?" The boy felt each piece of rock hit and lodge into his skin. "Ow!" the boy exclaimed. He started screaming. Gabe stopped throwing the rocks. The boy turned his head left, straight, and right. There was nothing there. He let out a gasp and dashed away from the tracks. His screams echoed through the woods. And the scream echoed in Gabe's mind. That boy. That boy was screaming. He remembered who he was when he saw the face. That boy was his brother. He stared in utter shock. How could he not remember his own little brother?

"What was that?" questioned Tommy.

"I have no idea. Could he really not see us?"

Lily jumped in, "Wait," she yelled. "More people are coming. What's all that stuff in their hands?"

"I'm not sure. It looks like flowers, candles, and maybe some picture frames?" added Sarah.

"Why are there so many people here? Nobody ever comes to the tracks."

"Wait, hey, Jay, isn't that your dad? And Lily, isn't that your mom and your sisters? And whoa, wait. . . . Is that my mom?"

The kids stood there stunned. Why were their families here? And why were they crying? Tommy's mom stood there, tears raining down her cheeks. Lily's sister didn't understand what was going on, and Jay's dad was fiddling with his hands. Tommy ran up to his mom and tugged at her sweater, "Mom, Mom?! What's going on?!"

No answer.

Jay went up to his dad, "Yo, Dad, can you hear me?"

Slowly, all five kids stood across from their parents, trying to get their attention. That's when Gabe looked at what the parents were setting up. Near the tracks lay many different colorful flowers, candles melting in the heat, and most important, pictures. Pictures of five smiling faces. Pictures of five children. Pictures of the same five children who were just playing hide and seek and saw that boy run away in tears.

"Mom, what is this? What happened?" Tears welled up in Gabe's eyes.

"They were such good kids, weren't they?" one voice said. Nods and sniffles came from everybody.

"Too bad we don't get to see them grow up." Tears were streaming down the parents' faces. "If only that train never came by."

Thumper

Cheryl Costa

WINTER SOLSTICE, SUNDAY, DECEMBER 21, 1941,
7:27 A.M., BLUE MOUNTAIN LAKE, NEW YORK

She was just an ordinary cadaver, like many of the ones the coroner had seen over many years. She had a whitish look. From the lividity of the corpse, the doctor could easily see that the deceased clearly had been lying on her back, at or about the time of death. All the blood had settled in the body's bottom, making for a purplish back, buttocks, and back of the legs. The doctor walked around the marble autopsy table, quietly observing the body for any unusual marks or other sign of foul play. There were none. She whispered, "What killed you, Helen?" The doctor moved to the head end of the autopsy table and stood staring at the decedent's head. She carefully opened the mouth of the dead woman, bent over, and sniffed near the mouth. "Ahhh, almonds," she mumbled.

She stepped over toward her cabinet of drawers and removed a large syringe with a very long needle. Then she stepped back over to the autopsy table and plunged the needle into the chest and withdrew the blood that was present in the stilled heart. After removing a quantity of blood, she deposited the blood sample in equal amounts into four test tubes.

After running several chemical tests, the doctor was content with her medical assessment. *Foul play*, she thought to herself as she stepped over to her typewriter and typed the cause of death on the death certificate:

homicide. After typing the cause of death, the doctor turned and faced old Mrs. Helen Johnson. "Who murdered you, Helen, and why?"

She hung up her rubber apron and stepped over to the morgue's sink and washed her hands. After drying them, she picked up the telephone receiver and tapped the cradle twice to signal the town switchboard operator. A few moments later, Patty, the operator, answered. "Morning, Doc!"

Dr. Julia Forman Smith greeted her neighbor. "Good morning, Patty. Please ring young Sheriff Williams. Since it's early Sunday morning, let's assume he's still at home and hasn't left for church yet."

"Any word on what killed Helen?" Patty asked.

"Now Patty, you know I can't talk about an unannounced death. Just put me through to Sheriff Williams."

Julia heard a click and the buzz of the phone ringing at the other end. A child picked up the receiver, and Julia heard a voice. "Sher-riff Ted Williams's residence, can I help you?"

Julia recognized the voice of eight-year-old Tabatha Williams. "Good morning, Tabatha. This is Auntie Julia. I need to speak to your daddy."

"Okay," the child said before she dropped the phone receiver on the table or perhaps the floor and ran off and yelled. "Daddy! Daddy! Aunt Julia wants you!"

Moments later, the disciplined, deep voice of the sheriff spoke on the phone. "This is Sheriff Williams."

"Good morning, Ted. Julia here. I've got that death certificate for you," Julia said.

"What are we looking at, Doc?" he asked.

Julia began, "Well, Ted, let's meet over at Ernie's Diner for coffee, and I'll fill you in on the details." Then she said in a serious tone. "But in my professional opinion, it's another obvious case of Martians."

There was a pause, then the sheriff remarked, "Not those darn Martians again. Damn! Okay, I'll see you at Ernie's in about ten minutes." Williams hung up.

ERNIE'S DINER

Abby Samson, Ernie Sampson's wife, saw Dr. Smith enter the eatery carrying a Sunday paper she bought from a news box outside the diner. Dr. Smith caught Abby's eye and pointed at an empty booth in the diner's corner. Abby thought to herself, *Doc's here on business.* She stepped over to the booth. "Hi, Julia, what's up?"

Julia did not even look at the menu. "How about coffee, three eggs over easy, bacon, with wheat toast, please?"

Abby gave her a curious look. "Are you expecting a guest?"

Doc Smith nodded in the affirmative. "Yes, you might bring a carafe of coffee for me and Sheriff Williams. He'll be joining me shortly for a meeting."

"You got it," Abby said as she walked off with the order.

Julia scanned the newspaper's front page as the diner door swung open, ringing a small bell. In walked Sheriff Ted Williams dressed in his uniform khaki shirt, sporting his badge, and wearing a white Stetson. He glanced around the diner and saw Dr. Smith sitting in the corner booth.

As the sheriff slid into the out-of-the-way booth, he asked, "Hey, Julia, what's the deal with the Martians?"

Julia smirked. "I figured Patty was snooping in on the switchboard. I didn't want to give away the details of the crime."

The sheriff nodded with a wink. "That was good thinking. She's the biggest gossip in town," he moaned.

The sheriff was about to ask for the autopsy details when Abby walked up to the booth. "Morning, Sheriff. Any breakfast?"

The sheriff just responded, "No, Abby, I'll just have coffee and perhaps one of those nice donuts over there."

"Glazed or regular?" Abby asked.

"Oh, I'm a growing boy; I guess I'll have glazed. Oh, hell, make it two glazed donuts in a bag to go."

Abby walked away. Ted got back to business. "Okay, what happened to Helen?"

Julia, with a straight face, remarked, "I've declared the case a homicide."

Sheriff Ted sat back with a questioning look on his face. "Doc, I didn't see a mark on her body."

"No, there weren't any marks. But when I opened her mouth, she had the smell of almonds. I ran a blood test. Somebody poisoned her with cyanide."

Sheriff Ted had a disturbed look on his face. "Who the hell would want to poison a sweet old lady like Helen?"

Julia gave Ted a grave look. "I was asking myself the same question. This is a tiny town. I cannot think of anyone who has a grudge against Helen Johnson. But it is not for me to guess. As sheriff, that is your bailiwick. You're the investigator. I simply did the blood test and signed the death certificate."

Ted gave her a curious look. "You mean you didn't do a complete autopsy?"

Julia shook her head. "No, the cause of death was pretty obvious to me, and I confirmed it with a couple of chemical tests on the blood. I didn't see any need to be cutting up a seventy-five-year-old lady who was probably a couple of greasy dinners away from a heart attack anyway."

The sheriff nodded his head in agreement. "I see your point." Then Ted added, "What if we need a full autopsy for the New York State Police?"

Julia gave him professional assurances. "I'll keep her refrigerated until you tell me if it's needed or not," Julia responded.

"How are you going to proceed?" Julia asked. Ted took a sip of coffee and thought for a few moments, then suggested. "Well, first I'll find out if anybody benefits from her death. Perhaps somebody might want her property, perhaps an inheritance or a big insurance policy. Perhaps she has some hidden wealth we do not know about. I'll find out what it is."

"What about all those boarders staying at that big old house of hers?" Julia asked.

The sheriff snorted a laugh. "French House? That place is a hundred years old. It can't be worth much. Back in 1931, toward the end of Prohibition, Helen told me they raided the speakeasy in the house and shuttered the place. Helen bought the place at a sheriff's auction for not much more than a few hundred dollars' worth of back taxes on the property," Sheriff Ted explained.

Abby brought over the glazed donuts for the sheriff in a small paper bag. "Here's your donuts, Ted."

The sheriff just smiled and winked at Abby before she left. "By the way, Julia, I was looking at the Sunday paper this morning. Did you see that article about the government calling up doctors to support the war effort for the various medical corps? Do you think they'll be calling you up?" the sheriff queried.

Julia answered with a perturbed look. "No, I have heard nothing about that. Besides, they'll never call me. I'm a woman and I'm barely tolerated in the medical profession. I'll be long dead and buried before women finally get to serve in the military medical corps."

Twenty-Eight Years Later . . .
Wednesday, June 25, 1969, 10:15 a.m., Lucy's
Restaurant, Blue Mountain Lake, New York

"First, let me thank each of you for putting up with a long, boring road trip to get here. Welcome to New York's Blue Ridge region. I think this is going to be the most intriguing ghost hunting case this team has ever worked on," Professor Ralph T. Parker remarked.

Maryse Gosselin spoke up in her moderate French accent, "I want more coffee before we start this case briefing."

Parker nodded and glanced over to Charles (Cassandra) Grover. "Cass, could you step out and get our server's attention?" The effeminate seventeen-year-old politely nodded and exited the private room.

A few moments later, Grover returned. "Our server will be here shortly with more coffee and to take our brunch orders."

As Cass returned to his seat, photographer Sherley Beggs, a twenty-something African American woman, spoke up. "Professor, is our client going to pay us mileage? My God, it was nearly three hundred miles to get here from Queens!"

Parker held up his arms in a "whoa!" gesture. "The owners of the site are being very generous in compensating our team. Both for our forensic work and our travel costs."

"Thank God," moaned Joshua Trotter. "Chuck and I drove nearly 350 miles to get here from the southern tier." Cass winced at being referred to as "Chuck" and got up and left the dining room.

Madame Maryse Gosselin gave Joshua a scowling look. "Monsieur Trotter, may I remind you that we as a team agreed to not call Mademoiselle Grover by her male name or honorifics? As she is one of two team psychics, we need her relaxed and quiet to perform her tasks."

Trotter stood up, obviously irritated. "Okay, team, I'm having a tough time stomaching Grover's fairy princess secret identity. Professor Parker, I will work this job and I'll play along with this charade, but after this investigation gig . . ." He paused and remarked with a huff. "It's me or the fairy princess. One of us will have to go."

Professor Parker held up his hand and remarked, "Joshua, I know that it's difficult to accommodate the kids' inner feelings. We need his or her special talents, and I think for our mission and our ghost hunting tasks, we can be polite and accommodate this eccentricity. She's a sha-man. Every one of them I've ever met is squirrelly in a variety of ways, for God sakes!"

Joshua spoke up, "But Chuck isn't a girl!"

Professor Parker had a serious expression on his face. "Hey, they screened the kid down at Johns Hopkins, and the diagnosis says the kid is a transsexual woman. That is as much as I can openly talk about."

Joshua Trotter responded vehemently, "As I stated, it is me or the fairy princess. I'll let it rest there for now, so we can get on with this paranormal mission. But all I'm saying is, we need to sort all this out before our next expedition."

Professor Parker addressed Madame Gosselin, "Madame, could you please bring Cassandra back to our meeting?" Gosselin left the room. She returned with the teenager a few moments later, and it was obvious that Cassandra's eyes were wet with tears. The kid just quietly sat down, opened a notebook, and was ready to put pen to paper.

Professor Parker began the paranormal expedition briefing pitch. "Our effort today will be to survey a structure and property of a resort facility called the French House. The principal house is well over one hundred years old and began operating as a resort guest facility after

World War II. Management informed us that, for years, it seems that the place has been haunted by one or possibly multiple entities. But the most common nickname for the entity is 'Thumper.'" The team members nodded their heads, grinned, and chuckled.

Professor Parker continued with his briefing. "This is because the entity has knocked on walls, obviously in some attempt to get someone's attention. Over the years, the entity has startled and frightened various lodgers, as management explained to me, although no one has ever been hurt." He paused for questions, but no one spoke up. "The French House management historian informed me that, during the Prohibition era, French House was a country club of sorts, complete with a hidden 'speakeasy' stocked with plenty of Canadian booze. Unknown individuals shot and killed several people during that time. Just before the end of Prohibition, revenue agents boarded up the place. A few years later, a Mrs. Helen Johnson purchased the property from the county for back taxes and reopened French House as a hotel and rooming house for seasonal workers. Someone murdered her in 1941, at the start of World War II. The woman's estate lawyers sold the property to an equity company just after the war ended. The current management organization is a descendant holding company several times removed."

Medium Madame Gosselin raised her hand politely. "Monsieur professeur. Why now? What has changed?"

Professor Parker assumed a troubled look. "In the resort this past spring, something pushed a gentleman down a flight of stairs. Several guests and a staff member observed the pushing event. The current management of the French House read about our team in that article that was written about us in the Sunday edition of *The New York Times* a few weeks ago. They wrote a formal request for us to conduct one of our studies and perhaps find a resolution for what the lingering spirit might be up to, or what different lingering spirits need in order to move on. At the very least, they asked if we could do something like a soul rescue. Questions?"

"Will we be doing our standard tasks? With photography, surveying, and walking around various areas of the house doing the psychic touchy feely stuff?" Joshua asked.

"Yes, in a manner of speaking," Professor Parker remarked. "Management is going to give us a brief tour of the facility, and they'll lead us to places of elevated activity."

Cassandra raised her hand. "I recommend we tack some little signs on those spots. So we can remember these particular areas and give them special attention. For all we know, there's something hidden in a wall someplace or under the floorboards that the ghost is trying to get our attention about."

Joshua Trotter responded with a snorted, dismissive laugh at what Cassandra said. Madame Maryse Gosselin ignored Joshua Trotter and gave Cassandra a nod of concurrence.

WEDNESDAY, JUNE 25, 1969, 1:00 P.M., FRENCH HOUSE RESORT, BLUE MOUNTAIN LAKE, NEW YORK

Tabatha Williams-Young, senior concierge and French House property historian, gave Professor Parker's team a very thorough tour of the legacy French House Resort building. As she led the tour, the two psychics, Maryse Gosselin and Cassandra Grover, tacked yellow three-by-five cards with notations on various walls and doors where one or both of them psychically sensed issues that they felt needed closer examination.

At around 3:00 p.m., Maryse Gosselin was quietly revisiting all those yellow three-by-five cards and wrote detailed impressions in a journal book. As she visited each yellow card, she annotated a number on the yellow card on the wall and matched that number to whatever impression she wrote in her journal book.

Meanwhile, Cassandra Grover, using a dowsing rod, was walking a pattern in a side yard on one side of the legacy 177-year-old building. As she carefully swept the dowsing rod back and forth, she marked the path she was walking by, dropping a yellow ping-pong ball about every yard. When she was done, she had mapped out a rectangle that extended from the legacy building about forty feet and was about twenty feet wide.

When she was done, Joshua Trotter commented, "You must have found an old foundation."

She shook her head. "I think it's a room, and someone is living there."

Trotter shook his head. "That's nuts, kid. I tell you it's probably just the outline of an old foundation, nothing more."

Cassandra simply asked, "Mr. Trotter, please get your Line Marker machine and lay down the lines where I've set down yellow ping-pong balls. Meanwhile, I need to speak to the professor and resort management," seventeen-year-old Cassandra said.

Thirty minutes later, Cassandra led the professor and Tabatha Williams-Young, the senior concierge, from the resort out to the lawn where she had dropped yellow ping-pong balls an hour before. The balls were still present.

Professor Parker glanced at the teen psychic. "Why didn't you ask Joshua to mark the pattern with his field marker?"

She shook her head in frustration. "I did, Professor. But he kept grousing at me that what I was sensing was ludicrous."

Parker got red in the face, "Damn it!" Then he looked at Mrs. Williams-Young and apologized for his swearing. "Sorry!"

She grinned. "Hey, I'm management. I entirely understand." Then she took an interest in the teen. "Professor, is she drunk?"

Professor Parker looked back at Cassandra and observed she was twirling around in a dancing fashion. He grabbed her as she looked as if she was about to fall down. The teen fell into his arms, seemingly delirious.

Again, Mrs. Williams-Young spoke. "Is she drunk or on drugs?"

The professor, with an urgent look on his face, gently shook the now limp teenager. "Who are you? Tell me who you are!"

Cassandra, in a delirious, jubilant manner, shouted, *"I am Jesse! I am a friend of a friend who sent me! Are you the station master?"*

Professor Parker looked at Mrs. Williams-Young. "She's channeling a spirit! I don't understand what she means!"

Williams-Young spoke up, "'Station master'—that's an old Underground Railroad term. Tell her yes! Yes, you're the station master!"

"Yes, Jesse, I am the station master. You are safe here."

Cassandra became jubilant. *"I followed the drinking gourd and I'm now at the station. I am on my way to heaven!"*

Williams-Young whispered, "He's been traveling the Underground Railroad."

Then moments later, Cassandra broke out into song in a deep tenor voice. *"Swing low, sweet chariot, coming for to carry me home. Swing low, sweet chariot, coming for to carry me home . . ."* Cassandra, with an ecstatic look on her face, looked deeply into Parker's eyes. *"Mr. Station Master, I am hiding in your station and I want to continue on my journey to heaven!"* A few instants later, Cassandra collapsed into his arms and fell silent.

Mrs. Williams-Young looked at Parker. "My goodness! Perhaps our ghost Thumper is a runaway slave who's been hiding here?"

Parker carefully laid the unconscious Cassandra down on the grass. He looked at Mrs. Williams-Young. "Did you follow all of that?"

She nodded her head. "As the resort's historian. I'm relatively well read about the Underground Railroad." She gestured toward Cassandra lying on the lawn. "Should we call a doctor or take her to a hospital?"

Parker shook his head in the negative. "She'll be fine. Channeling can be exhausting. They call it a conduit overload."

Mrs. Williams-Young was about to speak when Cassandra spoke up. "Ma'am, would you mind if I dig a hole in your lawn? I believe there is a freehold room of some form underneath the lawn. I suspect someone walled up Jesse in the space to hide him and then forgot about him."

Mrs. Williams-Young spoke up. "The owner of French House during the early nineteenth century had been a station master on the Underground Railroad. If memory serves correctly, he died abruptly of a heart attack."

Professor Parker had a concerned look on his face and said, "Jesse's spirit may be stuck down there in that hiding space. Prisoners and others who are confined before they die often go through this."

Mrs. Williams-Young remarked, "Is there anything that can be done?"

Professor Parker nodded his head. "Yes, I could have Madame Gosselin and Miss Cassandra perform a soul rescue. But there are a few hoops we might need to jump through first."

Williams-Young gave him a quizzical look and gestured for him to explain.

Parker thought for a moment. "We need to open that freehold room under the lawn. Either with picks and shovels or with a backhoe if we had one."

Williams-Young smiled. "This is a big resort. We have a backhoe. What else?"

Parker seemed to grimace. "More than likely, we'll find human remains. Being from the mid-nineteenth century, it will most likely be a skeleton, but we will be required to call the coroner's office and the police. But they are used to finding ancient remains. It's newsworthy; however, some folks don't want publicity."

"We aren't responsible. It all happened before we were born. Besides, the news splash will be good for business. Anything else?" Mrs. Williams-Young asked.

Parker nodded. "With the absence of family, the remains of Jesse will have to be dealt with. The resort could purchase a plot in a cemetery—"

She cut him off. "I propose a proper Christian burial on the resort grounds with a suitable commemorative headstone for Mr. Jesse, whom we have found on this property. From the context of the resort, we're family!"

Professor Parker nodded. "That sounds like a plan. If you could arrange for a backhoe to work with Miss Cassandra and Mr. Trotter."

Mrs. Williams-Young twitched her head slightly. "Regarding Cassandra. What is his or her situation?" Parker took on a reserved look. "The Hopkins folks told me. It's simply a young woman trapped in a young man's body. Beyond that, we're getting into medical privacy territory." She nodded her understanding. "My grounds people will be with you in the morning."

WEDNESDAY, JUNE 25, 1969, 6:00 P.M., FRENCH HOUSE RESORT, PRIVATE DINING ROOM

Professor Parker's team enjoyed a delightful dinner of locally grown fowl. During dinner, there was a great deal of excited discussion about

Miss Cassandra's channeling findings and the psychic surveys Madame Gosselin performed.

Professor Parker explained that the resort was going to provide digging help in the morning. Mr. Trotter explained he had enlisted the help of the local fire chief and department to provide ladders and ventilation fans if the digging operation opens up an underground freehold space. Parker informed the team that he had reached out to the county sheriff's office, who would ensure a deputy would be present to inform the regional coroner about any human remains that might be uncovered in the underground space.

As Professor Parker finished his dinner briefing about the planned dig, Madame Gosselin spoke up. "My colleagues, I have found a spirit hot spot as well near the spiral staircase in the Grand Room. I would like to perform a séance in the Grand Room this evening after sundown."

Professor Parker looked across the long dining table at Mrs. Williams-Young, who was facing him on the far end. "Madame Senior Concierge, could you arrange for our team to have privacy to conduct our séance?"

Mrs. Williams-Young assumed a considerate manner. She looked over at Madame Gosselin and stated, "Madame Gosselin, puis-je participer à votre séance?" ("Mrs. Gosselin, may I join your séance?")

Madame Gosselin smiled broadly and nodded. "Oui, Madame la Concierge" ("Yes, Madame Concierge").

Mrs. Williams-Young turned to Professor Parker and declared, "I will make the necessary arrangements so that we will not be disturbed." She then looked over at Cassandra. "Miss Cassandra, will you sit on my right side during the séance proceedings?"

Cassandra had a moment's surprise. She then simply nodded in the affirmative.

Joshua Trotter addressed Professor Parker and remarked, "Ralph, as usual, I'd like to be excused from the séance festivities, as it is not my cup of tea."

Parker nodded. "Consider yourself excused."

Then the academic looked around the table. "Would anyone else like to be excused?" No one asked.

Parker put his hands together. "I ask that everyone be in the Grand Room at about 9:15 this evening to settle and prepare for the séance."

As everyone pushed back their chairs, Cassandra rose and stepped over to Madame Gosselin. "Maryse, since I channeled Mr. Jesse earlier, I might be ripe for another spontaneous event if Mr. Jesse is the spirit presence you sensed during your survey."

Maryse smiled, shaking her head in the negative. "Mademoiselle Cassandra, do not worry. I suspect your physical boy body attunement was suitable for the man's spirit resting in that underground space. My gifts perceived a distinctly feminine and angry presence in the Grand Room. I doubt you'll be affected."

WEDNESDAY, JUNE 25, 1969, 9:15 P.M., FRENCH HOUSE RESORT, LOBBY SPACE

All the séance participants had gathered in the lobby of the French House's legacy building: Professor Ralph Parker, Maryse Gosselin, Sherley Beggs, and Cassandra Grover. When Tabatha Williams-Young entered the lobby, she was on the arm of a tall, vibrant, gray-haired man. She addressed the paranormal research team. "This is my father, and soon-to-be-retired county sheriff, Ted Williams."

Mr. Williams spoke up, "I hope you fine folks don't mind me being part of your séance this evening. I realize that none of you know me, but I'm sincerely interested in whoever's spirit is bound to this space and hasn't moved on to their glorious reward."

Professor Parker introduced the individual members of his research team to the sheriff. He then moved to the business at hand. "Shall we retire to the Grand Room?"

Senior Concierge Tabatha Williams-Young nodded her head and commented, "Lynette Carmona, my assistant concierge, will remain outside the Grand Room to ensure that no one will disturb us."

Everyone entered except Maryse Gosselin and Tabatha Williams-Young. Madame Gosselin leaned into Lynette and stated, "My dear, no matter what you hear. No matter if it's shouting and screaming of any sort. Do not disturb us or allow anyone inside. When we finish or if we need something, we will open the doors. I do not care if you think the

Minions of Hell have marched into the Grand Room! No matter what, do not disturb us!"

Lynette nodded and answered, "Yes, ma'am!"

Maryse Gosselin smiled and simply said, "Merci," and entered the Grand Room.

Tabatha Williams-Young gave her concierge's assistant a firm business look. "What she said!"

Inside the Grand there were plenty of overstuffed chairs, couches, and loveseats. In one corner of the room was a round banquet-style table with six side chairs surrounding it. The top of the table was a simple polished, varnished dark wood. Placed in the center of the table was one large, fat candle that had three wicks, each of which was burning.

Maryse Gosselin stood behind one chair and directed a seating arrangement. "Dr. Parker, you will sit to my right. Sherley, you will sit to my left." She looked across the table and addressed the concierge. "Tabatha Williams-Young, you will sit opposite me. Cassandra will sit to your right, and your father will sit to your left." Maryse seemed to study the arrangement for a few moments, then remarked. "Gentlemen, will you please help the ladies take their seats?"

Professor Parker pulled out Maryse's chair and helped her take her seat. On the opposite side of the table, Sheriff Williams performed the same courtesy for his daughter Tabatha. Parker did the same seating ritual with Sherley's chair. Sheriff Williams followed suit by respectfully seating Cassandra. When both men were behind their own chairs, they pulled them out and took their seats. Once the two men took their seats, Madame Maryse Gosselin addressed the séance participants.

"In the movies, séance participants routinely join their hands by touching their little fingers together, person to person. I prefer holding hands. Therefore, I will join my left hand to Sherley's right hand, and she will join her left with Cassandra's right hand and onward around the table until Ralph connects his left hand to my right hand, completing the circle." She paused and added, "Once we connect hand-to-hand in a circle around the table, it is imperative that we do not break the circle. No matter what happens! Do you each clearly understand?"

Everyone around the table verbally acknowledged. Maryse then spoke to Lynette, who was standing by the door of the Grand Room. "Please turn off the lights and do not enter the room, no matter what you think you hear. Is that clearly understood?"

Lynette answered, "Yes, ma'am." She turned off the lights and exited the room.

The six members of the séance team were now in darkness except for the fat candle with three wicks sitting at the center of the table.

Maryse began. "I cast this circle to hold conversations with the spirits that dwell in this space." Maryse then joined hands with Sherley, who repeated the charge that Maryse had stated, and when finished, she joined hands with Cassandra.

Cassandra repeated the charge of casting and joined hands with Tabatha, who followed suit and joined hands with her father. Ted recited the declaration and joined hands with Ralph, who repeated the circle casting verse and finally joined hands with Maryse, completing the mystical circle.

Maryse took a breath and, with a tone of conviction, spoke. "I, Maryse Gosselin, call upon the spirits within this place to come out of your hiding places and come forth and share your truths, pain, and what binds you to this place. Come forth and speak through me."

Maryse waited. Then, after a few minutes of silence, she remarked, "I feel a lady's presence! Please speak through me, oh lonely one."

There was silence. Then Sheriff Ted Williams said in a greeting voice, "Is that you, Helen Johnson? Please come out and tell us who killed you."

Suddenly Maryse opened her eyes, and with a very different facial expression and vocal manner, spoke. "Teddy Williams, is that you?"

Ted answered, "Yes, ma'am, it's me, just older and grayer."

Again Maryse spoke. "Teddy, who's that lovely woman sitting next to you?" Ted smiled. "Helen, that's my daughter, Tabatha, all grown up."

"I would never have imagined! I've seen her here attending to the business of running French House," Helen Johnson said through Maryse.

Cassandra made a facial expression that suggested "get on with it." Ted assumed a business expression. "Helen, I never solved your murder. Can you tell me who killed you?"

Again Maryse spoke, but in the manner of Helen Johnson. "Lewis Taylor, that man from New York City, wanted to purchase the French House from me. But I refused. He visited me a second time, and again I refused. Then strangely, here I was in this place, walking through walls and watching everything change around me."

Tabatha spoke up, "Helen, did you push that man on the steps recently?"

There was a long silence, then Maryse spoke with Helen's voice. "There he was, walking through this beautiful place and that spiral staircase. Yes! I pushed him. I wanted him to die! After all, he killed me!"

Tabatha gave her father a concerned look. Then she addressed the spirit. "Helen, it has been nearly thirty years since you passed away. That man wasn't the Lewis Taylor that you knew. It was his son, Lewis Taylor Jr."

Helen answered back, "It looked just like him. I'm sorry I didn't mean to hurt him. It was his father I wanted to hurt."

Cassandra was concerned about the strain that the channeling session was putting on Maryse. Cassandra spoke up, "Helen, the vessel you are speaking through is becoming exhausted. We must bid you good-bye for now. Perhaps we'll speak with you soon."

Again, Maryse spoke with Helen's voice and manner. "I appreciate this opportunity. Good-bye to you Teddy and to all of you sweet people for now."

A few moments later, Maryse slumped over to her left, and Sherley prevented Maryse from falling off her chair.

Professor Parker called out, "Tabatha, could you get us a wheelchair? We need to tuck Maryse into bed. She is clearly exhausted."

Tabatha got up, walked to the door, and hit the light switches. Upon opening the door, she called out to Lynette Carmona to bring a wheelchair. Within a few minutes, Lynette returned with a wheelchair. Professor Parker and Sheriff Williams lifted groggy Maryse into the wheelchair. Sherley and Cassandra took charge of the sleepy mystic.

Cassandra addressed Lynette. "Please come with us and open up Madame Gosselin's room."

Lynette gestured to them to follow her. Sherley grabbed Maryse's purse, and Cassandra took charge of the wheelchair and followed Lynette out of the room.

Professor Parker looked at Tabatha and her father, Ted. "Well, there is your answer to what ghost pushed Lewis Taylor Jr. down the stairs."

Tabatha smiled and nodded. "I never imagined we'd figure it out. Not to mention how you did it."

Ted looked considerate for a few moments. "Helen Johnson's death was the only homicide case I never solved. Now I know the truth, but I don't have a shred of evidence that will hold up in court."

Parker assumed a curious look. "Sheriff, you talk as if you could still prosecute a case if you did."

Ted gave the professor a disappointed expression. "I would if I could. There's no statute of limitations on murder!"

Parker looked at Tabatha. "Is Mr. Lewis Taylor Sr. still alive?"

Tabatha answered plainly. "Yes, he is, and he's the CEO of the company that owns the French House and many other resort holdings."

Parker assumed a wily smile. "Madame Senior Concierge, tomorrow morning bright and early, Miss Cassandra and Mr. Trotter are going to be working with grounds folks of this fine establishment to open a suspected hidden chamber of historic significance. If they should find human remains, the county sheriff's office and the county coroner would most certainly be involved. Wouldn't that be a justifiable reason to get the senior management of the holding company up here to represent the stockholders? In case of public relations issues and potential legal concerns?"

Tabatha raised her eyebrows and commented in a sarcastic tone. "Oh, my yes! Such a situation would be far above both the resort management and my authority to deal with it properly!"

Professor Parker continued, "Conceivably, while those senior management folks are here, we could treat them to a séance. Maybe we could persuade the spirit of Helen Johnson to confront Mr. Lewis Taylor Sr. and get him to confess his sin."

Sheriff Williams burst out laughing. "I love it!"

THURSDAY, JUNE 26, 1969, 8:30 A.M., FRENCH HOUSE RESORT, WEST LAWN

French House Resort grounds men parked a backhoe at the edge of the ground markings that Mr. Totter laid down with his field marking device on the pattern that Miss Cassandra had dowsed and marked with yellow ping-pong balls. As the grounds men lowered the stabilization supports on the backhoe, a short distance away, a member of the local fire department had helped dress Cassandra with decontamination coveralls and was now helping to mount a Scott Air pack on her back. With everything in order for both Cassandra and an assisting firefighter, they patiently awaited the backhoe crew to dig into the lawn.

After the digger had started, he made quick work of it. About a yard down, the bottom of the trench fell away, revealing a yawning, dark space below. The crew used a few more backhoe scoops of dirt to enlarge the hole big enough for a ladder to be lowered and for the survey team to climb down into the space with their bulky breathing devices.

Cassandra thought she must have looked silly wearing a firefighter's hard hat and the breathing pack, but it was a required safety protocol. The firefighter descended the ladder first, then signaled Cassandra to come down. The two shined their high illumination lights around the space before proceeding further. After about ten minutes, Cassandra climbed the ladder to the top. She held her arm out with a thumbs up before stepping off the ladder on to solid ground.

She unstrapped her breathing mask and looked at the county coroner. "Suit up, ma'am. There's two sets of human remains down in the space." Then she looked at the fire chief. "Your man wants you to ventilate the space with fresh air."

After the firefighter exited the space, the fire chief ordered the backhoe team to enlarge the hole to allow for large-diameter flexible ducting to be lowered into the space to ventilate in fresh air with some powerful fans.

Of course, while all of this was happening, the regional television station news crew was videotaping all the activity. Also, print news reporters were wandering the grounds of the resort and speaking to resort guests and key managers of the French House Resort. By eleven o'clock, the county coroner's office had removed both skeletons from the underground space and was taking them both back to the county morgue for analysis.

It was about noon when a corporate helicopter circled the resort facility and landed on a remote lawn. Senior Concierge Tabatha Williams-Young met the corporate dignitaries in a golf cart. At the helicopter were Lewis Taylor Sr., CEO of the resort's holding company; Lewis Taylor Jr., corporate regional manager; and John Priest Esq., senior legal counsel for the corporation.

Once all three members of the senior management team had seated themselves on the golf cart. Lewis Taylor Sr. simply told Tabatha, "Take me to the damned circus!"

As the golf cart rolled toward the legacy resort building, Taylor Sr. asked, "Who authorized this fiasco?"

"You did, sir, after someone or something pushed Lewis Taylor Jr. down a staircase a few months ago," replied Senior Concierge Tabatha.

Taylor Sr. groused. "I thought you'd be hiring a private detective, not a silly team of ghost hunters."

Senior Concierge Tabatha answered, "Sir, *The New York Times* did a huge *Science Magazine* article about them. They're supposed to be the best at this sort of thing."

Taylor Jr. spoke up, "How did they discover that hidden underground room that's been dug up?" Again Senior Concierge Tabatha answered, "Miss Cassandra, one of the team's psychics, found it!"

Taylor Sr. griped, "Madame, you allowed the digging up of the lawn on the word of some dingbat psychic?"

Senior Concierge Tabatha simply replied, "Sir, I think it's important to point out that she found an important historical discovery. The current public visibility has caused a drastic increase in reservations!"

"Very well. I want to meet this Professor Parker and that psychic who found the underground room!" Taylor Sr. remarked.

Tabatha swallowed hard. "Certainly, sir."

At the dig site, Senior Concierge Tabatha stopped the golf cart. As the executives got out of the cart, Tabatha gestured to Professor Parker to join them. As Parker approached, Tabatha introduced him, "This is Professor Ralph T. Parker of Onondaga University."

Lewis Taylor Sr. spoke up and extended a handshake to Parker. "Pleased to meet you, Professor. I didn't know that colleges taught ghost hunting."

Professor Parker seemed to grimace. "Actually, they don't, sir. I'm a professor of anthropology. It's the study of human societies and cultures and their development."

Lewis Taylor Sr., with an interested expression on his face, asked, "How does ghost hunting fit into that?"

Parker nodded in acknowledgment of the question. "Every human culture has stories, beliefs, and views about the afterlife. Our work is simply exploratory research to understand the phenomenon."

Lewis Taylor Sr. had a thoughtful expression and remarked, "The old Irish priest and pastor at my church would argue that, when we die, we're judged by God. We either go to heaven or we go to hell, period. Your thoughts, Professor?"

Parker maintained a professional posture and commented. "With all due respect to Roman Catholic doctrine, my research and study of the afterlife beliefs of many world cultures, as well as my team's research, suggest that the afterlife is much more complex than most people think."

At that moment, Senior Concierge Tabatha returned, with Miss Cassandra in tow. Professor Parker made an introduction. "Gentlemen, this is Miss Cassandra Grover. She is our shamanic psychic."

Lewis Taylor Jr. and the corporate lawyer both became amused upon sight of the effeminate teen. As Cassandra extended a handshake, Lewis Taylor Sr. did not accept the courtesy. He seemed to study the teen for a moment. Then he addressed Professor Parker. "If memory serves, shamans are some form of a tribal witch doctor. Professor Parker, how the hell do you expect me to take all of this spooky stuff seriously when you introduce me to a witch doctor who doesn't seem to have a handle on what damned gender he, she, or it is?"

Cassandra turned away from Taylor Sr. and walked away.

Professor Parker did his best to maintain his composure and replied, "Mr. Taylor, every culture with shamanic individuals typically describes them as unique, colorful, and a blend of gender expression. It's the nature of things, it seems. I assure you, she's among the most talented I've known."

Taylor Sr. spoke up. "So she found this secret room. What has that yielded?"

Parker explained, "Apparently, back in the day before the Civil War, the French House was a part of the Underground Railroad and helped slaves seeking freedom and a life in Canada."

Taylor Sr. cut to the chase. "How does that explain why something or someone pushed my son down a flight of stairs?"

"Frankly, it doesn't! It was simply a side discovery during our site survey to find the cause of that pushing event," Parker explained. He then added, "We can show you why the pushing event occurred. But it will have to be done this evening under cover of darkness."

Lewis Taylor Sr. huffed, "Are you saying I have to stay overnight?"

Parker shrugged his shoulders. "Yes, if you and your son want answers. We've arranged for a séance with Madame Maryse Gosselin. We believe that Madame Gosselin's séance will provide answers to all of your questions about why your son was spiritually accosted."

Mr. Lewis Taylor Sr. addressed his attorney, remarking, "John, if you are pressed for time, I can arrange for my pilot to fly you back to Manhattan."

Attorney John Priest simply answered, "I would like to hang around to make sure something fraudulent isn't being perpetrated on you and your son."

Lewis Taylor Sr. looked at Professor Parker. "Okay, Professor, we'll stay the night and will attend this séance." Then he addressed Senior Concierge Tabatha. "Please arrange suites for me and my colleagues."

Tabatha nodded her head. "I'll see to it immediately, sir."

THURSDAY, JUNE 26, 1969, 9:15 P.M., FRENCH HOUSE RESORT, LOBBY

Lewis Taylor Sr. entered the lobby of the legacy building of the French House Resort. Standing in the lobby was Senior Concierge Tabatha Williams-Young. He gave her a curious look. "Where is everyone?"

She smiled. "A séance requires some meditative and ritual preparation. Professor Parker's team has done the preliminary aspects. You will see my father and my assistant concierge, Lynette Carmona, who are taking part in the séance circle, sitting in front of you. Your son and your legal eagle are sitting behind my father."

Lewis Taylor Sr. nodded that he understood. Then Taylor Sr. asked, "Is there anything I need to know before I enter your spook house?"

Senior Concierge Tabatha simply said, "The function is already in process. We have darkened the Grand Room; it is now lit only by candlelight. Are you ready to enter, Mr. Taylor?"

He smirked a little. "Sure, Tabatha. Nothing you can show me in there can hurt me!"

She dimmed the lights in the lobby and simply remarked to the corporate executive, "Come, I'll show you to your seat."

As the two entered the dark Grand Room, the concierge led the CEO to an empty chair behind the assistant concierge. As Lewis Taylor Sr. took his seat, he noted his legal counsel, John Priest, seated to the left of him. Upon being seated, Lewis Taylor Sr. looked at the participants seated around an enormous banquet table. Looking to his left, he saw Sheriff Ted Williams glancing at the table, looking counter-clockwise. He next saw Professor Parker, and then at the head of the table, he saw an elegant older woman who seemed in charge. As he looked past her, he saw a younger African American woman he didn't know. The next person at the table was the effeminate person who had been the psychic who found the haunted underground room in the yard. Finally, in front of him was Tabatha's assistant concierge, Lynette.

Suddenly, he heard a strange voice call his name. "Lewis Taylor, how dare you come back to the French House! I told you then and I'm telling you now, I'll never sell it to you."

Taylor Sr. looked up. With shock, he saw a semitransparent manifestation of Helen Johnson in the air above the séance table, looking the same way she did on the night he killed her on December 20, 1941. Taylor Sr. shouted, "This can't be! Helen Johnson, you are dead. You died in 1941! I know! I was there! This has to be a trick of some sort. Because you are dead, dead, dead!"

The ghostly apparition floated closer. "How can you be so positive that I am dead, dead, dead, as you say, Lewis?"

Taylor pointed at the apparition and barked. "Listen, I gave you the cyanide myself, you crazy old bitch. I put it in your tea; I watched you collapse and fall on the floor. Helen, you are dead! I watched your last gasp on the carpet! Lady! You are dead!"

The ghostly apparition came to within inches of Lewis's face and smiled broadly, "So are you, Lewis Taylor!" A moment later, Taylor clutched his chest, collapsed, and fell off of his chair.

A voice in the darkness yelled, "Lights! Someone call the paramedics! Now!"

When the lights came on, county coroner Thomas Quinn went down on his knees and began performing cardiac chest massage on Lewis Taylor Sr.

Meanwhile, the city mayor, the county prosecutor, and the county commissioner were in a quiet conference. When they disbanded, Sheriff Ted Williams spoke: "Lewis Taylor Sr., you are under arrest, and you are being charged with first degree murder related to the death of Helen Johnson on December 20, 1941."

The coroner, still performing cardiac chest compressions, remarked, "Ted! Are you crazy about charging him? He might not survive this heart attack!"

Sheriff Ted simply answered, "Either way, I got my man, Doctor. I got my man!"

A MONTH LATER
Saturday, July 26, 1969, French House Resort, West Arboretum
Professor Ralph Parker wore a black suit. Madame Maryse Gosselin and Miss Cassandra Grover both wore black dresses, stood quietly and respectfully with about five hundred other people, and watched as an African American minister officiated a Christian rite of interment.

The decedents were Jesse and Nellie, two long dead and forgotten escaped slaves who had traveled the Underground Railroad seeking the freedom of Canada more than a century before. They were now being properly laid to rest with their names sandblasted into a granite tombstone, names that were only recently found on French House historical documents. Resort management had asked Cassandra, the psychic who discovered them, to deliver a speech. She respectfully declined, pointing out that the interment was Jesse and Nellie's special day and not hers.

CHAPTER 3

The Woman in the Picture

D. M. Delgado

Summer arrived. Nicole decided to visit her grandparents at their house adjacent to White Lake that was just over the brim of the Adirondack blue line. She wanted to change the hustle and bustle of the city for a quieter environment. Every time she came back, she recalled with fondness the good times she always had during this time of the year at their house. She would get together with her sister Val to play pranks and enjoy adventures along the shores of the dark, crisp lake waters. They would play soccer in the backyard with Marcio, the neighbor's son, and more than once those games resulted in a broken window or a broken water pipe. They would hit the ball so hard that they would often scare Grandma, so much so that she used to shout, "You broke something again!"

Grandma always forgave them, even with the backyard wall all marred at the end of the day with the dirt marks of each ball hit.

This time Nicole was coming with Melissa, her friend from college. Nicole had told Melissa about White Lake, the town where Nicole's grandparents lived since they were kids, where they formed a family and raised their children. Nicole also had described the beautiful Adirondack Mountains that surrounded it, where breathing fresh air, hiking, climbing the mountains, and going to the other lakes to enjoy the scenery are part of the plan of many tourists who visit this area. Melissa was excited.

Nicole and Melissa had arrived by train to Utica where they were waiting for Grandpa. They stood by the front door of Union Station, when he showed up in his old blue Chevy pickup truck. He was in a bit of a hurry.

"Hello, Grandpa, it's good to see you again," said Nicole as she smiled and waved.

Grandpa exited the truck. "Hello, Nicole, my little granddaughter," he said as he gave her a hug and a kiss.

"This is my friend Melissa, Grandpa. Remember, I told you I was bringing her to visit."

"Of course I do. I was waiting for you both. Melissa, nice to meet you."

"Do you mind if I call you Grandpa?" Melissa came closer and gave him a hug.

"Of course, Melissa, you can call me Grandpa," he answered with a smile.

"I am so sorry for being a little late. I stopped at the market for some tomatoes and cucumbers. Your grandmother needs them for a salad she is preparing for you."

Nicole nodded and said, "The dinner that Grandma is preparing . . . mmmm. Melissa you are going to taste the best food in this world."

Melissa smiled as she rubbed her hands together.

They loaded their backpacks into Grandpa's Chevy truck and continued on their way to White Lake.

On the way home, Grandpa told his stories of the old days when White Lake was a pure fisherman's paradise and free of jet skis, loud music, and party barges.

They arrived home as the sun hung on the rim of the pines and the sunbeams kissed the day good-bye. The house was a stone, hand-built beauty more than two hundred years old, but it kept its charm intact as if it had been built only a few years ago. In the past, a well-known politician of the city had lived there. In addition, the summer made it especially beautiful because the branches of vines crept up the stone, and their green leaves were growing above the windows.

Grandma was looking through the front window of the house when the truck parked. They entered the house, and Grandma welcomed Nicole with a big hug and a kiss on her cheek.

During dinner, they all laughed. The grandparents were happy to have their granddaughter back to stay with them for a few days, and Nicole was delighted to be spoiled. The grandparents called her little Cleopatra, because of her jet-black hair and because there was an Egyptian relative in her ancestry.

After dinner, Nicole invited Melissa into the living room. It had an especially old-time atmosphere. The room's beautiful fireplace preserved the original style from before the Civil War; above it there was a big shelf where you could see many pictures of the family. Nicole always asked Grandma about each one of them, like where they were taken, how long ago, who the people were in the black and white pictures. Nicole observed that the people in the pictures were enjoying a day in the summer. They were posing in their swimsuits with their radiant smiles and youthfulness in full bloom. Nicole and Melissa were talking about how cute Grandma looked in her twenties and how quickly a lifetime flies. They laughed about the fact that they looked just like Grandma and her friends in the picture and that, someday, which still seemed far away, they were going to have gray hair on their heads and wrinkles under their eyes.

Nicole turned to Grandpa and asked, "Tomorrow we want to go to White Lake for a swim and spend a few hours there. Could you take us there and pick us up later?"

Grandpa answered, "Sure, Nicole, but if you want you can take the truck. I won't need it."

"That would be great, Grandpa, so you wouldn't have to bother picking us up. Thank you."

"I'll stay home and help your grandmother prepare some refreshing drinks and a delicious dinner for when you come back."

The next day they left the house for White Lake just before noon, carrying a volleyball in their bags, along with some treats, snacks, and drinks for a few hours at the beach. They had on their bathing suits covered with T-shirts and shorts, and of course, they wore comfortable sandals.

The lake was only a five-minute drive down route 28. When they arrived, they found a good place to park. At this time of day, they noticed that theirs was the first vehicle parked there, possibly because it was Monday. Still it seemed strange that in the summer there were no people to be seen at the lake. They grabbed their things and walked to the lakeshore to find a nice spot.

They decided to walk around the lake a bit to enjoy the surroundings and the beautiful scenery. They had to be careful as some were private camps with protective owners. As they walked, they talked about the feeling of tranquility they felt, which was very different from the noisy atmosphere of the city. After a few minutes of walking, they found a nice private spot with some big stones and several trees behind them that pro-vided a nice shade, which would help protect them in case they needed to get away from the sun that was burning on a typical hot summer day.

The solitude of the place gave them a sense of privacy and peace at the same time; for a moment, they thought that the beauty of White Lake was like enjoying a little piece of heaven on earth. The typical sum-mer crowd was nowhere to spoil the quiet of the water and wind in the pine trees.

They decided this was the right place to stop, so they placed their things on top of the rocks and sat for a long time enjoying the scenery while talking and laughing about the fun things they did together the previous summer and what they were planning to do this summer.

Then Melissa said it would be good for them to get some exercise, so they started playing volleyball. They didn't have a net so they just vol-leyed it back and forth to each other. After about ten minutes of playing with the ball, Nicole hit it so hard that it bounced off the rock they were on and went into the lake. They quickly ran to catch it so the current wouldn't carry it away.

When they were in the water looking for the ball, they heard a woman's voice in the distance say, "Hello." It was a whisper. They both turned to look where the voice was coming from when they saw her. She was standing on the shore of the lake. Her hands were on her hips, and in her pose they could tell she was waiting for them to speak to her. She was wearing a swimsuit with a peculiar design, one of those that young girls wore in the late 1960s with psychedelic colors.

Her hair was reddish in color, and although it was wet, you could clearly see that it had a bob style, quite different from what girls their age wore. Her complexion was fair, but she looked a bit pale as if the sun had not touched her in a long time.

When they approached the woman, they realized that she was a young girl, possibly around their age. The woman looked at them and said, "Hi. I'm looking for my boyfriend. Have you seen him around?"

Nicole replied, "No, we haven't seen anyone else since we arrived. We have been alone all this time."

"My name is Christine."

"I'm Nicole, and this is my friend Melissa."

"Nice to meet you. I was passing by and saw you girls. I was swimming in the lake while my boyfriend was relaxing on those rocks. When I came out of the water, he was gone. I decided to look for him. I thought he was nearby."

"No, I'm sorry, we haven't seen your boyfriend," said Nicole. "We just got here. Maybe he walked off before we arrived. I'm going to get some water, and I'll be right back. I'm very thirsty."

Melissa approached the rocks where they had left their bags but did not find the bottle of water. She thought she had placed it there. But suddenly she remembered that she had taken out the water bottle when they were in the truck and forgot to put it back in the bag. Melissa went back to them and said, "I left my water bottle back in the truck. I have to go back to get it."

"Yes, I saw you drinking water in the car. It's a good idea to go to the truck to get the water. I'm thirsty, too, Melissa."

"Okay, Nicole. Sorry, Christine, I'm going to the truck and I'll be right back."

"Okay, Melissa," replied Nicole.

Christine went back to talking to Nicole. "As I was telling you before, I came with my friends Marie, Roxie, and Pam to celebrate our last outing as friends because I am going to study in the south and the girls are going to study in other cities. Our graduation was only two weeks ago. My boyfriend came to pick me up. He and I wanted to stay a little longer, so the girls left and we stayed. He was a little tired, and I told him I was going swimming for the last time. When I came back from swimming, I couldn't find him."

"Oh, sorry, Christine," replied Nicole. "As I told you before, we didn't see your boyfriend come by, but in case we see him, we will tell him that you are looking for him."

"Okay, thanks anyway," replied Christine. "You and Melissa enjoy your day at the lake. I'm going to keep walking around as I'm sure I will find him."

"I'm sure you will find him. You know how boys wander. It was nice meeting you. Have a nice day."

"Thanks, bye," answered Christine as she wandered away.

"Bye," said Nicole as she walked straight to the rocks to retrieve the ball she had recovered in White Lake. She picked up a mat to sit on the sand, and when she turned to go to the shore of the lake, she looked both ways and Christine had disappeared. It had only taken seconds for Nicole to get the mat to sit on the beach, and it was impossible for someone to walk so fast as to vanish like that.

When Melissa returned, Nicole asked her if she had bumped into Christine on the way. Melissa replied that she had not seen her again. Nicole ended up telling Melissa how Christine disappeared in a few seconds.

Both were quite surprised by what happened but decided not to give more importance to the matter and continued enjoying their day at the lake. They returned home at dusk. The grandparents were waiting for them with dinner ready. When they sat down at the table, Nicole immediately told them about the woman and how she had disappeared after talking to her.

They had also found her haircut and swimsuit strange as she didn't look like she was wearing the current fashion but, rather, a style from decades ago.

Grandpa asked them if the woman had said her name and what she looked like.

When Nicole told them the details, Grandma turned pale, and Grandpa told them that the woman always showed up in that area asking for her boyfriend and that people described her just as Nicole had. There were comments in the White Lake area about the same experience with this woman's appearance and that in town they knew the story of a young woman who had drowned in White Lake while her boyfriend was on the shore taking a nap.

Grandma quietly got up from her chair and said she would be right back.

When she returned, she brought a photo from 1969 that she had taken with her friends after graduation, and that was the last time the four friends were together.

When Nicole saw the photo, she felt her heart beat faster and said to her grandmother, "Yes, that's her. That's Christine! The woman we saw at the lake. She was wearing the same swimsuit as in the picture."

Nicole was cold with fright and so was Melissa.

Grandma held the picture to her bosom and smiled while a little tear came down her cheek, finding its path through her wrinkles. "She was my best friend at school, and, yes, she drowned in the lake. We had heard many times comments about a woman who appeared on the shore of the lake, but now I believe it is true. You didn't know anything about this, and I had never told you anything. I'm going there tomorrow to speak to my friend."

Everyone remained in absolute silence.

CHAPTER 4

Imaginary Friend

Marie Hannan-Mandel

Caseyville, New York. I've walked that house in Caseyville many times in my mind in the thirty-five years since we left. I never thought I'd do it again. I'd loved that house on the edge of the Adirondacks best of all the ones we lived in—and we moved around a lot. You do that when your father is a surveyor for a road builder.

It was meant to be—me having our old house back—I mean, how providential? I had money to buy a house, and I wanted to move back to upstate New York, and there it was, for sale. And I loved it every bit as much as I had as a nine-year-old. This was the first house I remember living in—a ranch with three bedrooms, a small kitchen, and a garage attached to the house by a covered walk. And it was mine.

"Hi, Mom," I said when my mother drawled "hello" through her landline phone. She refused to have a cell phone. I'd told her she soon wouldn't have the option—that phone companies were getting rid of landlines—and she told me that was ridiculous.

"Oh, hello, Bonnie. How are you?" She sounded distracted, and I knew she was pacing her kitchen, picking up a cloth, wiping counters, pottering around, her freedom to roam assured by the extra-long phone cord she'd purchased in the 1980s. Do they even sell those anymore?

"I bought a house—*the* house," I said.

"You did? That's wonderful."

I waited.

"What house is this?" she asked, grunting slightly as she scrubbed what was probably an imaginary stain on the plastic of her countertops.

"Our old house." What was it about me that, even in my forties, I still needed my mother to validate my every action?

"Which one, dear?"

"The first one, the first house in the woods. My favorite one."

Her butt crashed onto the rickety wooden kitchen chair, sending that unmistakable protest down the line. Mom never sat down unless there was a problem. "Why are you moving all the way up there? You have a lovely apartment in the city and a good job. Is it a summer house?"

I was flattered she thought me capable of affording a second home.

"No, I want to get out into the country, and I love the woods. You remember that house; it was so gorgeous and it's all redone. The back porch is now three-season with proper windows and screens. It's just lovely."

"It doesn't make sense. What are you going to do for a job?"

I didn't even answer that. How many jobs, good jobs, would I have to get before she stopped thinking every job I had was the last one I'd ever get?

"I loved that place. The woods right out the back. And my friends, Randy and Terry. And, of course, my imaginary friend. I loved Sarah best of all." I was smiling as I thought of them.

"Imaginary friend? You didn't have an imaginary friend," my mother corrected. "Why are you making up stories?"

"Just because you never saw her—well, no one did but me—doesn't mean she didn't exist. You know what I mean."

"I don't know what you're talking about, dear. Anyway, I have to go. It's time for *Cold Case*." My mom's favorite cop show waited for no one.

"Okay, well, I just wanted you to know," I said, though she'd hung up before I finished.

I was fully moved in a month later and had discovered that both Randy and Terry had left the area as soon as their parents died. They'd gone to

Florida, and now that I thought about it, Randy and Terry—two theatrical boys who played house with me and loved running around with nothing but their tiny bathing trunks on—would be a good fit down there.

I got my real estate license and joined the only realtor in the area, William B. Cecil and Company. I don't know why I hadn't done this earlier—all that time wasted being a party planner, a children's book editor, an administrative assistant—I just loved wandering around houses appraising and advising and enjoying the hunt right along with my clients. This was the job for me.

"You're Bonnie, right? Bonnie Beacon," a woman with a long nose and close-cropped yellow hair said when she came into the office. I'd been there a few months by then. She crossed to where I was sitting, and I stood up.

"Yes?" I smiled. I didn't owe anyone money, and I wasn't fooling around with anyone's man, so I figured I could admit who I was.

"I'm Teresa. Teresa Bryant. Well, now I'm Teresa Mason, but I was Bryant." She held out her hand, and I shook it.

Bryant was my friend Sarah's last name. Yes, I'm the type of person who would give an imaginary friend a full name. After all, how could I berate her, as I had felt compelled to do at least twice, without using her full name? "Sarah Bryant, I can't believe you did that!"

"You don't remember me," Teresa said.

"I'm sorry, I don't. I have a terrible memory." A total bald-as-an-egg-in-a-basket lie. I have an excellent memory.

Why would I remember her, anyway? More to the point, why did she think I should? No one around here seemed to know I'd ever lived here. None of my first-grade school friends even lived around here anymore, as far as I knew.

"Well, I was behind you in school."

Was she trying to make me feel better about not recalling her, or worse for being older than her?

"Is there something I can do for you?" I asked. I sat down again and motioned for her to sit opposite me. I didn't like her knowing me when I didn't know her. It might give her some kind of advantage, but I wasn't sure what.

"Yes, yes, we're looking for a house," she said as she sat down.

"We?" I said.

"Me and George, my husband. He's not here. He's at work. He works over in Plattsburgh. He's a stone cutter." She beamed at me.

"Do you have a house to sell?" Selling a house was always the better end of the deal, and when you could do both, well, that was the jackpot.

"No, but we have enough saved for a big deposit." Her smile burst even wider. She was missing all the back teeth on the left side of her mouth. She had all her front teeth, and her right side seemed populated. I'd never have seen the hole if she hadn't shown so much gum. Had she no friends? Who let her wander around without teeth? You could have no teeth and no smile, but no teeth and a huge smile was foolhardy to say the least.

"What kind of a house are you looking for?"

"Well, I'm so mad that we missed out on the house on Heartbreak Trail," she said.

"Which house?" I pushed my seat back slightly and leaned as far away from her as I could.

"You know the cute one with the dark green shutters and the wonderful back porch that looks right into the woods?"

Was she testing me? She was talking about my new house—well, old house, but now new. I waited for her to speak again.

"It's just that I have a family connection to that house and, well . . . Anyway, I like that layout. Do you think the new owners might be willing to resell it?"

I studied her face for some sign that she was lying, but she seemed sincere. Someone who didn't bother covering her dental deficiencies might practice that foolish honesty in the rest of her life.

"Why didn't you bid for it when it was for sale?" I asked, pleased that she hadn't, or I would have had to pay more. I was pretty stretched financially as it was.

"We were away. My mom had died, and we were dealing with stuff. When we got back, it had been sold without us knowing." No big smile, no missing teeth, just tears in her eyes, but whether for her mother or the house, I wasn't sure.

"I'm sorry for your loss," I said without thought.

"Yes, she's the last of my family. My father's dead, and my sister's gone. It's just me. Me and George, of course."

"Of course. That's a shame." I only had my mother left. I was an only child, and my dad had died when I was in college.

"You could tell me who the new owner is, can't you?" she said, leaning forward over my desk.

"All that sort of thing is confidential," I said. I didn't know if it was, but it sounded like it might be.

"Well, we can always look it up on one of those find-people sites."

I didn't like the idea of that, of her roaring back in here with my name and asking me why I hadn't just told her I owned it. Not that it was anyone's business but my own.

"I own the house," I said.

"You do?"

She was not good at lying, but she tried. So much for being honest. That's why she pretended to know me. She probably wasn't even from around here.

"And I'm not interested in selling," I added. I got up and walked to the wall where we still kept house detail handouts. My boss assumed if a customer came in, rather than hunting on the internet, they'd want something to hold in their hand.

"We'd give you more than you paid," she said, not getting up.

"There are one or two properties here that are quite like the one you want."

She took them when I handed them to her, but she didn't look at them. She got up, turned and walked out, saying, "George'll be very disappointed." As if that was something that should interest anyone other than her.

That night, lounging on my couch on the back porch with what was probably my third glass of Dr. Pepper, I saw the figure running along my chain-link backyard fence. It wasn't the first time I'd seen someone back there, not always dressed the same way and indescribable beyond the color of the clothes. This visit was different than the others, though

I couldn't figure out why. I got up, pulled down all the blinds, double-checked the door and the windows and went to bed.

The next morning, being Saturday, I expected drop-ins, but not Teresa and a man I guessed to be her husband. I figured she'd been trying to get the skinny on who owned the house and wouldn't be back, but there she was.

"Hello again, Bonnie," Teresa said, plopping down into one of the two chairs facing my desk. She gestured for the man to take the other seat.

"This is George," she said.

"Nice to meet you," George said.

In case they actually were intending to buy something, I pretended that I wasn't surprised and wasn't annoyed to see them in front of me.

"Teresa comes from around here," George said.

I nodded. That cleared up one thing.

"I don't," he added.

I said nothing.

"She's waited a long time to buy that house, and it's a shame that we were just a few weeks late." He looked at me as if he made an ugly confession and was looking for absolution.

"Now that's a coincidence," I said. "I waited a long time to get back here and buy that house." That wasn't true. While I often thought about the house, I'd never thought about returning to it. Not until recently, anyway. But I wasn't about to weaken my moral claim by admitting this.

"You don't understand. Teresa lost her sister, and she needs to be there."

"Are you two the ones running along the fence at night, trying to scare me?"

They looked genuinely surprised.

"I lost my sister," Teresa said, looking down at her hands pretzeled in her lap.

"I'm sorry, but . . ."

Her name was Sarah, and she was nine," she said.

"Nine?" I stared at the ceiling, which was dropped, stained, and ugly. Sarah? Sarah Bryant? My Sarah Bryant?

"I say I lost her, that we all lost her, because she never came home. She's never been found."

"When was this?" I snapped my gaze back to Teresa's.

"She disappeared in 1986. July 1986. The 8th of July, 1986." She doled out the information piecemeal.

I calculated. The date was six months before we'd moved into the house.

"The last place anyone says they saw her was at that house. She was playing in the yard with the boy who lived there. His name was Patrick. Patrick Clumpy."

They wanted the house to . . .

"Why do you want the house?" I asked.

"Because that's the last place anyone saw her and that's where she'll come back to."

"That's crazy. Didn't the cops search? Didn't your parents?" And didn't my parents know about the missing girl? Why would you live in a house where another little girl went missing?

"Wait, was there another Sarah Bryant, younger than your sister?"

"No. No. Just Sarah. They did look. Everyone looked, but I don't think they tried hard enough. They just gave up." Her pain was palpable.

"Excuse me," I said as I got up, walked to the bathroom, closed and locked the door behind me. I had imagined a girl whom I had never heard of, and I made her the same age as me, which also happened to be the same age the missing Sarah had been when she'd disappeared three years before. We moved away—suddenly, it seemed to me. I cried for months in my new house in the new town. I pulled my cell phone from my pocket and called my mother.

"Why did you pretend not to remember Sarah Bryant?" I said without preamble.

"Well, hello, Bonnie, how are you?"

"You heard me, why did you pretend not to remember my imaginary friend, Sarah Bryant?"

"Now, Bonnie, you always overreact. We just figured that if we ignored it, you'd stop, and you did."

"Did you know a girl named Sarah Bryant disappeared from our yard?"

"No. Not until later, and as soon as your dad heard he moved us out," she said.

"Is that true?" I asked.

"Is what true?" She sounded as annoyed as I did.

"Look, it was creepy. You were creepy talking with that imaginary girl. You used to say she hit you, or she stole things from you. We didn't know about the other girl until later. We just thought that you were . . ."

"Crazy," I supplied.

"No, not crazy. We thought someone must have told you about the other girl and you got confused. And then when you got lost, well, that's when we knew we had to do something. That's when we found out about the other girl. Everyone thought it was happening again."

A loud tapping on the door, followed by, "Are you all right in there?" It was Teresa's voice.

"I got lost?" I whispered, not wanting Teresa to be part of the conversation.

"Yes, we looked everywhere. In the house. In the yard. And then we went way back in the woods, and you were there."

George had joined Teresa at the door, and his knock, and his voice, were considerably louder. "You okay in there?"

"Please leave me alone. I'm on the phone," I barked back at them. I heard fumbling movement and assumed they were going back to their seats, or maybe even leaving. Wouldn't that be nice, if they just left?

"What? Say that again," I said to my mother in my regular tone of voice.

"We found you all the way back in the woods, and you said you couldn't go home until Sarah said you could." My mother's voice was tiny, uncertain, scared.

I closed my eyes and memories of times with Sarah in the woods came back but jumbled and unclear. I wasn't allowed to leave the yard alone. I knew that. I'd been told that every day. But with Sarah I wasn't alone, was I? That's what Sarah and I agreed. Perhaps my parents knew of the first Sarah's disappearance? Or perhaps it was basic common sense, though I'd never known my mother to be sufficiently supplied in that department. Sarah and I would creep out of the yard and to the edge of the woods. I don't remember going in far and staying. I don't remember Sarah being mean to me. But why had I given her a full name to berate her? "Sarah Bryant, how could you?" I flopped onto the tall metal garbage can that wobbled under the assault but remained upright.

"Are you there?" my mother whispered.

"I don't understand any of this. Why didn't you tell me? If you'd told me I wouldn't have wanted to come back," I said.

"Told you what?"

That was a good question. What could they have told me that would have made any sense? And anyway, they weren't that sort of parents. They didn't ask how I felt or shared how they felt. I was fed. I was clothed. I was kept warm and dry. I was made to go to school; I was inoculated and nit combed as necessary. What more could they have done? What more would it have occurred to them to do?

I hung up on my mother, a relief to us both, I was sure. The little bell on the front door chimed, and I desperately hoped that meant the Teresa and George were gone.

I left the bathroom having checked that I didn't look as shipwrecked as I felt.

They were gone, and in their place was William, my boss.

"You okay?" he asked as he shucked off his coat and sat at his desk at the back of the office.

"Fine." I waited. Was he going to mention Teresa and George? He didn't.

My mother didn't call me back. And I didn't call her. I worked quietly until five o'clock rolled around, got up, and grabbed my coat and bag. "I'm leaving now," I said to William.

"See you tomorrow, Bonnie. Thanks." He waved at me, a genuinely nice man in a cutthroat business.

I didn't allow myself to think about the Sarah dilemma until I was home, changed into my pajamas, and sitting on the porch with the blinds up and the lights off. All but the little night light that made seeing what was going on in the woods possible. I wrapped a blanket around me, one made of half mohair and half polyester with green and red stripes that my mother had given me for Christmas the year before. I might as well be comfortable as I waited.

The figure came at around the same time as always, but now I could see clearly that it barely cleared the top of the fence. It had never occurred to me until now that I'd been short as a child. When I remembered my "past" me, I saw someone the same height as I am now. Not that I'd previously given the height thing any thought.

The figure wasn't running—well, not the way I'd thought. I now saw the movement was a prance, a dance, a bob, a weave. And this time she was wearing the last dress I remember seeing her in, her favorite pink chenille jumper. She stopped and looked directly at me. I couldn't see her face, but I knew she was focused on me, beckoning me to join her.

I wondered if Teresa really thought Sarah would come back. Wasn't it far more likely that Sarah had never made it beyond nine, had stayed that way, and had come to play with me when I was her age, the age she died? I wondered why Teresa thought she might be alive somewhere, living her best life. I wondered if Teresa knew that Sarah hadn't chosen to go away, hadn't wanted to never come back.

I could have gone to her, my kind, difficult, nasty, funny, devious little friend whose secrets I had kept, even from myself. I could have gone into the woods and stayed there until she told me I could leave. I could have done that. But I didn't.

Chapter 5

Retribution

G. Miki Hayden

Not only was the trial over, but the sentence had been handed down. Richard Abel was to live out the rest of his earthly days, or at least the majority of them, in Clinton Correctional Facility located in the Village of Dannemora, New York—the prison that practically backed onto the pristine, wild, overwhelming acreage of the Adirondacks.

That was, unless he could help spending any further time in this unholy haven of filth and rats and dangerous men—men like him. And he very much intended to help it.

Richard was angry. Yes, he had killed Queenie LaSheba with eighteen knife wounds, so said the state. Okay, they actually counted such things. But who had caused him to fly into a rage? Miss Queenie herself. Would he have stabbed her if she hadn't told him they were through? Undoubtedly not. So who was to blame?

But as the girl herself was dead, she couldn't answer for her fault. And Richard didn't mean to while away the rest of his life in Little Siberia here to pay for her stupidity.

He knew the prison. He had studied the prison in detail over the seven months from his arrest to his sentencing. And he was a survivalist and had spent a lot of time in the wilderness. And he was smarter than those who were running this place.

Did he miss Queenie? Yes, he missed her. But then again, that was her fault.

He slipped into the four-foot-wide niche in the wall. The alcove was slender. But he was small and something of an athlete. He had been told by a long-time resident here that this was how an earlier escapee had made his way out. Twice. He leaned on one side of the wall and lodged his feet on the other side. From there, he crab-walked up.

He had brought along an extra shirt so he could grab safely onto the barbed wire at the top of the wall. Then once on the roof, he jumped down the several feet to the ground. From there, escape was actually easy. He knew if someone else could do it, he could do it, too. All he had to make sure of was to actually get away, and get away fast. In seconds, he was gone—as though he had never been here. Like a ghost.

Maximum security? Not hardly. And he had his ways. He slipped into the back of a supply van carelessly closed and carelessly looked into on the way out.

🌲🌲🌲

Two days later, Richard had in his possession jeans rolled up at the bottom, a T-shirt and sweatshirt, a backpack filled with food, and a knife. He was walking through the wilderness on a pleasant, crisp, early fall day. But he couldn't fool himself that this weather would last. Within a couple of short weeks, the weather would turn raw, and he was going to be freezing and miserable in the inevitable rain.

Then Richard saw two bicycles parked off to one side of a backwoods trail. He heard voices laughing and shouting. Within a short ninety seconds, Richard was riding a bike under the pines as well as the maples— which would turn red not too long from now.

🌲🌲🌲

Richard was exhausted, and his body ached. He was certainly not used to quite that much exercise lately. But finally, he had approached not only civilization but also his breaking point. Yet no. He had no breaking point. He stopped at a gas station for a minute of rest and to use an air pump for his bicycle.

The attendant came over to him. "You just want to use the tire infla-tor for free?" the man complained.

Richard stared at him. He tried to restrain himself. One wrong move and he could wind up right back in Clinton. However, he wasn't very good at holding himself back, was he? He took off his backpack where he'd stowed the knife.

"Oh, never mind," the man said, shrugging. "Go ahead."

Richard relaxed. *Queenie could have saved her own life, too*, he thought.

"What's that grand building back over there?" Richard called, turn-ing and pointing.

"The New York State Lunatic Asylum," the attendant said, and snorted a laugh.

"Is it closed? It looks closed." The fencing around the property had a "no trespassing" warning.

"It closed down in 1978," said the man. "Except for the ghosts." He laughed again and left Richard to pump the air into his tire.

That majestic, old, and official-looking building was where Richard intended to spend the night. Perfect. Actually, it appeared to have been built around the same time as the prison at Dannemora, and Richard would now be an honored guest here for the evening. He'd have the run of the place without having to attend any type of bed check. Yes, he was more intelligent than the rest of them and always could find an inn for a visit and a meal and drink, as he pleased.

As he knew how to bust out of the lockup he had abandoned, he knew as well how to break into a shelter for rest and relaxation. Ghosts? He scoffed. He didn't believe in them.

Going around the back of the building, Richard chose a spot on the grounds to hide his bike and climbed up and over the six-foot fence. He walked around the outside of the asylum and used his knife to break a window. He hopped up, cleared the glass, and hoisted himself over into the place.

Nothing inside, really, or did he hear echoes? Clanking, moaning—just the wind? Was someone in here? Probably only noises from the street.

Though outside the afternoon was warm, inside a chill had settled in. Yes, the sun hadn't beamed in through the windows, moderating the early day temperatures.

No beds in what seemed to be a reception hall. Well, he could sleep somewhere on the floor, but he'd like to find a blanket. He thought about the lunatics who had lived here once and unexpectedly shuddered. He went further afield. Behind him, he heard the echoing of sounds. The wind invading from outside? A piece of machinery or some sort banging against the wall from a broken window or such?

He did find a blanket. Some hobo like him had left his behind. He settled in a corner and opened his backpack. Sausages, apples, and a bottle of wine. That was a fine dinner, and in the morning he'd put his hands on something else to eat. The world was his oyster, as he'd heard said.

He found a bathroom and wet his face with drips of water from a faucet, though the flow was turned off. He rinsed his mouth just a bit. He went back then to his hidey hole and settled his thirst with a couple of gulps of wine, followed by another couple of gulps. This was ideal, a virtual palace.

Then came something like a shriek—a machine of some sort or certainly something from the street—though he jumped a little, startled.

Images from another era invaded his head. He must have seen a movie on TV about an early asylum like this one. Lunatics.

He fell asleep. And he woke up in the deep dark of night. Crying. He was crying, for God's sake. He couldn't fathom it. Was he ill? He shivered.

God protect me. No, no, what a thing to think. What had he to do with God? He wiped his tears away with the blanket. Had he lost his mind? *Shut up. Shut up.*

A flash of light drew his eyes in the dark. A flash of white, was it? A lady? No. From where? Maybe a flash of white of the moon through a window. He closed his eyes tight. *Mother, mother,* his mind cried. Had he ever had a mother? No. His mother had died when he was two. *Queenie,*

Queenie. She was dead. So what? He certainly wasn't crying for Queenie. He drank another few gulps of the wine. Oh, he must be drunk after not having had any alcohol in all those months.

Soon he had to go to the head, but couldn't find his way in the dark and had to pee—somewhere. Then frantic for the blanket, he groped around in the dark and fell on the floor. He then crawled, arms out. The sound of howls rose in volume.

Who were they? The homeless must invade this place at night and drink and scream. Why were they screaming? He shut his eyes tight yet again. He was fine. Just a little drunk. And cold. He hugged himself.

"Richard!" Oh, God, the voice was Queenie's. He would know her voice anywhere. He opened his eyes. Pitch black still. He shut them again. That hadn't been Queenie, hadn't been his name. Just sounds from the street—boys, and maybe girls, drag racing. He knew himself, knew he had a great capacity to believe only what he wanted to believe, to believe only what was useful to his survival. So he disbelieved.

He searched for the blanket until he became entirely disoriented. How long before dawn? The thought that he'd then find his way out comforted him. But picturing himself back on the bicycle made his muscles scream. And that thought brought up the sound of the screams again. Surely he was hallucinating.

By some good luck he ran into the blanket as he crawled—and his bottle of wine. He drank three more gulps. He had always been lucky and was lucky now. He laughed out loud. He heard the echoes of his laugh in every direction.

The man at the gas station had been wrong. They hadn't shut the place. The lunatics were in here still. Richard hadn't gone upstairs and they were up there. He drank the rest of the wine and knocked himself out.

When he woke up again, he knew that Queenie was in bed with him. "Queenie?" he whispered. "Are you angry at me?"

He knew what she would have said if she had been able to: "You killed me in front of our daughter, Lucy. I would have forgiven you just for killing me, but not for killing me in front of our child. No. That I can't forgive."

Of course she was angry. Oh course she was. That struck him hard. Let morning come, and let him run away from this place of damnation. He slipped into unconsciousness again, blotting out the terrifying sounds that sent a bloodcurdling chill through his veins.

The nearby room was filled with a dim light when he opened his eyes, and he was eager to take his backpack—and blanket—and run to the window.

But he couldn't find the window he'd broken in through, and though he tried to break another window to make his way out, he somehow wasn't able to hit the glass hard enough with the knife.

The wine was gone and he had only half a sausage and an apple core left. He had to find a way out, steal some money, and buy some food. Then he'd make his way to Albany or New York City where the opportunities were countless. He roamed around for a while, trying to find water first—only drips from sinks here and there—and he couldn't find a hammer to break a window.

Really, was not another soul in here? Not another living human in this whole big place to let him out? He climbed up the stairs, exploring from floor to floor. Even if he could break the windows upstairs, they were securely gated and he'd never work his way out. Down to the first floor again, and he searched for the broken window he'd come in. That must have been some sort of dream or nightmare because he couldn't find that window now. He sobbed. He couldn't stand another night here with the sounds—in fact, the smells, the groans and moans . . . of the dead.

He lay down and rested. He remembered a fifth-grade teacher telling them that the human body couldn't go more than three days without water. People could manage without food for long periods of time, but not without water. They'd die of dehydration. He'd gone through the ninth grade and then quit school, seeing it as of no use to him.

Could he find a valve to turn on the water? He brightened. But try as he might to break into the basement, he found the place securely locked. And search as he might, he couldn't find a water valve in any of the kitchen sinks or bathrooms. No food, no water.

And day was going to drift off soon into the horror of night. And he had to secretly admit to himself that the night here was a ghastly, ghostly time of terror. A time of dread unimaginable even to one like Richard who resisted such thoughts, or believed he could.

Stuck for a way to approach this without exhausting himself further or using up the resources he still had within himself, he found another place to make a nest and rest.

The second night went no better than the first. Though he tried to refuse accepting the sounds tearing through his nervous system and the disturbing visions, both internal and external mutterings were worse than the miseries he had seen in Dannamora. *Forgive me, Queenie,* he ventured in a thought. Had she no understanding of his inability at self-control?

She came once more in the middle of the night and lay down beside him. But she had no light in her eyes, no light in her soul, just as he now saw he had never had a light in his. The rest of his life in prison? But no "rest of his life" seemed to lie ahead.

On the following day, he made a methodical search of the premises for anything that would be a help—a few drops of water, another blanket. He tried to go to the roof, but the exits were locked. This was a huge and exhausting place to be in. He gave up.

He supposed he had given up, though he never would have believed he was a man to simply give up. But what could he do? He thought. He thought about his life, which had not been kind in giving him anything but his intelligence and his grit. He still had his smarts, but his resolve had drained away. He drank some of the bitter urine coming out of his body. That was surely all toxins and of no help.

The third day, he knew he was fated to die, and did it matter? The body, the person runs on hope. Those beings who shrieked here in the night, perhaps, though dead, must still have hope of life. He no longer had. He had thought so much of his ability to survive, and he had been wrong. Now he had at last to admit he had been wrong.

"Queenie?" he asked, and now he spoke to her directly, out loud. He heard a rustling that told him she was there. One day after the other, the occupants here tormented him. Not just Queenie but the mad, the dead, the lunatics. And he would soon be one.

On the fifth day, he made one last superhuman effort, and with a single hand pushing himself up from the floor, he staggered up and toward the outer ring of the administrative area. "I'm sorry, Queenie," Richard whispered. When ever in his life had Richard said such a thing? Had he ever admitted a wrongdoing or apologized? Never that he could recall. On the verge of death, he saw an opportunity now, his eyes gluey with the tears of days.

There, ahead, finally, was the window he'd come in through. Queenie with his request for forgiveness, he didn't doubt, had set him free. He could climb out, but was such an attempt of any use? Was it too late to live?

He teetered his way across the floor and saw that something was out there. No! Some*one*. He looked out. A policeman. "Help me," Richard's hoarse voice called. The policeman staring back looked as if he had just seen a ghost.

As Richard took that in, he collapsed. Dead himself?

🌲🌲🌲

The first time Richard woke up he was in the back of an ambulance, a cop with a jaundiced eye on him, a fluid being dripped into his arm, and his vitals being monitored by an EMT. That answered that. He was alive. "Queenie?" he called. Where was Queenie?

The next time he woke up, he was in a hospital bed, his arm hand-cuffed to the bed frame. He would have laughed, except he couldn't. He coughed. Again, fluids were being dripped into him. Then his voice rose. "Queenie," he called.

"Who is Queenie?" the doctor asked.

"My wife," he mumbled. But he hadn't married her. His mistake. He squirmed with shame at his anger toward her, his treatment of her, the murder of her in front of their child. He cried.

Two days later, they transferred him back to Clinton, not to the general population, but to the separate mental health facility where the psychiatrist made much of his having seen the dead woman he had murdered . . . and the others. But he had seen—and heard—exactly what he had experienced.

Now the days grew heavy on him, and he stopped speaking about his time in the loony bin, the lunatic asylum, and asked to be returned to the main building, where he requested to work again in the laundry where he had worked before. He made sixty-two cents per hour and put aside the money for his daughter, Lucy. His dearest wish was to see her one day, but he couldn't expect that.

The other workers in the prison spent their money on packets of noodles, coffee, and smokes. He went without and let the earnings add up for Lucy. She would have the money for her schooling or whatever else. He wanted to go without so she could have . . . something. Queenie agreed, not that she said so exactly, but Richard felt she did.

Richard didn't speak of Queenie anymore, but she was there, day and night, whether he was in the laundry running the equipment, mumbling to her, or she was in his bed while he slept. Sure, she was a ghost, but she was his companion. He never could manage without her when she was alive, and he couldn't make his way in here without her now either.

Those who had been inmates at the lunatic asylum would visit him here, too. They would wake him while he slept; he would open his eyes and see them flash away in front of him, or he'd hear their footsteps. Why they had followed him here, he had no idea. Maybe just a chance for them to sniff at some life in the penitentiary. In fact, some of the prisoners would mention strange sounds in the night, strange sights.

Richard saw and heard the same that they did, but he never replied. What was the use? And he had grown familiar with it all. Not insensible of it, but adapted to it, as anyone would become accustomed to a headache that never went away or a constant feeling of anxiety.

And twenty years passed in this way, and Richard was able to send his $25,000 to Lucy, a great satisfaction to him. Then another five years went by.

Richard worked on his case with a series of criminal-law-knowledgeable inmates. He wanted a probation hearing, and one of his legal mentors suggested that he might have such a hearing after so many years and with (a) a clean record and (b) a good defense to his initial conviction: emotional distress or mental illness. He had killed Queenie due to the disturbance of her having told him she was leaving him. This was well documented in his original case file.

Not that he wished to leave the life he was now acclimated to, but his hope was that his daughter might be invited to attend the probation hearing and that he might simply see her. He had loved Lucy dearly when she was a child, but he knew, of course, the terrible offense he had committed against her. He longed to see her all the same.

To Richard's surprise, he was granted a parole hearing based on a brief his current "lawyer" had prepared for him. A date was set, and he found out that Lucy was entitled to attend and make a victim statement. He was both unutterably glad that he might see her and abjectly ashamed for what he had subjected a small child to. His child.

The days went by. His legal representative, so to speak, counseled him to express remorse. Indeed, he felt remorse.

The night before his hearing, sleep was elusive for him, and his ghosts stirred beyond their usual bounds with screeches in the night, footsteps here and there, flashes of light, unseasonable chills.

He washed in the morning but had no clothing to put on other than his prisoners' usual outfit. The prisoners were made to wear it not only as a mark should they try to escape—something he knew well about—but also as a mark of shame.

He was stirred up over this significant day. He couldn't be sure, though, that Lucy would come.

The corrections officers seated him in the hearing room, and he rocked back and forth to throw off some of his restless energy before the parole panel entered.

Was that pretty young woman Lucy? Of course she was, because she reminded him of Queenie, the ghost still stuck in her own youth as he saw her from time to time. He wanted to speak to Queenie, but he didn't want to look insane. He quieted himself with difficulty.

The parole panel set forth Richard's crimes: his grievous murder of the woman he loved—inflicting eighteen stab wounds in front of their child—and his escape. Then a quietude of twenty-five years. Had he not paid enough? But no. He didn't care. His head was bowed, but as much as he could, he cast a glance at Lucy, without being obvious. This would have to last him for his eternity.

At last they called for the victim's statement, Richard's heart pounded, and he turned a bit to focus on his girl. He was proud of her. Did he have any right to be?

She cleared her throat, and he braced himself to hear her condemnation. She was forever entitled to great bitterness.

"This is my father," she said. "The man I used to call 'Daddy.'" God help him.

"I speak to my mother every day." As did he.

"And she forgives him." Yes, that was so, or so he believed she did.

"As do I," said Lucy. Tears came to his eyes.

"I forgive you, Daddy, and I know as you've told the board here, that you're regretful over what you did." His eyes met hers to affirm her declaration.

"I want my father to be given probation." She looked with fortitude at the men and women on the panel. She looked at him.

"I want to take him to my home in a nearby Adirondack town where I recently came to live and where I'll look after him. We'll make up for all the years we've been apart."

Richard couldn't believe what she was saying. He heard the rustling of the ghosts, but their now still voices were quiet. What was all this?

The members of the panel themselves set up a clatter, more defiant than the usual outcry of the ghosts.

"Yes," said Lucy without hesitation.

"Young lady . . ." began a member of the panel.

The tears fell from Richard's eyes.

"This is what my mother, Queenie, wants. I know her words and her feelings, and I've come to join her in this. He is a different man, and we want him back." She sat.

The hearing was over, and the panel would come to a decision after consultation with one another.

A corrections officer hustled Richard out of the room.

For twenty-five years he had been sure of what each day would bring. But now? What would the panel conclude? They might think she was insane, that he was too great a risk to her safety. He himself wondered what she would make of him. Why she would want to live with him. And had Queenie actually spoken to her, the ghost he knew so well?

In his cell he mumbled to Queenie, waiting. For Lucy's own good, he must refuse. Or must he? What could he give to her? How would they feel, the two of them living with not just an imaginary ghost, but a real ghost, the ghost of his wife, the ghost of Lucy's mother. How could that be?

Then, that day, he had his first prison visit ever. His daughter came into the visitors' room and sat behind the window and they spoke. And they spoke with and about the ghost they both knew and loved.

Later that afternoon, the panel refused his release, but said they would meet again a year from then to once more consider the request—and Lucy had told Richard she would visit often.

After that day, the lunatic ghosts from the asylum vanished, yet Queenie remained as Richard's companion whether Queenie knew it or not.

His daughter visited. Lucy, at least, was not a ghost.

Chapter 6

What Mr. Hoover Knows

Marianna Heusler

My father said a lot of things to me before he died.

He said that I should try to be more like my mother, even though they had divorced years before. He said I should try hard to do the right thing, even if he himself didn't always. He said that I should try to be strong and to never forget that, despite everything, he loved me.

He never said that he'd be coming back.

And maybe he wouldn't have—come back I mean—if he hadn't died so violently, so disgracefully, shot down during that drug deal in the streets.

What happened next started the day after he was buried. I didn't go to the cemetery. My mother thought I would be traumatized for life, seeing my father in that coffin.

She didn't know what was coming.

On a chilly autumn day, I took a walk around Lake Placid. Frost was on the ground, and the dry, dead leaves crunched beneath my sneakers as I went. The air was so cold, puffs of clouds appeared with my every breath.

I found myself standing on the shore. Yeah, the lake was pretty and all of that, lots of tourists at this time of year, but to me, the lake had always been a scary place, a place I avoided.

People whispered that the lake was haunted by Mabel Smith Douglass, a lady who was supposed to have drowned here a long time ago. They didn't find her body for thirty years, and when they finally dragged her out of the deep, dark water, she was in pieces; her head and her hand fell right off.

I never believed in ghosts, but I felt as though someone or something had been calling me there. I stood for a while as the red and gold leaves swirled down from the trees. I wondered what would hurt more, dying by a gunshot wound, or drowning.

I once read that drowning was bad because your lungs burst. And being shot, well, if you died right away, that wouldn't hurt too much. Maybe.

I wondered if my father had died right away, or if he'd bled out on the blacktop, right outside that old train station. Did he lie there alone on the cold, hard ground, gasping for breath, drowning in his own blood?

I had to get away from there, from the water, from the dead leaves.

A few people were walking quietly, holding hands, smiling, as though they didn't have a care in the world, as if their father hadn't been a drug dealer and then, suddenly—dead.

I turned around to leave when I spotted a man in the distance.

He wasn't moving, just standing there, not really dressed for the weather. I was shivering in my sweatshirt, and there he was, wearing a T-shirt and a dirty pair of jeans. And he was barefoot, like some sort of derelict. Hey, this isn't the big city, and homeless guys, they don't make it at Lake Placid. The cops move them along because they don't want to scare off the tourists, who come from near and far to escape the problems of city living.

I started walking toward the guy, because there was something about him, something familiar.

And like a whisper of smoke, he disappeared.

"Hey," I yelled to no one in particular.

An older couple, a pudgy man and his skinny wife, stopped and stared at me.

"I was yelling at that man over there," I pointed to the distance.

The pudgy man shrugged. "We didn't see anyone." And then he shook his head, as if something was wrong with me.

Like the place wasn't known to be a place where ghosts camped out. I ran all the way home.

🌲🌲🌲

"I know this sounds crazy," I told my best friend, Luca, "but that guy who I saw hanging out on the shore, he looked like my dad."

"Your dad is dead," Luca said as he stuffed cheese doodles into his mouth.

"How can you be so sure?" I asked, reaching for a handful of my taco chips. "Maybe my mother just made up that story because she doesn't like to talk about my father. And, after all, I never did see him, not even in the coffin. Nobody did. My cousin, Aaron, told me that the coffin was closed, tighter than the liquor cabinet in our den."

"Because," Luca said thickly, his mouth full of orange crumbs, "this wasn't just about your mother. I mean, his being shot dead isn't something she made up. It was in all the papers because of the way he went down." Luca stopped for a moment of respectful silence. "Besides, you said yourself, this guy just evaporated into thin air. If the guy had been alive, where would he go so fast, especially if he wasn't wearing shoes?"

I had to concede that Luca had a point. "Maybe, maybe he came back to tell me that he was okay, not to worry because he was in a better place," I said, the chips feeling like a lump of cotton in my throat. "I mean, that place—by the lake—it's known to be a place where ghosts hang out."

"Only one ghost. That lady with the cut-off head. Let me ask you something." Luca had finished the cheese doodles and started on my taco chips. "After this guy left, did you feel kind of like peaceful?"

"Peaceful?" I almost choked. "No, I didn't feel kind of peaceful. I was kind of like scared bad."

Luca shook his head. "Then if it was your father, he didn't come back as an angel."

"How do you know so much?" I asked angrily.

"'Cause I read, man, I read."

I knew what Luca read, and it wasn't books or magazines or newspapers. What Luca read was on the websites he surfed. He was always on his iPad; sometimes he learned valuable information, but most of what he read was crap.

"Maybe . . ." Luca swallowed. "Maybe your father came back 'cause he wants something from you."

"Like what?" I asked suspiciously.

Luca shrugged. "You know what I'm betting?" he asked.

"What's that?"

"You haven't seen the last of him."

I hated arguing with my mother, partly because I could never win, and partly because I felt sorry for her. My dad left seven years ago, when I was six. He was supposed to have visitation rights, but he hardly ever visited. He was supposed to pay my mom child support, but he hardly gave her a nickel. Part of that was because he was in the slammer for dealing drugs.

So, my mom left me with an assortment of weird babysitters, while she went back to school to earn her degree in social work. Now, she was a high school therapist, and she thought she knew everything a person could know about kids and how they messed up.

But I understood that she had it hard. I was aware she worried about me. She didn't come out and say so, but she gave me a few hints about bad blood, like maybe my father's addiction habits and his devil-may-care attitude somehow ran in my blood, as if I were tainted or something.

She didn't like me hanging out with Luca because his older brother had been caught shoplifting. He'd only taken a charger for his phone, though, and Luca was too chicken to commit a crime.

My mother wanted me to join a church choir.

Right.

The fact that I couldn't sing a note didn't seem to matter.

"I'm not doing it!" I screamed at her. "I don't want to make friends with those nerdy kids."

"You having only one friend isn't healthy," my mother argued. "At the very least, you should reach out to other kids in your school. Join the chess club."

"I don't know how to play chess."

"Or the art club."

"I can't draw."

"I know how devastating your father's death was, and I know you're still grieving."

Here she was, trying to analyze me, so I couldn't tell her about the man at the lake, because then she'd think I was really nuts.

"I'm not grieving. I need some air."

I grabbed my phone and headed for the door.

"Where are you going?" she yelled after me. "We're not through!"

I was.

"Be careful out there," she cautioned, looking at me with concern. "It's going to rain."

Like I was going to drown or something.

▲▲▲

I headed for one of the trails around the lake. The evening was growing dark, and sure enough, it had started to drizzle. The dead leaves sucked at my sneakers, and the air smelled like maple syrup.

I couldn't go back home, not after I had left so dramatically. Maybe I'd call Luca and ask if I could come over. His brother Mario wasn't so nice, but his parents were never home, so we were able to eat junk food and play video games nonstop.

My phone was dead. I'd had forgotten to charge it, well, not really forgot, just couldn't find my charger. Maybe I could get Mario to steal one for me. I slipped and fell against a bush, a vine brushed against my face, and I let out a small scream.

I had to go home.

And then the phone rang.

I looked around, couldn't be my phone, but no one else was around.

At least no living person.

I answered.

"Alex?" The question came out like a whisper.

I thought it was Luca, trying to act all mysterious.

"What's up, man?"

"Mr. Hoover."

The moment I heard that name chills ran down my spine, and not just from the rain. I knew my caller wasn't Luca. Because no one knew about Mr. Hoover. He was the crazy clown my father had given to me.

"Who is this?" I could barely push out the words.

This time the voice was louder and clearer. "Ask Mr. Hoover. Mr. Hoover knows."

And then I was left with a dial tone.

I stared at the phone for several long minutes, feeling sick to my stomach.

Where had the call come from?

Not from my phone.

My phone was dark. And dead.

🌲🌲🌲

I never liked Mr. Hoover. My father gave him to me when I was six, and two days later my father was gone, out of my life. I wish he had taken Mr. Hoover with him.

I thought that Mr. Hoover was creepy then and not just because I connected him to my father's leaving. Mr. Hoover was about three feet tall with a big rubber head, a squishy, round nose, jug ears, and white tufts like cotton for hair. His straw-stuffed body was dressed in a purple and white jumpsuit with two matching pockets on either side. Plus his glass eyes really freaked me out. An eerie shade of green, they seemed to follow me wherever I went. When my father first brought the clown home, I propped it up on my dresser. The next morning, I found it on my toy chest.

The following night music was coming from his belly. I didn't recognize the tune, but it was an old-fashioned waltz. My mother heard me yelling and became angry and threw the clown back down into the basement. Mom didn't like him much either, most likely because my father gave it to me. And that's probably where Mr. Hoover was, where he'd stayed for seven years.

I didn't know if I was brave enough to go and get him now, especially since the order came from a dead person.

And I was alone in the house. I thought about inviting Luca over, but I knew that this was something I had to do by myself. Besides, Luca was hardly an asset.

I turned on the cellar light and trudged down the rickety stairs, clutching a butcher's knife. I knew I was being ridiculous because a butcher's knife wasn't going to kill someone who was already dead. But just in case.

The clown doll was on the other side of the cellar, the dark, dingy side by the hatchway. The door creaked open. Without looking left or right, I went immediately to the center of the room, stumbling over packed boxes, empty bird cages, broken lamps, wooden trunks, and several bent license plates. I reached up to pull the string attached to a naked bulb, hoping I wasn't going to spot any mice running around. The dim light created menacing shadows on the stone walls.

The clown was sitting in the corner, squatting, and squinting with those bright green glass eyes, as though he had something to say.

I kept the knife glued to my leg.

From the other side of the cellar, I heard the hollow sound of footsteps on the concrete floor. I whirled around, trying to decide what to do.

Then the music from the clown started again, out of the blue, that weird tune, which seemed to go around and around and make me dizzier and dizzier and dizzier . . .

I ran out of the cellar, thundered up the stairs, slammed the door behind me, and didn't stop until I was safe in my bedroom with the door locked.

"What is the matter with you?" my mother asked, taking off her raincoat and draping it on my desk chair.

So, I told her. I told her everything. I told her about the man I saw I thought was my father, I told her about the whispers I heard from my dead cell phone, and I told her about the mysterious music I heard in the cellar.

She told me that I needed to visit Dr. Springer.

I hadn't seen Dr. Springer since I was eight. She was a crabby, older woman, who always seemed to want to trip me up, who asked me a lot of questions and, when she didn't like the answers I gave her, kept firing statements at me, until she was satisfied.

"I am not making this up," I protested to my mother. "Luca will tell you."

"Luca!" she said sharply. "As if he's someone I might believe! And was Luca there when any of these ghostly visits occurred?'

I thought it best not to answer.

"Well, the first thing I'm going to do is get rid of that clown. You're too old for stuffed animals. and whatever you think is going on is all tied up with that clown."

"His name is Mr. Hoover," I blurted out.

My mother eyed me with suspicion. "I'm making an appointment with Dr. Springer," she repeated.

I didn't bother arguing with my mother, because maybe that was a good idea.

Maybe getting rid of Mr. Hoover would free me from the ghost of someone who might be my father. No reason to think that he was my father. He could be someone from the other side, someone like a devil, who was just playing with me.

Or maybe my mother was right. Maybe something was seriously wrong with my mind.

And that was the scariest possibility of all.

I woke from a deep sleep with that slow, spooky sound playing in the background.

At first, I thought the tune was part of a dream, but when my eyes opened, the muffled music didn't stop. I sat up and my heart pounded as I saw, in the inky darkness, the figure of a man, standing by my bed.

It's a shadow, I told myself. *Nothing but a stupid shadow.*

And it might have been except for the fact that the room was freezing cold, despite the hissing of the radiator.

I blinked and then opened my eyes wide.

The shadow was my father, but he didn't look like my father. He was transparent, sort of like if I should put my hand through him, it would come out the other side. And in his head was a gigantic hole.

Was I dreaming?

I had to be dreaming.

"Leave me alone!" I lashed out. "Why are you doing this to me?" When he didn't answer, I went on. "Mom was right. You were always a bad man. Even though you're dead, you're still a bad man! You're scaring me! You're trying to give me a heart attack, so I can join you!"

Then I heard a sound—a heavy sigh.

"Find Mr. Hoover," he said in a breathless voice. "Mr. Hoover knows."

And just like that, he vanished, taking the chill in the air with him.

I reached for the lamp. I slept with the light on the entire rest of the night.

And the next morning, which happened to be a Saturday, with my mother in the kitchen, talking cheerfully on the phone to my Aunt Betsy, I found the courage to go down into the cellar again.

But I left the basement door open.

Mr. Hoover was gone.

You got to help me, I texted Luca, happy I had found my charger, and happy my mother wasn't paying attention, just blabbing about what she was going to buy at the Alpine Mall. *We got to find Mr. Hoover.*

Luca didn't understand, and I couldn't explain it to him in a text. My mother hung up and then declared, "I'm going shopping with your aunt. But first I'm going to the tag sale at John Brown's Farm. It's for homeless pets. I'm going to drop off some things we no longer need or want."

I couldn't see everything she had tossed into a shopping bag. But what I did spot were some white tufts sticking out from an old quilt.

Mr. Hoover.

And I was going to buy him.

I ran upstairs and rummaged through my T-shirt drawer, underneath the lining. My mother never looked in there. She said it was messy and smelled like old socks.

I had exactly twenty dollars, saved from raking leaves and mowing out-of-control lawns. Once Mrs. Ross gave me twenty dollars to show her how to get on the internet and set up an email. But I spent that money on a used Apple watch, which broke in one day.

I waited a few moments, and when I heard the car start in the driveway, I called Luca. "You gotta meet me there," I said. "We gotta buy Mr. Hoover."

He asked who Mr. Hoover was, and I told him I couldn't explain right then.

Then I ran down to John Brown's Farm.

The day was nice. The sky was bright blue, the air crisp. Large crowds were lined up for hayrides, as shelter pets, hoping for a home, barked furiously in front of a sad looking scarecrow.

Then I saw Mr. Hoover. He was in the arms of a bratty girl. At least she had a pained expression on her face. So did her mother, who eyed me critically, frowning at my dirty sweatshirt and unlaced sneakers.

And where was Luca?

"I'm sorry," I muttered. "But that's my—" I wasn't sure what to call it. "My mother donated it to the tag sale. Without asking me. My father gave it to me and he's . . ." I paused for effect, "dead. Murdered. I'd like it back."

She wasn't impressed. Maybe she didn't believe me. "I'd like to be in Paris right now," the mother huffed, "but that's not happening."

"I'll buy it from you," I said.

The lady's eyes narrowed. "How much?"

I was about to say, "Twenty dollars," when Luca appeared and blurted out, "Twenty-five."

The lady held out her hand, and I whispered to Luca, "I only have twenty."

"I'll spot you five, if you pay back six."

"No!" the little girl screamed at the top of her lungs. "No! I want it! It's mine!" She hugged Mr. Hoover close to her.

I knew she didn't really want Mr. Hoover; she just didn't want me to have him. She was that kind of a girl.

"Sorry." The woman shrugged and started to walk away.

Suddenly the little girl screamed and threw poor Mr. Hoover on the ground. "He bit me," she said. She held out her arm and showed us a red mark.

Her mother looked aghast, and I didn't think that Luca's laughing was helping the situation.

Then a scrappy looking yorkie came running toward us and began to bark at Mr. Hoover. A minute later, he was no longer barking. The dog released a loud, high-pitched yelp, as he scurried away.

A frightened look ran down the mother's face, but she wasn't quite frightened enough. "Where's the money?" she demanded.

I gave her twenty; Luca gave her five.

I looked at Luca and Luca muttered, "You pick him up. I don't want anything to do with that creature. He might bite me next. And you better tell me what's going on."

So, I did. I had a feeling that Luca didn't believe a word I was saying, and I knew he was scared. Scared of Mr. Hoover and quickly becoming frightened of me.

He didn't even want that creature in his house, which sucked because it meant I had to hide him in mine. But Luca did manage to come over, and while my mother was out, we propped up Mr. Hoover and tried to talk to him.

At least I did.

Luca stood by the door, ready to flee at the least sign of anyone from the other side making an appearance.

"I'm supposed to ask you something," I said, feeling like a fool.

Mr. Hoover didn't make a sound, just stared at me with those glass green eyes.

"Do you have something to tell me?" I asked.

"He doesn't like that I'm here," Luca muttered. "Which is fine with me. I don't want anything to do with ghosts or . . ." He paused. "Crazy people. I'm gone."

I didn't want Luca to go. I needed him for moral support. But that was who Luca was. In times of trouble, he was as elusive as any ghost.

I covered Mr. Hoover with an old blanket, put him in the closet, and left the bedroom.

I thought about sleeping with the light on, but then I thought I was being dramatic. I wasn't only scared of Mr. Hoover but of the ghost of my father. I was afraid that he'd come back and give me more useless instructions.

I fell into a restless sleep and then I woke up when I heard someone breathing beside me.

When I switched the lamp on, Mr. Hoover was there, sitting in my chair, staring at me with a penetrating look that gave me the chills.

How the heck did he get out of the closet?

I didn't care. My mother had to see this, even if she thought I was insane. And just when I opened my mouth, I saw something I hadn't noticed before. A white piece of paper sticking out of Mr. Hoover's pocket.

I wanted to reach for it, but what if Mr. Hoover reached for me first?

I thought about how my father told me to be strong, so with one quick swoop, I leaned over and grabbed the paper.

I thought it was going to be some old, decrepit thing, but instead it was a piece of loose leaf paper. My head swirled when I recognized my father's writing.

I don't know if you'll ever see this. Because who's to say if one can come back from the dead? But I want you to know, Alex, that I was shot in that drug deal, not as a criminal but as an undercover cop—an informant. I'd been working for the FBI for some time, and no one knowing that was important. If you check Mr. Hoover's other pocket, you'll find my badge and my ID card. Remember, Alex, I love you, and I'll always be there for you.

I was hoping he wouldn't be.

I reached into Mr. Hoover's pocket and pulled out a metal badge and a wrinkled card. My father's picture and his badge number were laminated on cardboard.

I tried not to cry as I hid the badge and the card in my bottom drawer.

I wasn't afraid of Mr. Hoover anymore. I lifted him up and put him in bed beside me.

I guess you know the end of the story.

In the morning, he was gone.

But three years later, I still have my father's badge with his ID.

And my father vanished peacefully to the other side with Mr. Hoover.

CHAPTER 7

A Haunting in Wells

P. J. McAvoy

It's hard to recall how I felt at that first impression. Memory, we all know, can be deceptive. Years of nightmares and replaying the scenes again and again can affect the mind, coloring the pictures we keep. Did I have a sense of foreboding from the start? Dread? If I did, it's been long buried under the weight of what happened.

It was a beautiful Craftsman-style house that was built backward—that was the first thing I remember noticing.

When we pulled into the driveway, I craned my neck from the backseat to see around my parents. It was a large bungalow, with a sharp-angled roof and a wide dormer that came over the porch; only, the side that faced the street looked like the rear of the house. And the side that faced the lake, with its deep porch and wide steps down to the lawn and the dock, was what most people would call the front.

It was August 1989. I was fourteen years old. I had spent four hours crammed in the backseat of my parents' wood-paneled wagon with my younger siblings, Bobby and Kate, five and nine.

"It's right on the lake! It's going to be fantastic," Dad said. I was skeptical, having never been the outdoors type. Wells, New York, was a town so small it didn't have a stoplight. On the map it wasn't far into the Adirondack Park, but as we drove the towns got smaller and the trees grew larger, civilization fading behind our Ford with each passing mile. It was nothing like Putnam County.

We were here for two weeks, the house a rental my dad found in a PennySaver ad. Stepping out of the car, we walked up to the front back door. The 1920s house was painted dark brown with orange trim around the window and door frames. The key was hidden under a flower pot, as promised, and we entered. The living room was full of oak Stickley furniture, aged to a caramel brown. Birch-stick dining chairs and a roughhewn table added an antique, rustic appeal to the dining room. On the walls hung framed sepia-toned photos of men and women looking like pages from an Adirondacks history book—boating, swimming in bathing caps, sitting on a dock, showing off a proud haul of fish strung on a line.

My dad, ever the optimist, loved every bit of it. My mom seemed tired from the trip. Kate ran off to explore the bedrooms, and Bobby stuck close by me. He was always quiet, especially in new situations. An odd kid who didn't make friends his first year at preschool and preferred to sit alone. We had a lot in common.

"There's *four* bedrooms up here!" Kate yelled from the upstairs. "Three bunk beds!"

"Kevin, you're going to stay with me?" Bobby asked me.

"Yeah, of course," I replied. I knew he didn't want to be alone.

The house felt like nobody had been inside in years. Bobby moved closer to me.

"We need to open up some windows," Mom said, parting the curtains. But the house didn't seem to lighten much. The dark wood trim and forest green color on the walls absorbed light, giving the house an oppressive feeling.

"Would you look at this view?" Dad said from the back porch. The lake glittered in the afternoon light, a thousand reflected suns winking and beckoning us from the water's surface.

"This is going to be a great vacation," he said, tossing his arm around me and Bobby.

The notebook on the counter had instructions for renters. The home's owner lived about an hour away and the house had a telephone, but the notebook pointed out it was often out of service after a summer storm.

"Really roughin' it!" Dad said, with a grin. "No TV, no cable, and even the phone might not work. I might actually get to relax this week."

Aside from the usual directions on where to find things in the house and in town, the notebook also had two warnings. If there was a plumbing, electrical, or appliance problem, we were to call (or go to) the Wells General Store and ask for an Otis Sanford. We were not to try and fix it ourselves.

The second warning was for one of the bedrooms. There was a locked door to the attic that we were to stay out of.

We had all brought along plenty of books. I was in the middle of *Hatchet*, and I was terrified by the wild animals in it. I took after my mother that way. My dad used to say about my mom, "You could pay her to worry and you'd get your money's worth." Nobody ever said the word *breakdown*, but then again, they didn't have to. When she had to stay with my grandmother for a few weeks this year, it was clear enough. I'm sure Dad was hoping the vacation would help.

During the day it was picture-perfect. But at night the purple veil rolled down from the mountains and reclaimed the land. We had never seen nights so dark. The deep blackness was full of unfamiliar noises—strange animals, the creak of an old house, and the lapping of lake water.

🌲🌲🌲

Mom had a full-blown panic attack when we lost Bobby.

He wasn't having a good start to the trip. He spent his time playing inside with his toys, or complaining of being cold. When my dad would try and convince him to go outside, sit in the sun to warm up, he only shook his head. He wouldn't go near the water.

Kate was like Dad. She relished every minute of the outdoors. She caught two fish from the canoe on the fourth day, and there's a photograph of her holding them up proudly. In the background you can you see Bobby standing on the porch, in the shadow near the steps, holding a green truck.

The day we lost him he had been playing upstairs. I swear that's where I left him, but as Mom called and he didn't answer, I walked up to see if he had fallen asleep. He wasn't in the bedroom. We scattered to frantically check the house—outside by the lake, the dock, the garage, and the woodshed that housed the canoes. Nothing. Mom was starting to hyperventilate and flap her hands; Dad held both her shoulders and spoke softly to her, his nose an inch from hers. I held my panic in, not wanting to add to Mom's worries.

Twenty minutes later Bobby came down the stairs with the green truck. Mom cried and grabbed him and asked where he had been hiding and how come he didn't come when we called him.

"I didn't hear you. I was playing upstairs."

"But you weren't, honey. We checked all the rooms."

"I was there," he insisted.

"He must have fallen asleep under a bed," Dad said. But I had checked under the beds. And so had Mom.

🌲🌲🌲

The green truck wasn't ours. It looked like an antique, from the 1930s, with curved fenders and half-moon hubcaps.

"Where did you get this?" I asked him.

"I found it upstairs."

"Nuh-uh. I looked in the all rooms and didn't see it."

Bobby got quiet. "Do you promise not to tell?"

He leaned in closer to me.

"Will gave it to me. He had it upstairs."

"Who is Will?"

"The boy who lives here. He stays in the attic. He doesn't have anyone to play with and he's lonely. I don't have anyone to play with either."

My heart started pounding. Was Bobby losing his mind? He never had imaginary friends before.

"What does Will look like?" I asked.

"He has sandy hair. He's short. He has some toys and he says he'd share with me. He stays inside and told me to never go in the lake. He said it's not safe."

I thought for a moment before I responded.

"The next time you see Will, can you come get me? I'd like to meet him."

Bobby nodded. "He doesn't like new people. But I'll ask him. I gave him my Ghostbusters toy. He gave me this truck. We traded. So we're friends now."

That night I checked the door to the attic. When I tugged gently on the brass padlock, it gave way. I stared for a moment at the open lock, contemplating opening the door. What would I find up there?

I latched it shut and double checked that it would stay closed.

On the fifth day we saw a bald eagle. It swooped down over the lake, threw its claws in the water, but came up with nothing and flew off. Dad and Kate were in the canoe and cheered. I was watching from the dock, a fishing pole in hand but my mind a thousand miles away.

Mom and Bobby were sitting on the porch chairs, watching from there. She had her arms around him tightly, like the eagle might change its mind and decide to make a try for her little boy.

The Will stories were getting more elaborate. Bobby said they had gone hiking together, and Will showed Bobby his secret fort in the woods. He said they played checkers and told stories and hid from Will's sister. He said he met Will's parents. But he never left the house. *Maybe this was Bobby's way of dealing with a place he doesn't want to be*, I thought.

"I'm *not* making it up," Bobby said loudly one afternoon when I insinuated a little too directly. "Will is real and he doesn't like you and he's my friend!"

Bobby stomped up the stairs, my parents quieted by his outburst. This was the first time he had raised his voice to them.

79

We suddenly heard a crash and a shattering. My mom jumped up off the couch, and Dad walked briskly into the kitchen. He came back with shards of a mason jar.

"Must have fallen off the counter."

I went upstairs to check on Bobby. I peered into the room. He was in his bed, holding the green truck with his back to me; he looked like he was talking to someone. I stuck my head in further. He was alone on the bed but speaking quietly. I couldn't understand all of what he was saying. Only snippets.

"No, they don't understand. They said you're not real."

That's when I started to get very worried.

I tried talking to my dad.

He laughed. "Kevin, come on. He's just being a kid. A nervous kid who is dealing with some big feelings."

"No, Dad, there's something weird going on."

"He's anxious about starting kindergarten next year. This kind of developmental thing is totally normal; I see it all the time in my practice. Some kids deal with it differently. Yeah, there are times when I get a little concerned, but he's doing okay."

"He's not one of your pediatric patients. I'm telling you, I saw him talking to himself."

"Totally normal. Just be kind to him and give him a little attention. He's looking for some connections."

But Bobby didn't want to connect with me. Up until this trip he had clung closer to me than he did to either Mom or Dad, who both seemed wrapped up in their own worlds. He had spent the past two years as my little shadow.

Now, though, he shot me suspicious glances and clammed up around me. I could feel him pulling away.

Bobby and I always had each other. Until this trip.

"KATE! Did you track lakeweed into the house? I told you to dry off before you come in!"

Mom stood over the clump of milfoil and wet footprints. She waited for a response from my sister, but none came.

"Kate and Dad aren't back from town yet," I told her.

She looked confused.

"Did you go in the water today?"

"No, I've been in here."

"Where's Bobby?"

"He's on the porch," I pointed out my brother, who sat building a stack of his blocks and humming to himself.

She stared down again at the small puddles and plants.

"Well, where did this come from?"

A breeze blew in from the side window, puffing out the lace curtains and causing a door on the other side of the house to slam shut with a loud crack.

There was an old woman who worked at the general store, but she wasn't one of those kindly, matronly seniors. She was hard, thin, with a granite glare. Wiry black and white hair frizzled out from her head. Melda, they called her. Whether that was short for Esmerelda or a weird take on Amanda or "Elder," I didn't know. But she was there every day that we went into the general store.

"She looks like a witch," Kate said loudly, when we were back in the car. "Do you think she's casting spells on us?"

"Now stop," Dad said, offended. "Don't go judging people like that. She's helped us get all the things we needed."

When the sink sprung a leak, Dad called Melda and asked for Otis. "Oh," she said, the tone of her voice dropping. "You're staying at *that* house? I'll let Otis know. He should be there shortly."

Otis arrived in a rusty pickup. He fixed the leak. On his way out my Dad asked him about Melda, and he gave a thin smile. "She's been around here forever. Seen it all. Her daddy was some Buffalo big shot who had a summer home out here."

"What if this is *her* house and she hates us and is casting a spell to make us insane or something so she can get the house back?" Kate whispered to me that night.

"Why would that make sense?" I replied. "We're only renting the place."

"She's evil. She doesn't care."

The next day we saw Melda when we went into town. She glared at us from behind a copy of the Gloversville *Leader-Herald*.

"Evil eye," Kate whispered to me. "Classic witch trick."

"That plumbing all fixed?" she asked my dad.

"Yes, thank you for getting to Otis so quickly."

She kept looking at my dad. "You be careful there. I know the owner; she ain't gonna like if someone wrecks that house."

Dad gave a nervous chuckle. "Ha, no we won't wreck it! We're taking good care of the place."

Melda sucked her teeth and nodded. She turned back to her newspaper.

"Strange things sometimes," she said to herself.

Kate raised a convinced eyebrow at me.

Mom wasn't sleeping well. She was up a lot at night. I could hear her in the hallways. She would be bleary eyed in the morning, and Dad would make sure we were all quiet as she caught a few more hours of sleep during the day. She had gotten quieter, too. Spent all her time reading and seemed half in a fog when she did speak.

"Two weeks is too long to be away," he said to me. "I should have known. A week would have been enough."

We had only a few days left.

Bobby was taking an afternoon nap on the couch. I was reading at the dining table, Mom was upstairs sleeping, and Kate and Dad were out in the canoe. The loud ticking of the mantel clock was all I could hear as I got lost in my story.

Suddenly, I heard a shriek from upstairs.

I raced up the stairs and into the room my parents were staying in. My mother was frantically screaming from her window, her palms slapping the glass panes.

I looked down. From the window I could see the dock. Bobby was slowly walking as if sleepwalking. He was going to the edge of the dock. He didn't stop despite Mom's pleas. He walked right off the dock and into the water.

Bobby couldn't swim.

I sprang down the stairs, out the porch door, and down the dock; my heart pounded faster and faster, and I saw his little head bobbing in the water. His arms flung like windmills, trying to keep himself upright. He was spitting and trying to catch his breath, his eyes wide in fear. Just before I reached the end of the dock, his head sank beneath the surface.

I dove in and got a hand on him as I went by. I tugged up but felt resistance. Something was pulling him down.

I pulled again, and again something pulled back.

I held him tight and kicked hard against the slimy lake floor; it wasn't very deep here. Finally, he came free. I hoisted him by his shoulders to the water's surface. By then my mom was on the dock, and I handed him up to her. She was still making some kind of noise with each breath, but she got him up on the dock. He was sputtering and taking deep, violent breaths. She rocked him, pawing at his arms and crying, "What did you do? What did you do?" over and over again.

He told he us didn't remember walking into the water. For the first time, Dad looked pale and worried. His eyes traveled from Bobby to my mom. He saw her anxiety on my face and now Kate's.

"That's it. We're going to leave early. I think everyone's had enough vacation."

"*No!*" Bobby shouted, shocking everyone. "We can't go! Will said I have to stay!"

"Bobby, we are getting in the car and going home. That's all there is to it," Dad said firmly. My mom wiped grateful tears from her eyes.

The sky outside had turned dark, and a peal of thunder rolled across the lake. Heavy clouds hung low and were churning toward us above the tree line.

"Everybody, go upstairs and start packing up your stuff. We're leaving in thirty minutes. We'll try to beat this rain."

The porch door slammed shut with a loud *bang*.

The lights flickered.

"Goddamn storms," my dad muttered, going upstairs.

Kate ran up to get her things, energized by the excitement. My mom went into the kitchen. Bobby sat on the couch, a towel still slung around his shoulders, looking dazed. I sat next to him.

"He doesn't want to be alone. He doesn't want me to go," he whispered, under his breath. I took his cold little hand in mine. We sat for a moment.

The wind picked up and rattled the windows in their frames. I heard a thud outside and saw a broken pine tree branch had narrowly missed hitting the house.

Fifteen minutes later we had all the suitcases in the living room. A quick count and Dad and Kate started hustling them out into the car. The rain began, not a gentle summer shower but angry bullets of water fired down from the sky. The wind was now making small whitecaps on the lake. Choppy ripples of waves tossed the tied-up canoe against the dock.

We heard two loud beeps of the car's horn, and my father got out and kicked the door shut in a fit. He came inside. "Great. Just great. The car won't start."

"He's not going to let me go," Bobby said quietly. "He told me. He needs a friend. Mom," he said, looking into my mother's face, a mask of sheer terror written across his features. "I don't want to be Will's friend anymore. I want to go home."

At that moment, the power went out.

The rain whipped sideways at the windows. A bolt of lightning struck a tree on the far side of the lake, releasing a tremendous flash of orange light followed a second later by a house-rattling boom.

Kate jumped, clutching me.

That's when I felt an ice-cold chill go through the air. The whole ground, and my sanity, seemed to be slipping away from underneath me. It felt like January on this August afternoon. I looked and saw my mom was shivering. Kate's arms erupted in goosebumps.

We could all see our breath in the house, as if we had walked into a freezer.

"We're going to wait in the car," my dad said. "Let's go, everybody calmly and slowly."

But it was like we were glued to the spot. I couldn't move. My legs were like concrete. I tried to force one of them to just take a step, but it held heavy in place.

My mother looked like she was about to pass out.

Bobby shook violently as he sucked in deep breaths, like he was having an asthmatic attack. The windows were blurry with condensation, droplets of dew from the air fogging them from the inside.

The sky was now black as if it were night, even though it was only four in the afternoon. Veins of white lightning lit the clouds. The white-caps surged more angrily. We all managed to step closer together, and my dad lifted Bobby off the couch, making him stand with us.

The condensation began to drip from the side windows. I looked over and watched in horror. It was as if someone was writing with a finger on it. I blinked, not believing what I was seeing.

Words began to appear. Three words.

THE BOY STAYS.

We heard the front door open. A flash of close lightning lit the room, and we saw a figure in the doorway. Standing inside the house. A silhouette of frizzled hair and sharp, angular features.

My mother shrieked as Melda walked into the room, dripping from the rain.

The old woman looked wild eyed at us, like a Greek Fury come for her revenge. My father stepped forward, putting himself between us and her, this gaunt specter who looked like she crawled out of the lake. She eyed Bobby, watching him shake and convulse with fear.

"That is enough, William!" She yelled at him. "That's enough."

The howling wind seemed to falter.

"Mama told you not to scare the boys and girls. You get back in that attic or I'm going to tell her."

A tree branch slammed into the side of the house. She spun in a circle, now looking around the room.

"I am *not* joking! You listen to your sister or you're going to be in big, big trouble."

A kitchen cabinet door swung open and a plate sailed out, shattering on the floor. We all recoiled.

"*Oh*, that's it! Now you're in for it," she howled, completely unhinged. "No more tantrums and get back upstairs, this instant! Or so help me God, I won't come back again."

All at once every cabinet door simultaneously opened and slammed shut. BAM. BAM. BAM. Three times. The surface of the lake surged up monstrously, as if something huge and ancient and evil was about to emerge from the water. A bolt of lightning hit the water right off the dock, the light and the tremendous sound of thunder overwhelming my eyes and ears, deafening and blinding me. My mother fainted and her collapsing weight pulled us all to the ground. Kate cried out loudly as we fell into a heap.

🌲🌲🌲

I don't know how much time passed—it could have been five minutes; it could have been fifty. I sat with my eyes screwed tightly shut, afraid of what I might see if I opened them, holding my father, mother, brother, and sister. Someone was sobbing. I couldn't tell who. All I remember is the light seemed to return, and the screeching wind stopped. I heard a bird chirp in the distance.

When I opened one eye I could see the sky was getting lighter. The room had returned to a normal temperature, the fading condensation retreating from the windowpanes. Melda stood looking out the rear porch door, her back to us, staring at the lake and the dock, mumbling something.

I think my dad stood up first. Then Kate, and slowly, the rest of us. He kept patting Bobby's front and back, to make sure the boy was okay.

"What was that?" he asked Melda.

"It's the lake that took him, but the house that won't let him go," she said, clearly enough for us all to hear. "I don't know if it will ever let him go."

She turned to look at us, her eyes dead and empty, speaking softly. "I said I would watch him. I was sitting right here on this porch, and only left for a second. Went upstairs to get a book. When I came back . . . he was gone. We looked everywhere. Took Papa two hours to find him. He was floating under the dock."

We all stared in disbelief. Mom gripped Bobby tighter.

"I don't understand," my father said. The scientist, the doctor, looking for a rational explanation for what he had just experienced.

She tilted her head, her gaze falling upon Bobby. Still speaking, barely above a whisper.

"I've often wondered, *Is it really him?* Or a cruel echo of what happened, sent to torture me? And what will happen, once I'm gone?"

The old woman shook her head slowly, as if trying to wake from a daydream. She blinked and turned her gaze to my father, eyes shaper now.

"Do yourself a favor and don't come back. He's got a long memory and a short temper. Whatever you think you saw, best to forget it." She motioned with her head for us to leave. We turned to walk out, the five of us together.

Melda spoke one last time as we got to the front door.

"Just make sure your boy leaves the green truck. He's going to want that back."

Bobby was holding the truck absent-mindedly in his hand. He gave it a horrified look, and then carefully put it on the floor. A grin crawled up the side of Melda's mouth.

"It always was his favorite," she said.

Chapter 8

Bertha

Margaret Mendel

My experience started when I was very young, maybe four or five years old. I'd wake up in the middle of the night and see a dog in my room. We didn't own a dog, and I wondered how it got into our house without my parents knowing. The golden spaniel would wag its tail, sit on its haunches, and sometimes come up close to me and sniff at my feet. Occasionally, too, I would wake up and a strange woman, an old lady with hair piled on top of her head, would be sitting in the chair where my mother sat to read bedtime stories to me. This woman didn't say anything and simply looked at me. And she never got out of the chair.

In the morning when I told my parents about these occurrences during the night, they said I had been dreaming. They assured me that no one could have gotten into the house. But these nighttime sightings continued for years and well into my college days. My visitors were different human characters and different animals, and though they were never threatening, when I told my friends about them, everyone agreed on the creepiness of such an event and were glad that this didn't happen to them. Some friends suggested that ghosts had lived in my childhood home.

Then, over the years, and especially after I'd married Don, a very logically minded man, and we had settled into the Upper West Side of New York City, the nighttime visitations stopped.

It's not that I didn't believe in ghosts; I just never thought about them and figured the odd incidents were really dreams. Ghosts, as far as I was concerned, were the stuff of fiction. And ghost stories were something that either scared the heck out of the reader looking for that kind of entertainment, or if the ghosts were kind and gentle, they gave comfort to the bereaved.

Well, my concept of ghosts was shot all to hell the day I caught one in a photograph. I realize now, you don't catch them, but they ensnare the unaware. They make you feel crazy, and you start looking for them everywhere.

Let me back up a bit. This last year was hell for me. The misery started when I caught my husband, Don, in bed with a young lady who lived down the hall from us. But finding him in bed with another woman was the easy part of the separation, because the bickering over assets turned into a real dog fight. Don had always been a penny pincher and closemouthed about bonuses and raises he'd received through his job. I suspected, though I could never prove it, that Don had secretly squirreled away funds. Sure enough, a forensic accountant helped me uncover Don's several secret bank accounts.

As the divorce proceeded, the judge, not happy learning about the hidden money, and the fact that I was the offended party, ruled in my favor, and I was awarded the lion's share of our savings, as well as the total of the secret bank accounts. Don would keep our one-bedroom Upper West Side co-op, and I was granted the cottage in the Adirondacks that we had recently purchased.

As soon as the final decree papers were signed, the money transferred into my bank account, and the cottage signed over to me, I high-tailed it out of town and headed for my new home in the Adirondacks.

I was now to live in a lovely, just-renovated lakefront cottage in the lower Adirondack region, less than a three-hour drive from the city. The owners had been eager to sell. Don and I had never asked why they were in such a hurry to rid themselves of the place, and we easily negotiated the price in our favor. The purchase took place a few weeks before I had found Don in bed with the neighbor. So, we'd never had a chance to stay even one night in the cottage.

Now this fine little place, nestled in a dense forest, was all mine, featuring a delightful, contemporary open-concept design with a small kitchen and a cozy living room combined. The house had two bedrooms— one to sleep in and the other I'd decided to turn into the study/workroom I'd always wanted. Large windows on either side of the front door faced out onto the lake, only a short walk from the cottage. A charming porch stretched out along the front of the house, and I called that my veranda.

My new home came unfurnished, and the first week I slept in a sleeping bag on an air mattress. The only drawback to the cottage was the clicking, snapping, and other odd sounds my new home made in the night. This wasn't anything to lose sleep over, but a couple of times the noises were akin to the sounds of someone walking around in the kitchen. The third night, I actually got out of my bed when I heard something rustling in the other bedroom. I wanted to make sure someone wasn't in the house with me. But nothing was there, and I went back to my sleeping bag.

I'm a freelance writer and photographer, and the first thing I did, besides hooking up my coffee machine, was set up a work area in the second bedroom. Before I left the city, I'd purchased a couple of do-it-yourself shelves and an easy- to-assemble worktable. All I really needed was my computer with Photoshop, and the very expensive printer that I treated as though it cost a million bucks.

But other than my workspace, this cottage needed furniture. I wanted a country look. So, I opted to shop at a local general dry goods store in the area that also sold used furniture. That didn't leave me with a lot of choices. Two couches were available, one I liked and one I hated. Easy choice. A pleasantly overstuffed armchair then caught my eye, and it went perfectly with the couch. After that, I fell in love with a round, authentic-looking Adirondack coffee table, with some weathering, which made it even more appealing. Then, too, while shuffling through a stack of quilts, I spotted a sign that read, "Handmade double-bed frame, constructed from a yellow birch tree on my property. Make an offer."

"Is this for real?" I asked the store owner, who had been following me around tallying my purchases.

"Yep, Mr. Fuller comes around with his handmade things from time to time. He's kind of a loner and doesn't want anything to do with the local craft dealers. So, he brings things to my shop. You interested?" she asked.

When the store owner pulled the headboard and footboard away from the wall, I knew right away I had to have it. The rough woodsy construction was exactly what I was looking for. After a few minutes calculating what I'd probably already spent, I made the store owner what I thought was a reasonable offer.

She cocked her head, gave a slight smile, and said, "It's yours."

The store owner added up all my purchases and handed me back my credit card. We confirmed a next-day delivery, but when I gave her my address, her demeanor changed. She raised one eyebrow, gave me a quizzical look, and said, "You renting or are you the new owner?"

"Owner," I replied.

"Can't seem to keep anyone in that place for very long."

"What do you mean?" I asked.

"Oh, it's nothing. It just seems a lot of folks want that place, and then quickly don't want that place. Go figure," she said.

"Something wrong with it?" I asked, my heart sinking.

"Probably just the wrong people making too quick a decision, and changing their minds," she said. "Ralph, my husband, could tell you more about the house. He grew up around here. Expect delivery tomorrow afternoon."

We arranged that her husband, who would do the delivery, would also put the bed together.

"Well, nice to meet you," she said. "My name is Tracy. Welcome. Come by for a visit and a cup of tea when you're settled in."

"Nice to meet you, too," I told her.

Satisfied that I'd had a good day of shopping, I stopped at the local grocery store to pick up some food and then headed back to the cottage. This was a perfect day to sit by the lakeside and eat lunch. The weather was ideal. The trees were just starting to change colors, and I could feel a hint of a chill in the air. I had no doubt in my mind that autumn would be beautiful up here. As I sat on a large boulder at the lakeside munching on a peanut butter and jelly sandwich, a very pregnant, scruffy looking dog came out of the underbrush. She slowly walked along the water's edge, then came closer to me. But I could tell her interest wasn't in me, because she was looking directly at my sandwich.

"You hungry?" I asked and reached out with the remaining half of my lunch. The dog hesitated at first. Then she cautiously walked toward me and gently took the offering, eating the peanut butter sandwich in one gulp.

Funny how humans sometimes talk to animals as though they might expect an answer, and I said, "You live around here?"

Of course, I received no reply, and the dog turned and walked back into the woods. "Well, see you later," I said.

Early the following afternoon, Ralph showed up with a pickup truck loaded with the items I'd purchased. And he'd brought a helper with him, a skinny, long-haired boy-man—couldn't tell which—who was half the girth of Ralph. I wrongly supposed that the larger man would do the bigger share of the heavy lifting, but the skinny, long-haired guy was the one who did most of the work.

Ralph didn't say a lot at first, and in no time the truck was unloaded. The last thing they brought into the cottage was the yellow birch bed frame and the mattress and box springs I'd also bought.

As Ralph and his skinny helper began to put the bed together, Ralph said, "They did a great job of fixing up this old place. I remember when it wasn't much more than a broken-down fishing cabin. Lots of feet have tromped across this floor," he said as he handed the skinny guy a bag of screws and a screwdriver.

"As the story goes," Ralph said, "this place used to be a speakeasy. I'm talking back in the 1920s, in my granddad's days. That old man told some wild stories about what went on back then. A woman, Bertha, ran the business. She was a bossy, hard-living woman who took no nonsense from anyone. Granddad had a lot of respect for her and said she could be as mean as a cougar or as gentle as a lamb. She kept a working whiskey still somewhere in these parts. All sorts of folks would sneak out here in the dead of night looking to carry off some booze, and I've heard tell that plenty of trouble could show up on the roads in and out of this place.

But Bertha kept a real close watch over her territory. She carried a pistol in a pocket of her apron and had a shotgun at the door. The big trouble came when a Canadian rum-running gang, with a lot of fire power, tried to take over her business. She was a sweet lady, but she supposedly killed a couple members of the gang. That's when this part of the Adirondacks wasn't so peaceful. But the law never intervened out here, and Bertha held on to her establishment as long as she could. But one day, she up and disappeared. Granddad said she probably was killed out of revenge. And she was never seen again. Some folks speculated back then that Bertha's buried out in the woods somewhere or maybe was dumped into the lake. And no one ever did find that still. After a while, things changed when Prohibition came to an end, and the old speakeasy just became a fishing shack." Ralph smiled in a friendly way.

"Now these days around this pretty lake, instead of whiskey, we have RV parking spots, camper facilities, and summer rentals. This is the time of the year folks start closing their places for the winter. In a week or two it's going to be pretty quiet around here. Tracy said you were going to be here year round. If you like the wild and quiet, you're in the right place."

Ralph shoved a hefty-sized screw into the sideboard of the bed frame and worked the screwdriver. "Yeah, my folks started running a general store and secondhand shop when I was a little tike. My dad always said part of the job was like being a welcome wagon for the newcomers and sometimes it was like publishing a local newspaper. We know when folks get married, when they have babies, and if their babies die. We sell them things, and we buy their stuff. We know when they're upgrading and when they are downgrading. Sometimes folks give up prized possessions to pay the rent, sometimes to hide a gambling problem or a drinking addiction. Sure as hell, folks come and go. But Tracy and me, we're like those boulders you see stuck in the mountains; we aren't going nowhere."

Ralph got up from the floor, screwdriver in hand. He gave the bed a good shake. "This is one solid bed," he said. "It's strong enough to hold an elephant. Old man Fuller's work is no joke. His goods probably will outlive us all."

The skinny guy and Ralph packed up their tools.

"You couldn't tell by the way it looks now, but a lot of history resides in this old place you just bought," Ralph said. "It's really all dressed up and fancy now. Hope it suits you. By the way, Tracy threw in a set of new sheets for the bed. She's like that, likes to give welcoming gifts to the newcomers. Come by the store when you're settled in. We'll help acquaint you to the area."

"Thanks, I will."

So far, the skinny guy hadn't said a word, but as he got into the pickup truck, he pointed out into the westerly expanse of the lake. "Looks like we're going to have a storm. Might be a big one," he said and closed the pickup door.

As they drove away, a gust of wind blew up from the lake. The top of the fir trees whipped wildly back and forth, and a deep rumble of thunder sounded in the distance.

I love a good storm. Even as a kid, storms excited me, and I watched as the blue sky turned gray, and craggy black clouds moved closer to me. A shard of illumination lit up the western sky as a bolt of lightning split open a dark cloud. The shrub that grew on the other side of my parked car rustled and shook as the wind reached down to the earth, and the rain, which had started as a light mist, quickly turned into a downpour.

I ran to my veranda and stood under the overhanging roof as the rain splashed everywhere. The storm moved closer. The lightning strikes became more frequent, and understanding storms as I did, I knew standing in an open area wasn't safe. As I turned to go into the cottage, something caught my eye as a flash of lightning filled the darkened sky with a bright amber glow. I saw the dog that I'd fed my sandwich to the day before creep across the path that led to the lake and disappear into the underbrush. This was no night to be out in the open, but the animal didn't seem to have much choice in the matter.

The storm came even closer, and I went into the cottage as a crash of lightning lit up the darkness. By the time I'd gotten into the cottage, my pant legs were soaking wet. But the wet was a good wet, a fun wet, a storm wet, and I loved it.

Once inside, I felt as though I had come home. The couch and over-stuffed easy chair were a natural fit for the room, and the Adirondack table couldn't have been more perfect. I made a cup of coffee and plunked myself down onto the couch. The storm made the silhouettes of the young saplings outside my windows and the shadows of the hearty old fir trees appear to be dancing across the illuminated sky. The storm was a delicious entertainment to watch as I sipped my coffee.

After a while, I became restless and went into my newly established workroom. I hadn't taken a lot of photographs yet since moving up here. It felt as if most of my time had been spent shopping and recuperating from the nastiness of the divorce. Silly me—I thought a few days out of the city would get me back to my old self. But the disappointment and hurt lingered. It might take me longer than I'd thought, or hoped, to recover from all that had gone on in the last year.

The photos I'd taken in the previous week had been downloaded to the computer, yet I hadn't looked at any of them. I opened the computer. I had several dozen new downloads. Some were practice shots of the trees and river in the morning light, my favorite time of the day. A couple of photos were of the little flower garden just outside the front door. I remembered one afternoon following a painted lady butterfly around the garden. It was a fine specimen, with its orange and black markings. The hollyhock that grew at the side of the cottage was in the end stage of its flowering, and the butterfly kept returning to the last blooms on the top of the flower's stalk.

A crack of thunder sounded overhead. I had been so involved with the photos that the storm had become like background music. But this time the rumble of thunder was so close that my cottage vibrated, and it sounded was though buckets of water were being thrown against the window in my workroom.

The storm lingered overhead for quite some time. The lightning flashed repeatedly, and the thunder rumbled with an amazingly powerful gusto. Then the storm sounded as though it was moving away, and I returned to my computer screen and the butterfly.

As I enlarged the photograph with the butterfly, a curious image appeared to one side of the hollyhock. At first, I thought I was looking at a refraction of the sunlight on the lens. My lenses are very well cared for, so I know this was no distortion from a smear. I enlarged the photo a little more, and I couldn't believe my eyes. What I was looking at was a face. Blurry, but it was a human image. Yet the figure appeared nearly transparent. I used a magnifying glass to heighten a closer view. The image was real. It was the face of a woman, and she was looking directly at me.

My heart raced. What the heck was this? I looked again. My eyes had not deceived me. I saw a woman, a ghostly image of a woman standing next to the hollyhock. Both the butterfly sitting on a leaf of the plant and the reflection of the woman's face were undeniable. I quickly went through the other photos that had recently been downloaded. The woman's figure didn't appear in any of the other photos.

The storm wasn't totally over yet. A slight rumbling of thunder sounded in the distance, while bright lightning illuminated the windows from time to time with soft quick flashes of light. The rain had calmed somewhat, but the windows still ran with water.

My cottage felt different somehow now as I heard the storm moving away. This was the first storm of my new beginning, and I felt as though I was being cleansed. A peacefulness came over me even after the startling discovery of the ghostly image of the woman.

But then, as quickly as I'd felt the calm and peace, came a clamor, clanking, and even something that sounded like gunshots emanating from the walls of my cottage. A ringing sounded in my ears, and a heady smell of body odor wafted across my nose. Then it sounded as though the front door of the cottage had been opened and slammed shut. And yet, I was totally alone. Something crashed in the kitchen. I rushed to see what might have caused this. I turned on the light. Nothing. Nothing at all. Laughter and murmuring voices then filled my ears with a raucous drunken revelry as the windows facing the lake displayed the turbulent water in an eerie amber glow from a flashing lightning strike.

And then I heard a faint scratching at the door. But how could I have heard this scratching with all the noise coming from the walls of the cottage? Yet, there it was. Softly, scratching. And then a whimper. The sound was not a human one. I leaned my ear against the doorsill. Again, I heard the soft scratching and the high-pitched, whiny whimper.

I opened the door only wide enough for a mere breath to slip into my cottage. And I saw, through that very slim crack, a dog sitting on my doorstep. It whimpered again and scratched at the door, as though begging, entreating me to open the door wider. And as I did, for I couldn't resist those begging eyes, the dog, as miserable as any dog could be that had endured this storm, stepped into my cottage, dripping wet, yet as gracious and elegant as any animal might be in such a state.

I quickly went for a towel and dried the dog. Startled as I was by the crazy noises that continued to come from everywhere in my house, when I rubbed the rainwater from the wet animal, I was aware of the small bubbles of wiggling jelly kicking around in the dog's insides. She was pregnant. And as far as I could tell from the activity going on in this female's body, these pups were about to be delivered; with or without me, they were on their way.

The raucous noises continued to rebound from everywhere in the cottage. Crazy as it was, with the storm, the dog giving birth, and the ghostly photograph of the woman by the hollyhock, I was not unhinged. Everything made sense to me. I remembered, as a child, the confusion of all that I saw in the night, but back then I believed in everything. Anything was possible. Nothing frightened me. As an adult, I had learned not to accept what I couldn't understand and live in denial. Now, as I settled into my newly purchased overstuffed chair, I listened to the trailing end of the storm and the quieting of the strange sounds now softly coming from the cottage walls, and I accepted it all.

I'll never know what brought those extraordinary events on that night during that thunderstorm. I could venture a guess. But in the matter of ghostly images, what is there to say, because they are not of this world. Yet, I think I always had an accepting bone in my body for believing in unworldly beings. They had come to my childhood bed. They'd sat in my mother's chairs. They'd even smelled my feet. So, now I live in a mix of real and otherworldly. I no longer push away what I do not understand but accept that I am a part of it.

The glorious mountains of the Adirondacks and the multitude of lakes and ponds enclosed within the Blue Line now feed my photography. My cottage is alive to me, and it breathes with the seasons. I'm settled in and very comfortable. The dog that gave birth during the stormy night is now my companion, and I've named her Peanut Butter. Her pups are growing strong, and Ralph and Tracy have found homes for them when they are ready to leave their mother.

The quiet of the lake and surrounding forest with the absence of summer vacationers has lured the wildlife out into the open. Deer, skunks, and even a badger and a fox walk along my pathway to the lake for a drink during all hours of the day and night. I hear wild animals call in the night, and sometimes Peanut Butter becomes agitated and calls back to them, a warning not to enter her territory. I've also realized that the ghostly woman standing next to the hollyhock plant is most likely Bertha. I can't know what really happened to her, though it is evident to me that she is still very much a part of this area. I live in her speakeasy. We share a delight in possessing our surroundings. Over the last months I've made peace with many things, and I know now that I am exactly where I was always meant to be.

Then one day, just before a heavy snow was projected to hit our area, I took a photograph of my sweet cottage in a beautiful afternoon light, a magic hour of light that is a gift to the photographer. Such a moment doesn't last long, but it is glorious and precious because it doesn't happen that often. That evening when the snow began to fall, I downloaded my latest photographs onto the computer. And I wasn't surprised to see Bertha in one of those photographs sitting on my veranda in the companion chair next to my Adirondack rocker. Strong and healthy, not translucent, Bertha looked right into the camera. At me.

CHAPTER 9

Ghost Bear?

W. K. Pomeroy

For the first morning in six months and twenty-two days, hours away from anything resembling a real city, Burton allowed himself to breathe and feel like a real human being again.

Looking out at the mist hovering over Fourth Lake through thick prescription glasses, he saw out past the metal dock about sixty feet before a wall of fog made it impossible to make out any details. The island easily visible later in the day had vanished into a gray-white cloud. He found it oddly beautiful in the dim morning light, almost mysterious, while entirely natural, then . . . the scent of rotting garbage assaulted his nose, making his stomach feel queasy.

It took him a moment to realize where the putrid odor had to be coming from. He moved cautiously down the wooden stairs from the porch deck to the ground level. Something did not feel right.

The way this camp had been built, even a tall person like Burton could comfortably walk into the storage area beneath the cabin, which was supported by unpainted concrete blocks.

When he saw the trash had been ripped from the secured heavy plastic containers, he immediately guessed an adventurous racoon or perhaps even a whole family had found their way in.

He put his hand out to examine a long tear across the side of one of the thick gray bins. The rip seemed much too big to have been caused by a racoon.

How in hell did I not wake up with a bear doing this much damage right beneath me?

He had not allowed himself anything to drink last night, and his medicines if anything tended to keep him awake rather than put him to sleep.

He decided to call the camp's rental agency, rather than the police or the park rangers, at least for this first incident.

The next morning, dawn broke with the same thick cloud of fog encroaching from the lake. Out on the porch, Burton sniffed at the air. Fresh delight entered his lungs and nothing else. Below the porch no new destruction shattered his peaceful moment. Burton dismissed the incident from his mind and set about surviving the day.

After a productive morning working on compiling his thirteen hand-written journals into something that approximated the beginning of a book, he decided to take advantage of a beautiful late spring afternoon by eating his lunch out on the dock.

He carefully balanced a paper plate the packaging claimed to be "heavy duty" with one hand, trying not to let his roast beef sandwich, handful of Lays potato chips, and three juicy dill pickles spill while holding onto a glass of herbal iced tea in his other hand.

He almost made it to the edge of the water when he saw it; impressed deeply in the gravel-like sand, right next to the stone step-up onto the aluminum dock that extended into the lake, was a paw-print more than double the size of his foot.

Putting his food down on the dock he ran back up to the cabin for his cell phone.

Staring at the print through the camera app, Burton did a quick mental inventory of all the bear prints he had seen in his life in person or doing research online. His experience put the number around twenty. None were anywhere close to the size of this one.

Ten days later, after several long conversations with all the local enforcement agencies, and four more incidents with destroyed trash containers, Burton felt some satisfaction when an Adirondack Park ranger finally knocked on his cabin door.

"Hello, sir, are you Mr. Aimes?"

Burton nodded.

"I'm responding to your reports of a dangerous bear sighting?" The little patch above the man's badge displayed his name, Ranger Randall T. Ameris.

"Thank you for coming," Burton said as he stepped out onto the porch. "Let me show you what's been happening."

He led the officer down into the area below the porch. Burton noticed that, despite being taller than him by a couple inches, the officer walked like a hunter, barely making a sound.

"The damn thing keeps ripping into the garbage cans, even when they are sealed and chained. There wasn't even any food-trash in them this last time."

"But it found food in them before, right?"

Burton nodded.

"This one has a good memory." Ranger Randall knelt next to the heavy-duty metal cans that had replaced the plastic ones and examined the gashes. "Looks like you've got a big one, too. Why don't you just keep your garbage inside?"

Burton's guts twisted. "Yeah," even in his own head his protest sounded weak, "I tried that a couple days. It roared when there were no cans down here. The sound almost gave me a heart attack."

Randall nodded. "Maybe some loud noise to scare it away, like a radio? Most of the time a bear is way more afraid of you than you are of it."

"By the size of this one's claws, I don't think it is afraid of much."

The ranger ran his fingers along one of the long rips in the middle of the trash receptacle. "I see what you mean." He chuckled under his breath. "I'd love to see one this big. Reminds me of Nyah-Gwaheh."

The way the ranger said the word with a ring of reverence sounded odd to Burton's ears. It was the same tone he'd heard when a young

103

priest introduced him to Cardinal Joseph a decade earlier for an article about the problems increasing the size of Catholic congregations. "What is Nyah-Gwaheh?"

Randall's voice quieted a little, like he was remembering something from his childhood. "It is a Haudenosaunee legend of a monstrous bear, so large the strongest braves could not pierce its hide, so powerful it could kill a deer in one swipe, so hungry it almost starved the tribe before the most powerful warriors united and drove it into the sky."

"You wouldn't happen to know where I can find a tribe of warriors to drive off my bear, would you?" Burton let a little laugh escape at his own joke. It felt good to be able to laugh.

"'Fraid not, sir, but if you really think this is a dangerous bear, I'd suggest you get a trail cam so we know what we are really dealing with."

"I'm from down near Utica. Where would I get one around here, or do I have to drive all the way back?"

"There are a few places in Old Forge. I like Mountainman the best myself."

"Okay, I'll try that. Anything else I can do?"

"Get your trapping license, and get a few bear traps."

Burton couldn't tell if the ranger was serious or not. He wasn't the first one to suggest a bear trap, nor would he be the last.

Burton slid the chip into his laptop computer to look at what the little camera he'd purchased had picked up sometime during the night when the newest garbage cans had been ripped into again.

He expected to find a bunch of files on the screen's directory, but he found only a single fifty-three-second video file. He clicked the "Play" icon. A faded black-and-white picture of the underside of the porch came into focus. Something had tripped the motion detector to make the camera start recording, yet he saw no bear, no racoon, not even an oversized rat.

He heard a deep guttural growl just before a wide slash appeared on the brand-new heavy plastic trash container with nothing in it.

Still no bear or other animal appeared on his monitor.

It was not until hours later, watching the video for the fifth time, that he realized the camera he had purchased didn't record audio.

♣♣♣

As soon as the man picked up, Burton blurted, "Darin, I need your help."

"Excuse me, who is this?"

"Burton Aimes."

"Who?"

"I did that story on you and that . . . eccentric woman after all those bodies were dug up on Exley Avenue."

"I . . . ummm . . . that was a pretty busy time."

"I interviewed you at Rio Grande over a long lunch. We ate at the booth in the back corner."

"Oh, yeah, I remember you now." The younger man's voice still did not sound completely sure.

"Are you on a case right now?"

Darin hesitated a bit too long before answering, "I've got a few irons in the fire, but I could be available."

"I'm staying in a cabin up at Fourth Lake. I've got something weird I think you and Louisa might be able to help me with."

"Who the hell is Louisa?"

"That silver-haired woman with the scar eyebrows."

"You mean Lulu."

"Yep, that's her." Burton struggled a moment then remembered the woman's last name. "Lulu . . . Jonesh, right? The press called her a spiritualist."

"Mr. Aimes . . ."

"I told you before, please call me Burton."

"Burton, you do know that woman is completely nuts, right?"

"I remember, but I find myself in a situation that is more than a little nuts."

"Tell me about it."

Burton started to speak, hesitated, and then restarted. "I'd rather tell you both, face to face."

"I'm not even sure where she is staying right now."

"If you two can get up here, I'll pay you double your normal rate, just for the consult."

"I don't know . . ."

"Plus gas and expenses."

Darin paused, then let out a deep sigh. "What's the address up there?"

The afternoon had turned overcast by the time Burton finished his show-and-tell on what had been happening. The three of them sat at an all-weather round glass table with an oversized umbrella over it off to the side of the porch.

Burton had almost forgotten how odd Lulu looked. The deep scars where her eyebrows once had been made her face look somehow alien, like one of those original *Star Trek* races; close to human, but not. It felt like she had been talking nonstop for an hour.

"Mr. Reporter-Man has got something that looks like a bear, but isn't a bear, not there when it should be, but claws through things, leaves impressions in the earth like a real live animal, and does violence like a person, but animals don't have ghosts like people do, at least I don't think they do. They don't talk to me like people-ghosts, at least they haven't so far, or maybe I've learned to ignore them, the last set of pills the people at that big brick house gave me even quieted the people-ghosts for a while, made them all go down to this really soft whisper that I can't quite understand, maybe if I didn't take the red pills I'd hear the ghost bears singing, or if I didn't take the aqua pills I could understand all the backwards lyrics. What do you think, Detective Mercury? Is that what I should do? Overall, it seems like a bad plan."

Darin's expression clearly read, *You see what I mean, she's crazy.* His voice had a resigned quality. "Look, I get that the video glitch is weird. The image you took of the paw print on the shore definitely looks like some kind of big animal. I do get it that this is all strange."

Burton nodded, without replying.

"I'd really like to take your money for this job, but please, Mr. Aimes, can you tell me what the hell you think I can really do about any of it?"

Burton's answer came slowly. "I don't know. I came out here to relax and write."

"Having something mauling the underside of your porch doesn't sound too relaxing, nor does setting a bear trap where you or people visiting you might accidentally step in it."

Burton dipped his head to look Darin squarely in the eyes. "I guess I thought if this all were something normal you could figure it out."

"Maybe I could."

"And if it was something, well, for lack of a better word let's say, *supernatural,* then she could help you figure it out. I remember from our interview you were good at surveillance. How about you do that for a night or two?"

"And if I don't find anything?"

"You still get paid, plus expenses."

"I have your word?"

Burton paused then mumbled, "It's not like I've got kids to leave my money to."

Darin cocked his head to one side as if he thought he had misheard something. "What did you say?"

Before he could respond, Lulu started back in. "He said he had no kids, though that isn't quite true. A long time ago he had a daughter, cherubic girl with puffy pink cheeks who liked to dance, swirled and swirled around for hours without end, but she and her mom in the blue flower dress died; a sad, awful, messy accident. Nobody's fault. Like a beautiful butterfly for short seasons, beautiful and gone, no cocoon and g—"

Darin put a hand over Lulu's mouth.

"I guess I can keep watch a couple nights. Do we really need her?"

"Just in case."

Lulu's cat-like tongue licked the palm of Darin's hand where he held it in front of her mouth.

He reacted instinctively, dropping it to rub her saliva off on his khaki pants.

"Just in case. Mr. Reporter-Man said just in case. I'm the insurance policy, the gifted one who keeps on giving, the listener in dark places where no one wants to hear—"

Darin cut her off. "The one who never knows how to shut up when she should."

♣♣♣

Burton slept better that evening than any night since his first at the cabin. A light rain drowned out many of the normal forest sounds.

Darin kept a watchful eye on several monitors set up in the back of his Windstar van. The different angles generated by the hidden cameras he had positioned strategically under the porch should have covered every direction.

Lulu had taken three Diazepam pills, which allowed her to pass out on the pull-out couch in the main room.

As the first beams of golden morning light illuminated hot dust in his rented bedroom, Burton woke to go to the bathroom, run a comb through his fading gray hair, set his glasses atop his nose properly, and take his morning medicines.

He tip-toed into the kitchen, trying not to disturb Lulu's soft sleep breathing on the couch.

He poured a pitcher of filtered water into the coffee maker and listened to its reassuring gurgle for a second before heading out the door to go check on Darin.

The outside air did not smell of rot. Since they had not put any garbage out the previous night, there was no reason it should.

He walked up the slight hill to the parking area. Fifteen feet away from the private investigator's two-tone brown-red mini-van, he heard a growling sound. Burton overcame the animal fear that temporarily gripped his stomach when he realized what the roof-rattling nasal sound had to be: Darin's snore.

Burton considered banging hard on the door and shocking the man awake. *It would be really funny. On the other hand, no one other than the two of us would see it.* He had not resolved the internal debate, when his thoughts went a different direction. He noticed the van leaning a little oddly, like one wheel had been parked in a hole. Any thought of a prank went out the window when he moved to the other side of the vehicle and saw the back passenger tire had been shredded.

"Darin, wake up." He tapped gently on the side of the vehicle.

Almost immediately, the side door slid open. "What is it?"

Burton pointed at the back tire.

"What the hell?" Darin hopped out of the van. First, he examined the flattened tire, then the ground around it. Only a single oversized print had survived the previous evening's rain, and even that was half full of water. "How did I not hear something doing that?"

Burton shook his head. "If I knew that, I wouldn't need your help."

Around the little breakfast bar in the kitchen Burton and Darin spoke in hushed tones, trying not to wake Lulu.

"The trail camera didn't activate at all last night."

"That makes sense; I didn't see anything on the monitors."

Burton refrained from saying, "*while you were awake.*" "I don't get it. Why would it go after your van?"

"Have you pissed anyone off lately? I mean going after my tire seems more like a human thing than a bear thing.

"You saw the print."

"People have been known to fake prints." Darin put his hand to the side of his head as if something had jogged loose. "The fact that you keep finding only one print also points more to a person than an animal. Maybe someone who knows how to edit video tinkered with your trail cam, and that's what . . ."

"It doesn't explain the roar that woke me up or that I heard the first time I played the video."

"The one at night could have been something someone recorded." Darin paused. "I can't explain the other one though, unless you imagined it."

"I didn't! It was a real as you talking to me here."

Burton's raised voice elicited a high-pitched groan from the couch.

Both men turned their heads to see Lulu half roll so her head squished into one of the pillows.

Darin lowered his voice to a softer whisper. "Okay, let's assume you didn't imagine it."

"Because that's the truth." Even with his volume low, a hint of anger crept into his response.

"Then there have to be some electronics in here; probably both a mic and a speaker."

Burton nodded, following Darin's logic. "And probably a camera, too."

Darin nodded his head toward the porch door.

They both stepped outside.

The beauty of the view struck Burton. Even on a gloomy morning with dark rainclouds all around, the lake and the island had a certain pull, that if he had been a painter he would have wanted to capture on canvas.

Darin kept his voice down despite the relative safety of the deck. "I'll do an electronics sweep after Loopy wakes up. No need to hurry that annoyance." He took a deep breath of the moist air. "I had another thought about motive. Could the owner want you out of here for some reason? Like maybe they got a better rental agreement after you signed up?"

Burton started to dismiss that possibility, then stopped and took a moment to consider it. "I did call the rental agent back when all this started. They were really apologetic. They put in the heavier cans, and said they'd pay for any others when it kept up." He shook his head like he was trying to get the thought out of it. "No, it doesn't make sense that it would be them."

"Then who? Do you have any ongoing exposés?"

"No." He paused, deciding how much of his personal trauma he wanted to tell this man. "I had my last byline about four months ago on the website. Not many even saw that last piece. I don't think I left any serious open grudges behind from that part of my life."

Darin shrugged his broad shoulders. "Well, it was just a thought. If we could figure some kind of normal motive, then . . ."

"Where am I? Where am I? *Where am I?*" Lulu's rising screams interrupted everything.

The two men hustled into the building.

The white-haired woman sat on the edge of the coauch with her back as stiff as a board. Her wide-open eyes, with tiny pinprick pupils, darted around as if a predator would catch her at any moment.

Darin clasped her hand gently in a way that showed much more kindness than Burton had ever seen from him. His kept his voice deep and soothing. "It's okay. You are safe. You are at Mr. Aimes's cabin at Fourth Lake. Take a deep breath. No one here is going to hurt you."

She inhaled deeply before letting it out in a big whoosh.

Her eyes focused on Darin's. The flush in her cheeks began to fade. It looked like she wanted to speak, yet her moving mouth produced no sound, almost like her earlier scream had used up all her words.

"Take your time. Don't stop breathing. You are in a safe place, near water. It's so calming and relaxing."

Her chest heaved up and down a few more times. The panic in her eyes eased. Her posture began to relax a little. The voice that came out of her mouth sounded more like a little girl than that of an older woman. "They don't want us here."

"Oh, shit," Darin cursed without taking his focus off Lulu's eyes. "Who doesn't want us here?"

As if time made everything move in slow motion, she turned her head toward Burton. "They don't want us to interrupt his end of *laulhá*."

"My what? My life?" Burton heard the panic in his own voice.

That light little girl voice replied, "No silly, your *laulhá*, your only-ness. It's so simple. You just have to . . ." Her voice trailed off to silence.

Burton kinked his neck like it needed to crack. "Nothing about this is simple."

"Sure it is." Lulu's voice and rambling energy sounded like the woman he had met previously. "You just have to understand that everyone is what they are, until they aren't anymore. Sometimes chronicling other people's yesterdays don't add up to todays. If we keep moving forward without mixing everything up, we'll see who got to where and how, but bears in the sky can't be real today unless someone really wants them to be, like a little girl without her voice. Do you understand what I'm saying?"

Burton took off his glasses and cleaned them on his shirt. "I have no idea what you are talking about."

Lulu turned back to Darin. "Did I forget my morning meds?"

He released her hand. "I'm afraid you did."

🌲🌲🌲

A little after noon Darin concluded his sweep for cameras, speakers, and other electronic surveillance tools.

While Darin had been walking around waving the wand that looked like something TSA used to make sure people could not hijack a plane, every little beep allowed Burton a flash of hope that a rational explanation for everything existed. Every time Darin shook his head or told him it was just the satellite wire, the baseboard heating element, or an ungrounded outlet, the hope shrank.

Eventually Darin shrugged his shoulders again. "Sorry, dude. If someone's using AV tech in here, it is better than my scanner tools."

"Thanks for trying. I'll pay for one more night of surveillance, then maybe I'll just find another cabin."

"Fair enough."

Lulu wandered in from the porch holding an empty iced tea cup. She moved toward the refrigerator. She talked without looking at him. "They didn't really want you to leave, just us. I think they'll follow you if you leave, but they won't follow us—not even the great bear. That's weird. I can barely remember. When you make the star trip, it'll be better if it is from here, without the warriors chasing you though. Whoever the warriors are. War-E-Ors, is there an *or* to war? Everything seems to be electronic today, even what my mom used to call ice-boxes." She opened the refrigerator door, pulled out the pitcher of iced tea, and refilled her cup. "The storm will be here in a little less than an hour." She shifted her focus to Darin. "Can I watch it from out there? I promise not to rip my clothes off and run out in it again."

Darin responded without any humor in his voice. "As long as you promise. We don't want any of Mr. Aimes's neighbors calling the police."

"I promise." She crossed her heart, went back out on the porch, and sat in one of the Adirondack chairs facing the water.

Occasional thunder accompanied their dinner. Sheets of rain descended from the sky, splashing into Fourth Lake more like an invasion of tiny pebbles than a combining of water sources.

For a pleasant change of pace, Lulu seemed to be listening to something far in the distance without talking.

Darin swallowed a bite of moose meat stew. "I hope the rain doesn't short out the cameras tonight."

"They're pretty well covered down there."

"For a normal rain you're right, but look at it out there; half the time wind is blowing the raindrops sideways."

A flash of lightning crackled across the sky over the lake, searing the image into the back of Burton's eyes for a long moment. "I see your point. We can go down and look them over after we finish eating." He pointed to Lulu's almost untouched bowl of stew. "My famous moose stew not good enough for you?" He grinned at the unintentional rhyme.

"Tasted fine, better than fine even, tasty for meat. Now be quiet, I'm trying to figure out the song."

Darin's face betrayed a hint of concern. "Lulu, did you take your dinner-time meds?"

She glared at him.

"You need to take them."

"They get in the way of the music translation, transposing, transition from something to nothing and back again, or is it the other way around?" She began humming something that might remotely have been musical.

"Come on, Lulu, you need to take them."

"You take them then, not going to understand anything right if I take them. Not going to picture the big see, or is that bass ackwards, too?"

Darin began to open the purse containing all Lulu's pills. "Which ones are for dinner time?"

She moved too quickly for anyone to stop her, grabbing the bag out of Darin's hands. "I can do it. I can. I know which ones. You don't." She took out three prescription bottles, opened them, and removed a pill from each.

Burton could have sworn she had four bottles the night before, but figured one of them might have been her sleep medicine.

"Give me ten more minutes to listen, please, then I'll take them, cross my heart and hope for pie."

Darin almost smiled. "I'll give you five minutes, then Mr. Aimes and I need to go check a couple things."

"Okay dope-yay. We got a deal." She held out her hand, and Darin took it gently and kissed the back of it.

"Thank you, Lulu."

🌲🌲🌲

Trying not to slip on the wet stairs, Burton carried a metal breakfast-in-bed tray with a big plastic bowl containing all the leftover stew down to the area under the porch where Darin went to check his equipment.

Water flowed across the cement floor less than a finger-width deep, not even deep enough to drown a mouse.

Darin looked up when Burton ducked under the cover of the porch. He held one of his surveillance cameras in his hand. "This is the only one that got wet, and it's working okay."

"Nice."

"It's letting up a little now, so I think they'll be good for the night."

"Good to know." Burton looked down at the big bowl of stew. "While I was cleaning up, I got an idea. I thought if I put the rest of the meat from tonight's dinner down here out in the open where the bear wouldn't have to tear anything open, maybe we'd get a better pic?"

"It can't hurt."

"Where's the best place to put it?"

"The lenses are all focused on your trash cans, so right in front of them."

"Sounds good." Burton set down the food. "What do you think, will the rain make it more likely or less likely that we'll see something tonight?"

Darin's familiar shoulder shrug communicated "*we'll see*" as clearly as any words could.

Burton awoke with that odd sensation of being someplace else, someplace unfamiliar; like he'd physically been in a dream and just transported back to the real world.

Steady rain pounded on the tin roof without the punctuation of thunder. The rat-a-tat sound felt comforting, until he realized a higher-pitched noise accompanied the patter. He let the sound come into focus, tuning out the rain. It did not work at first. Only when he listened to the song in the rhythm of the raindrops did it clarify for him: a lullaby, a love song, a ballad without words in the strictest sense of language.

He stepped out of bed forgetting to put on the clothes he had laid out to jump into if the bear made its presence known. As he moved down the hallway wearing only his underwear, the unsong grew clearer without actually getting louder.

Lulu stood in front of the couch with that same stiff posture he'd seen before. The spiritsound came from her. Her open eyes did not seem to recognize him as he got closer. She stared up toward the roof not moving, yet singing.

She still looked like Lulu, yet for the first time Burton saw her as beautiful.

He wanted to reach out and touch her. He lifted his hand. Something deep inside at a primal level made him feel afraid. He blinked his eyes twice, wondering if she might disappear. When she remained, oh so gently, he put his hand on her cheek.

Her skin felt soft, smooth, and warm—not at all what he would expect from Lulu. Touching her reminded him how long it had been since he had caressed a woman's face; not since Raelyn. Perhaps his thinking of her opened the portal. Perhaps she had been calling to him from the beginning. He didn't understand it. He only knew that she was there.

Hello husband. His wife's voice became part of the unsong.

"Rae?" He knew her, was sure of her, but could not quite make himself believe.

Yes.

He had so much he wanted to say. It all tried to boil up out of him at once. What he said was "I love you."

I know.

"I've missed you so much."

We've been with you.

He started crying then. "Dove is with you?"

Yes, she is.

It almost overwhelmed him. For the briefest of moments, he almost forgot . . . they died. "I'll be with you soon."

We know.

"The doctors said a year at most. That was more than six months ago."

We know. That is why we came to be with you.

"You came?"

We followed you here, near the water's edge, where the veil is thinnest.

"I don't understand."

Thank you for feeding Nyah-Gwaheh. He was so hungry, he kept chasing us away from you.

"Nyah-Gwaheh?" He asked the question before the memory of the park ranger's story kicked in. "The bear spirit?"

Yes. Once these were his lands and your need let him return.

"My need?"

For us.

"I do need you."

And now, as long as you feed him, we will be with you. You don't have to rush to be with us.

A sense of shame washed over him as he thought of what he had planned to do after he finished his memoir.

He felt her begin to fade away from him. He grabbed onto something that didn't make sense to him.

"If the bear is a ghost, why does he need food?"

Her answer felt like laughter, not just his wife's laughter, but also his daughter's.

The great bear isn't a ghost. He was chased into the sky, but at heart he is still a hungry bear.

Her answer didn't make sense to him, but he accepted it because it came from her. The rhythm of the rain began to change, and again he felt her shifting away.

"Don't leave me. I need you."

We will help sustain you. We always love you.

"Are you sure you don't need us here anymore?" Darin seemed truly distressed about driving away and leaving Burton in this weird place, especially after last night's stew mysteriously vanished without anything being picked up by the cameras.

Burton leaned into the van window. "I'll be fine. I cannot thank you two enough." He looked at Lulu one last time. It was an odd phenomenon that even though she had reverted to her crazy fast-talking self, she somehow still had a beauty to her that he had not understood or appreciated before. "Now you'd better go cash that check before it bounces."

The corners of Darin's mouth pulled up in a half grin. "Don't worry, I will, and if you need anything," he waved his hand around at the cabin and the open sky, "of this nature . . ."

"I know who to call."

As they drove back to civilization, Lulu talked and talked and talked, even after Darin turned the radio up to eleven.

Two years later, Darin found himself reading Burton's obituary.

He apparently died peacefully from complications of a virulent form of leukemia. According to the obit, he published three books since they had parted ways, one of which briefly made an appearance on *The New York Times* best-seller list.

I guess he lived a good life after we left him. Ghost bear or no ghost bear, he was a pretty cool guy, and he paid well. I'll have to remember to tell Lulu about his passing the next time we meet.

Chapter 10

The Great White Stag

Lorena A. Sins

Lake Placid, 1897

Samoset stood behind the rough plank table set up in the backyard of the Northwoods Inn and stared down at a severed bear's paw that lay upon it. It was a big paw. The black claws that curved out from the equally black and glossy fur of the paw were long: the longest was almost as long as Samoset's little finger. He touched the claw, then picked up the paw with his right hand and gingerly laid in it his left. It felt heavy and cold but still pliable. He held it gently, as he might hold the hand of a dying grandmother. He thought he could feel the ghost of life in the paw; it was inert, but in a different way from a stone or a piece of wood. It was moving and alive once. "My relative. I'm sorry," Samoset whispered to the spirit of the bear.

Suddenly, a meaty hand, as well padded as a bear's paw in September, clamped down heavily on Samoset's shoulder. "He was a big one, wasn't he?" a voice, bluff and hearty, asked him.

Samoset turned his head to look at the man addressing him, though his ears and nose both told him who it was. If the voice hadn't been unmistakable, the odor of whiskey, cigars, and strong cologne would have warned him of the presence of J. Winston "Stone" Ballinger of New York. As a guest at the Northwoods Inn, where Samoset worked as a tracker and guide for those who wanted to hunt in the North Woods but lacked the skill and competence to do so safely and in comfort, Ballinger was Samoset's employer at the moment, and the Algonquain guide thoroughly despised him.

Samoset placed the paw carefully back onto the table next to its mate. "Yes, he was, Mr. Ballinger," he replied. To himself he thought, *You are like a rabid wolf, killing all living things that come in your path.* Samoset was a hunter himself, killing moose, deer, and bear each fall and bringing them back to his family's cabin so his mother could preserve the meat for the winter. But he never killed more than his family needed. They were thankful to the animals who fed them and would not kill only for the pleasure of it. This white man was very different.

"Not as big as the one I shot back in July, though. A monster, that one was. Once his pelt has been properly prepared, that one's going in my office in Manhattan. Full equipment intact, Natty my boy: fangs, fur, and claws there in my office for all eyes to see." He chuckled. "Should give my business rivals a turn, seeing the monster my gun brought down." He picked up the paw that Samoset had just set down, examined it briefly, then tossed it back on the table. "The hide of this one will do for a lap robe in my new automobile, but I want you to boil down the paws and extract the claws." He looked up sharply. "You fellows know how to do that, eh? Leahy told me that you do."

"Mr. Leahy told you right, Mr. Ballinger," Samoset replied. "I can do that for you." He liked Tom Leahy and was glad for the job that helped him help his widowed mother support his younger siblings, but Leahy liked to tell tall tales to his guests about the secret woodcraft knowledge of the "Injuns" he hired as guides in the summer. Samoset disliked having to "put on a good show" as Leahy put it. He did not tell Ballinger that the extracting of claws from a bear's paws among his people was done by the hunter who had stalked and killed the animal, and that the claws, strung into a necklace, were worn to honor the bear as much as to celebrate the hunter.

"I'm going to give them to my nephew, have 'em made into a necklace like you Indians wear." Ballinger walked around in front of the table as he spoke and stood with his hands on his hips, watching as other guides who were also employed at the hotel unloaded a moose and several deer that Ballinger had killed earlier that week on the shores of Lake

Placid. They had been carried out of the woods to the road by the guides and loaded on one of the hotel's wagons to be hauled back to where they could be properly processed. Some of the choicest cuts of meat would find their way to the guests' tables, and the hides and the particularly good heads of moose or deer would be preserved, but most of the meat was wasted, thrown out to the resident dogs of the inn.

"Nine years old, he is, and mad—just mad—about cowboys and Indians, ever since I took him to see Buffalo Bill's Wild West Show at Madison Square Garden. He and his chums are always playing Custer's Last Stand." He chuckled. "Driving my baby sister wild herself, what with ambushing the parlor maid and tearing up her knot garden that she's so proud of. Mind you," he said, turning around and cocking an eye at Samoset. "All the boys want to be the Seventh Cavalry. But they take it in turns to be the Indians. Can't have the Battle of Little Big Horn without Indians, can you?"

Ballinger seemed to expect a reply, so Samoset said, "No, sir, you can't."

Ballinger was silent for a moment. "No, you can't," he finally echoed. "You fellows got the best of us there, didn't you? Old Sitting Bull and Crazy Horse." He inhaled deeply, then let his breath out in a huge explosion. "Well, a bear's claw necklace, just like Sitting Bull wore, will make it less of a hard pill to swallow when young Winnie has to play Indian during the lads' games." Then quietly, almost to himself, he said again, "You got the best of us there."

Samoset didn't know who Sitting Bull and Crazy Horse were. He had heard of the famous Battle of Little Big Horn that had happened more than twenty years before because his father had told him that, as a boy, he had been beaten, then spat upon, by a gang of white men when news of the battle had reached back East. Even as an older man, his father had been confused about the incident. Why had they beaten him for what had been done by people he did not know? Neither Samoset, nor his father, nor any of their kin had been at that battle. Samoset had heard once that a Mohawk, the enemies of Samoset's people, had fought on the side of the white man Custer. If that was true, Samoset thought that he would have fought against the Seventh Cavalry, though he did not know what the fight had been about. But Ballinger seemed to want an answer again, so he cut his musings short and said, "Yes, Mr. Ballinger."

"Right, then," Ballinger said briskly, with the air of a man who has decided on a course of action and means to waste no time pursuing it. "Get along, then, and start with the boiling. And once you get the claws out, Natty, set about making that necklace. Use some teeth from that buck I shot up by Copperas Pond, as well. I shan't want that head mounted; I have a better one I got last year on the Southern Tier—a twelve-pointer! He's hanging in my study." He gave Samoset a wink. "My new wife won't have it in the bedroom. You know what women are." He strode off in the direction of the path leading to the front of the hotel, but then stopped abruptly and tuned back to Samoset. "Oh, and I shall expect you back here in the morning, at 7:00 a.m. sharp. No lazing around, my good fellow. I want you to go out with me this coming hunt. I want to see what I can find to shoot at over around Whiteface Mountain."

"Yes, sir," said Samoset, who woke up three hours before 7:00 a.m. every day, whether or not a white man who couldn't be bothered to call him by his real name needed him to find animals for the white man to shoot at. "I'll be ready."

"Good," Ballinger answered. "I like you, Natty. You're a good listener."

Early the next morning Samoset was waiting, sitting on the bottom step of the stairs that led up to the front porch of the hotel. He was working at one of the bear's claws with an awl, slowly and carefully making a hole through which a cord could be passed. He looked up at the sound of Ballinger's voice; the hunter had just emerged onto the porch through the front door.

"I tell you, Allie, you must learn to let a man do what he's bound to do. I am bound to hunt. It's in my blood. My father was a hunter, and his before him. I'll not let a woman's tears get in the way of my God-given right as a man!"

"But must you kill so many, Stone? You've killed such a great mound of them! Bears and deer, and those big droopy-nosed things." The woman's voice was as thin and plaintive as the call of a white-throated sparrow after the man's gruff thunder.

"Moose, Allie. The 'droopy-nosed things,' as you call them, are moose. And you've left out the two bobcats and the coyote I shot down at Old Forge."

As the couple walked across the inn's porch arguing, Samoset slipped the claw and the awl into the possibles bag he wore slung crosswise over his right shoulder and under his left arm. Then he shifted noiselessly across the step into the shadow of the large lilac bush that grew next to the inn. He didn't want Ballinger to think that he was eavesdropping on him and his wife. Guides had lost their jobs, and worse, for less than that.

The couple was closer now, standing at the top of the porch steps. Out of the corner of his eye, Samoset could see the white, slender form of Mrs. Ballinger. He ducked his head so that he could no longer see her.

"But why must you kill them at all?" she asked her husband. "Your study and the front hall are lined with heads already, and you have that great skin in the library. Must you take more?"

"My dear Allison," Ballinger began. Samoset gritted his teeth at the condescending tone in which he spoke to his wife; it was the same tone he used with Samoset. He had heard it the first time when Ballinger had decreed that "Samoset" was too hard to remember, so he would call his guide "Natty" instead. "Like Cooper's leatherstocking, you know— Natty Bumppo. I dare say you've slain a few deer in your time, haven't you, my boy?" Samoset had never heard of James Fenimore Cooper or his books. He hated being called by a name given to him by a white man. Ballinger went on: "The forest is teeming with wild beasts. Why shouldn't I shoot them?" He chuckled, the ultimate expression of his complete satisfaction with himself. "One might say it is God's mandate that I should take as many of His creatures as I please. Doesn't it say in the Book of Genesis that He gave Man dominion over all the creatures of land, sea, and sky? I am following in Adam's very footsteps, surely!" Samoset heard the thud of Ballinger's own footsteps as he strode across the wooden planks of the porch.

"Hunting began after the Fall, I'm sure," Mrs. Ballinger replied. "Killing can't have been allowed in the Garden of Eden! How could it have been, when the creatures God made are so beautiful? Leave them for a few days, I beg you! It seems sinful to kill so many, and just for sport, to have your photograph taken with the largest of them."

"Nonsense, Allie! However many I shoot, twice as many again are being born each spring. Now go inside and find some of the other ladies to converse with. When I spoke to Mrs. Aldridge last evening at dinner, she assured me that she is a great hand at whist; no one better, she claims. You might try her in a game, see if her skills live up to her boast. Now I," he went on, punctuating his words with a smacking sound that Samoset thought must be the planting of a kiss on his wife's cheek, "am going hunting. I shall return in two weeks, my love. Farewell!"

Ballinger thudded down the porch steps and started a little in surprise when he noticed Samoset in the shadow of the lilac bush.

"Oh, Natty. There you are. Come along, then. I see that the teamsters have finished loading the wagons."

As he followed the white man to where the wagons stood, burdened with all that the client hunters would need for a comfortable sojourn in the North Woods, Samoset looked back at the inn. Mrs. Ballinger stood on the porch, gazing anxiously at her husband's retreating back. For an instant, the guide and the woods-widow locked eyes. *You are my relative,* Samoset said silently in his mind to the woman to whom he would never speak. Then he turned back to follow her husband to the wagons.

🌲🌲🌲

A week had passed since the hunting party left the Northwoods Inn, and Ballinger was in a rage. Despite the guides' best efforts, no wild game animals had presented themselves to be killed by his gun. The party had begun scouting for game close to the shores of Lake Placid, usually a rich source of killable trophies, his guides assured him. But their efforts had garnered nothing. Samoset and the party's other tracker guides, captained by a wiry French Canadian named LeFranc, searched diligently along the familiar game trails but found no tracks or scat fresher than five days at the least.

So, at Ballinger's command, as the wealthiest and therefore the most powerful of the client hunters, the teamsters had moved their two wagons, loaded with camping gear and weaponry, along a rough forest road, farther from the lake and closer to the grizzled mountain looming above it. Still they found nothing. Samoset was puzzled, and a little uneasy. Why, at high summer, were there no deer grazing in the small grassy meadows that dotted the forest near the lake? Why no bears, round with summer fat, trying to glean a few more pounds of flesh from the forest to sustain them through the long, frozen silence of the North Woods winter? Why no moose, standing up to their great, knobby knees in beaver meadows, strings of dripping bright-green waterweeds hanging from their pendulous muzzles?

The other clients and their guides, disheartened, remained at the camp they had set up near the road that led back to the Northwoods Inn, but Ballinger insisted on continuing the hunt to a place they hadn't ventured yet: the land upon the mountain's flanks. LeFranc advised him against looking for game up on the mountain. "No deer gonna go up there, no bear, neither. Too much good eating down below."

"We've *looked* down below, you fool!" Ballinger stormed. "They aren't here. Logically, then, they must have gone up the mountain."

"That ain't logical, Mr. Ballinger," LeFranc replied, respectful even as he contradicted. "Not if you the bear or the deer. Where they went, I don't know, but I bet my mustaches they didn't go up on ol' Whiteface. Nothing up there but wind and frost."

Ballinger's jaw jutted out in a way that was familiar in boardrooms throughout the city. "Go up there I shall, my good man," he said. "And I'll take my prey, too. You may take me at my word."

The lead guide mulled this over, chewing on the ends of the mustaches he had so recently staked. "Better take Samoset, then," said LeFranc, "'E's the best tracker we got."

So now Samoset climbed up the mountain's flank, dutifully searching for sign of bear or deer as he went, although he agreed with LeFranc. No game would go up there: not in the summer when there was so much forage nearby on the lower level, and not in winter. Whiteface Mountain was home to the snows alone.

Whiteface stood alone, apart from its mighty brothers to the south, like a warrior standing before a gathering at the council fire to speak his mind. So many of the great peaks of the Adirondacks now went by names the white men had given them when they, latecomers to this land, had arrived. But "Whiteface" was not too far off in meaning from "Wa-ho-par-te-nie," the name Samoset's people gave it: "It Is White." Summer or winter, the great mountain's color was what struck humans at first sight: the pale gleam of the granite slides that scarred the mountain, like bolts of lightning turned to stone, from peak to base, white of snow up where only the wind walked in the winter. White was a color for spirits, and although it wasn't forbidden for people to walk on the mountain, Samoset felt a sense of unease because of the task he had been given. If the mountain didn't want Ballinger to have the animals it watched over from on high, he should take note of the warning he had been given and leave. Samoset was now at its base, following the twisting path of stone formed by the wind-flattened branches of the stunted spruce trees: the only plants, other than mosses and sparse, tufted grass, that could thrive on the stark mountainside. He scanned the granite for signs of game, dutifully following his employer's orders, though Samoset knew, wise tracker, only a god could leave a track in that blank and unforgiving stone.

Some way behind him Ballinger huffed, so winded already that he had no air left with which to grumble. Samoset purposely kept up a pace that was more than the city hunter could manage comfortably. Better not to have the silence of stone and wind broken by his complaints. The weight of the rifle and ammunition that he carried added to the trouble he had keeping up. The rifle was new: the newest, best, and therefore the most expensive to be had, and not to be trusted to the hands of a mere Indian guide. Optimistically, Ballinger carried far more ammunition than he would ever need, even if every buck in the mountains had converged on the slopes of Whiteface. Samoset carried nothing but his knife and possibles bag; he was there only to find the game, not shoot at it, and if Ballinger did kill something, it was Samoset who would have to pack the gutted carcass out to the road where the wagons waited. He owned a gun, and knew how to use it effectively, but he did not want the added encumbrance of a rifle. He neither knew nor cared about the quality and cost of Ballinger's rifle, though the hunter had discoursed at length on the subject to the other hunters around the campfire at night, when the clients drank whiskey and the guides prepared for the next day's business. Samoset's own gun was old, one he had purchased thirdhand from LeFranc. A rifle like the one Ballinger carried was far beyond his means.

Samoset heard a thin trickling sound and paused, scanning the moss under the creeping boughs of the stunted spruce trees that clothed the slopes. He quickly spotted what he was looking for: a thread of water, flowing down the rock under the vegetation and gathering in a tiny hollow in a level place on the stone, before overflowing the little basin and continuing on its journey to the lake below. He knelt and, pushing aside the spruce branches, bowed his head to drink from the little pool, more to give Ballinger a chance to catch up than because he was thirsty. After he drank, he remained with his head bowed and one knee pressed to the granite, offering reverence to the mountain. *I am here, my relative. I thank you for this water.* His eyes scanned the moss and damp grit that served as mud here, made by the sparse soil of the mountain flank, and he saw what he had been looking for, ever since they had established their base camp on the road that passed between Lake Placid and the mountain. A deer's hoofprint, pressed into mud and moss. At first he had failed to see it for what it was because of its size; it was as big as a big moose track, but with the unmistakable shape of a deer track. On his hands and knees, Samoset crawled upward, careful not to spoil the first track he'd found, searching for more hoofprints. They were hard to find, but they were there. He was sure that a deer, a giant of his kind, had come this way not long before.

As he searched, Ballinger came up behind him. "What, have you lost something? Am I to pay you to creep about like a child? Stand up, man, and give an account of yourself!"

"See! Tracks!" Samoset slid aside from the stag's trail to show the hunter the clearest one. "Deer. A big one. He is going up the mountain. Not long ago!"

Ballinger bent and squinted at the marks Samoset pointed to. "That? Pshaw! Too big to be a deer. Moose, maybe, or likely you made that showing yourself, crawling around like a drunkard!"

Samoset scrambled to his feet, excited now, for all his uneasiness, with a hunter's joy in pursuit. "No! It's not a moose! Moose don't make sharp points like that! And look," Samoset walked carefully beyond the last mark he'd found, scanning the ground anxiously. "Here! Right here! You can see it, clear as the mountain!"

Ballinger came up and looked; there was a patch of real, deep mud, wet from a recent rain, and a hoofprint was there, centered as precisely as though an artist had placed it there. "My God!" Ballinger whispered. "He must be a giant! I must take him! Here, Natty, you keep tracking him and don't lose his trail! And be quiet! I don't want him frightened off by your noise."

Samoset kept his opinion to himself about whose noise was most likely to frighten the deer. He was almost excited as the hunter, but at the same time, his uneasiness at the sight of the giant tracks had returned twofold, overcoming his hunter's excitement. A stag of such size, and on the slopes of the mountain, might well be a messenger from the gods of the high places. How they would view the shooting of their messenger by the city hunter, Samoset did not like to think. So he thought instead of how many pairs of boots and how many lengths of woolen cloth for winter wear his mother might buy for his little brothers and sister with the bonus he might get from Ballinger at the end of the season if the man managed to shoot the huge deer.

He moved carefully along, scanning each inch of ground before stepping over it. Ballinger followed closely behind, almost treading on Samoset's heels in his eagerness to sight the deer. The tracks were hard to spot. Even though he was walking up the steep slopes of the mountain, the stag's strides were extraordinarily long, and the distance between each hoofprint was greater by far than that of an ordinary buck. And often, when a hoof had fallen on bare stone, there was no track at all. But what LeFranc had said was true: Samoset was the best tracker employed at the Northwoods Inn, arguably the best in the northern reaches of the mountains. By bent moss and dislodged pebble, he followed the gods' messenger with certainty.

Suddenly Ballinger gave a sharp hiss of indrawn breath, and Samoset felt himself being shoved roughly off the track of the mighty stag. Not having to peer constantly at the ground searching for tracks, Ballinger had seen the creature first. "Look!" Ballinger whispered. "My God, look at the rack on him! And he's white, pure white!" As Ballinger pushed past Samoset, the guide did look, and he knew that his uneasy feelings were right, for surely such a creature could belong only to the gods. The stag stood above them on the mountain slope, and to Samoset it seemed that he was staring directly at the two men. But he did not run, not this chief of all deer in the mountains. His antlers rose high above his head, stark as the branches of an elm tree in winter; they stood out against the pale granite of the slope of the mountain, for they gleamed with a strange, silvery brightness. No less brightly did his silver-white coat gleam in the thin sunlight. Even his hooves seemed to glow. Only his eyes were dark as they gazed down on the men. He saw them as clearly as they saw him, but still he did not run.

Ballinger set his stance for firing and raised his rifle to his shoulder, sighting carefully along the barrel. Despite his excitement, he took his time preparing for the shot. He was shooting uphill, a difficult position from which to hit a target, since the shooter had to know how to make allowances for the pull of gravity on the bullet. But Samoset had seen the man shoot. He knew that Ballinger would not allow gravity to play him any tricks. The hunter was a practiced shot.

Samoset could not let Ballinger shoot the stag who was the gods' messenger. Whatever happened to the man himself, such an act could bring the gods' anger on all the people living in the mountains of the north. Ballinger could go back to his city, but the folks who made their homes among the mountains had nowhere else to go. So the tracker threw his weight into the right side of Ballinger's back. At the same time, he grabbed at the gun barrel with his right hand, hoping to knock it down and spoil the shot. In this he was successful. His attack had taken Ballinger off guard, and the bullet ricocheted off the stone and flew off with a zinging whine, lost among the ice-carved pebbles of the slide.

Samoset had been prepared to meet Ballinger's fury, but the face he turned on the tracker was twisted with more than human rage. His eyes were mad, and Samoset thought, *This is what a demon in the preacher's white-man hell must look like.* And that was all he had time to think, for without a word, the hunter drew back the stock of his gun and slammed the butt of it into Samoset's right temple. He fell, sprawling back down the mountain, landing with his feet higher than his head. He, too, never spoke a word.

Without giving the fallen tracker another glance, Ballinger turned to face the place on the slope above where the deer had been, and to his amazement and joy, he saw that, somehow, it was still there. It stood as it had stood before, standing full-flank presented to the hunter, with its head turned to stare at him. Not daring to breathe, Ballinger again raised the rifle and fired. The bullet took the stag in the flank behind the shoulder, where the powerful heart pumped. Ballinger watched with maddened glee as the great antlers sank, the mighty head dropping as the deer fell to its knees. The hunter waited for the hindquarters to fold. He could see the blood blooming on the white coat where the bullet had struck. But then, incredibly, the deer staggered back to its feet. It turned and ran unsteadily up the mountain. Even after it was out of sight, Ballinger could hear its hooves dislodging stones as it ran. One of the loosened rocks clattered down to come to rest at Ballinger's feet.

Ballinger cursed in a way that would have made the demons in hell proud. He stumbled up the rock-strewn slope, slipping on his hands and knees, to the place where the stag had stood, searching for blood spoor. There was none to be found. He crawled back and forth along the spot, cursing more violently than before, but in the end, he stood up, defeated. He would need a tracker to help him pick up the trail of the wounded deer. His mind went to Natty, and he turned around to look for him and demand that he track this deer, to the very gates of hell, if he must.

He was surprised to see the tracker lying motionless on the mountainside. For a moment, he didn't recollect what had happened: Natty spoiling his shot, himself turning on the Indian in a white-hot fury. Then he remembered. His bowels became heavy with fear as he scrambled back down to where Natty's body lay. He was only an Indian, it was true, but if the blow to the temple, however well deserved, had killed him, it could still cause a scandal back in the city, especially if his business rivals got wind of it. Natty's eyes were open and staring, and when Ballinger gingerly gripped the man's chin and turned his head to get a look at his right temple, the ghastly, discolored indent, just the shape of the butt of Ballinger's gun, made it necessary for him to go over behind a boulder and relieve himself of the watery looseness gripping his belly. When he had finished, he walked back to what he was quite sure was a corpse and laid his hand against its chest. No heartbeat, no breath. Natty the Indian tracker was dead, and J. Winston Ballinger had a problem.

He stood up from crouching over the body and thought. Then he turned to search the ground. In a moment he found what he was looking for: a stone that his hand could get a good grip on. He knelt again by Samoset's body, then, aiming carefully, he brought the stone down on the corpse's temple as hard as he could, obliterating the dent left by the rifle butt. He struck twice more to make sure that there was no sign of the first wound, then tossed the rock aside and stood up again. He walked back up the slope to where he had dropped the rifle, then picked it up and fired off three shots in rapid succession: the signal that the hunters staying at the Northwoods Inn were told to use if they got in trouble in the forest. Ballinger then sat down on a boulder and waited, looking out at the other high peaks far off in the distance, and at Lake Placid, the sun's mirror, reflecting back its glory in a sheet of molten gold. He was careful not to look at the body lying on the stones.

The sun had dropped considerably lower on the horizon when Ballinger heard a whoop off in the distance. He fired the rifle again, then whooped back in the direction the call had come from. Soon a small group of men came toiling up the slope: the four guides besides Samoset who were on the expedition, and two of the younger, more adventurous clients. LeFranc was leading them.

Ballinger walked down the slope to stand near Samoset's body as the group approached. He began talking before any of them had a chance to give the body more than a cursory glance. "A terrible thing has happened, men. Just terrible. Poor Natty—we were tracking a stag up the mountain, and a right monster he was, too. Pure white like snow, and sixteen points on his antlers if there was one. And Natty—well, he fell. Put a foot wrong on a loose rock and it turned under him, and down he went. I was looking at the deer, taking my shot, then when I looked back . . . there he was, lying just as you see him now. Great dent in his head, must have struck it on a stone."

LeFranc knelt beside his fellow guide and looked at the wound. Then he pressed Samoset's eyelids down over his staring eyes and rested his hand gently for a moment on the cooling face. "It surely does look like what you said, Mr. Ballinger. *Pauvre garçon*, side of 'is head's all caved in. Like a stone would do." He stayed kneeling, gnawing on his mustaches. "Funny thing, though. Samoset was sure footed; most Injuns are. I've seen 'im dance out on a log jam in a river and back again, just for fun; 'e never move a one of 'em. Nimble as an otter, 'e was. I can't see how 'e woulda tripped on a rock." LeFranc looked sideways at Ballinger. "'N if 'e did fall, 'e knew how to fall so's to take no hurt. These young boys, they raised in de woods, fallin' outta trees an' jumping off boulders an' what. They know how to fall. So do I, so does any man who lives in de forest. Dis wound, she deep and wide. Half 'is head crush in. Like a stone would do, but more like two, three stones. Musta bounced pretty hard on 'is way down."

"Well, I tell you that he fell," Ballinger replied angrily. "This stag, he was enormous. The poor lad was probably taken aback at the sight of him and made a misstep. You said yourself that a stone would cause such damage. How many stones he hit is no business of mine." Then he remembered: the stag. The ultimate trophy of his career as a hunter. "Look, that deer's still on the mountain. I shot him and hit him, clean in the flank. He's dead up there; I'll wager anything you'd care to match. We have to go up there and find him!"

LeFranc frowned. "No, sir, Mr. Ballinger, we can't go after no deer right now. A man is dead, *mon ami*, my friend. We gotta take Samoset down off this mountain, an' we gotta do it soon. The sun, 'e settin'. We got no time to look for a deer."

Ballinger felt the white-hot rage descending again and fought it back with all his will. "I tell you that we *must* go after that stag. An animal like that—it comes along once in a lifetime, if that. I will have my trophy!"

"So whereabouts was this *monstre* when you shot 'em, Mr. Ballinger?" LeFranc asked, still kneeling by the body.

"Right up there, just beyond and to the right of that boulder shaped like a bear's back," Ballinger pointed.

LeFranc nodded. "Henri! Eddie!" he called to two of the younger guides. "Get on up there, see if you can find a trace of 'is blood, this *grande bête* Mr. Ballinger shot!" The two young men went quickly but carefully up the slide to the place Ballinger had indicated. They scoured the ground beyond the bear-shaped boulder as the sun dropped lower and the shadows grew longer. Finally, Henri called down to the other men.

"Sorry, Anton! Nothing up here! Not blood, hair, or tracks."

Rage like wildfire leaped up in Ballinger's brain. "Idiots! You couldn't track a train if you started from the station. I tell you he *was* up there, and I shot him! If you weren't a pair of suet-brained fools you'd see blood there!" he shouted, forgetting that he himself had searched for, and failed to find, blood spoor.

"Well, sir, you can do as you like. This country is free, so they say. But me, I'm taking *mon ami* down offa dis *montagne*, dis mountain. My wife, she de cousin of 'is *maman*, so 'e's like blood-kin to me. I will take 'im down." He raised his voice so that the guides ranged in a loose group on the slide could hear him. "You men, you do what pleases you, eh? Stay with Mr. Ballinger, look for 'is *fantôme* if you like. Me, I will take our friend back down the hill, take 'im back to his *maman*, so." He stood up and began straightening the corpse's limbs to make it easier to carry. Two of the other guides came forward and solemnly helped him lift the body onto his shoulders and arrange it like they would a deer carcass that had to be humped out of the woods on a man's back. Then without another word, he moved steadily off toward the valley floor. The other guides fell in behind him, Samoset's funeral cortege. The two client hunters cast uneasy glances at the shadows creeping out from behind rocks and boulders and fell in behind the guides. Ballinger fumed, but there was nothing he could do, unless he wanted to stay out all night with no fire or food on the mountainside. Angrily, he followed the other men.

It was October, and Ballinger could not sleep at night. He spared no thought for the murdered man: the thought of Samoset had faded from his memory once the threat to Ballinger himself was overcome. There was an inquest, of course, but the sheriff and the coroner, both white men, took Ballinger's word about what had happened. No one in the town of Lake Placid wanted to do anything to alienate the wealthy men from New York City who brought so much custom to the mountains, and who left so much of their money behind them after they left. LeFranc had been difficult, it was true, repeating what he had said about the severity of the wound in Samoset's skull and how unlikely it was that the young woodsman would have fallen on terrain he had walked on all his life. He was quiet, however, after Ballinger gave him a generous sum of money "for the poor lad's mother." LeFranc didn't like it, Ballinger could tell, but he took the money anyway and, thereafter, held his tongue.

The thing that haunted him was the thought of the white stag. After the wagons, one carrying Samoset's body, returned to the inn, his presence was required by the sheriff for his testimony about the accident, and he didn't dare not be present when the other men who had come up the mountain in search of him and the tracker were questioned. By the time he was able to go back to where he'd shot the deer with one of the younger guides (LeFranc suddenly falling ill when Ballinger had told Leahy to tell the man to be ready to go out with him in the morning), there was no sign of the stag. He'd had the guide scour half the mountainside searching for the carcass, but there was nothing. Now, night after night, when he closed his eyes to sleep, he saw the creature as clearly as if its image was being projected on the insides of his eyelids. He saw it standing, the statue-like majesty of the beast; he saw it sink to its knees again with the blood from the wound he gave it blooming on its side. Most maddeningly, he saw it rise to its feet when it should have fallen, then trot unsteadily off up the mountain, leaving behind nothing more than the stones it had sent tumbling with its hooves. And he saw it as it should be: its head and glorious rack mounted on the wall in the great room of his mansion, its silvery hide spread on the floor before the fireplace in his study.

As his frustration grew, his temper grew shorter and shorter. One morning, back in the city, after he had berated the servant who brought him and his wife breakfast for letting the coffee grow cold in the kitchen, then roaring at her when he'd burned his mouth because the fresh pot was too hot, his wife had had enough.

"Honestly, Stone, we shan't have a servant left to us if you don't stop scolding them for every little thing!" Allison had told him crossly, after the waitress had fled, barely managing to keep her tears at bay until she'd left the room. "You need to get whatever bee is buzzing in your bonnet out, before you send us all mad!"

Four additional months of marriage had done much to transform my wife from a shrinking violet to a stinging nettle, Ballinger thought sullenly.

"I don't call a scalded tongue a mere bee in the bonnet, Allison!" he snapped back. After a pause, during which he sulkily stabbed his scrambled eggs with his fork and Allie folded her linen napkin into increasingly smaller squares, Ballinger spoke again.

"I *am* sorry, Allie, but you know how I can't stand leaving matters unfinished. I keep thinking about this summer . . ."

"Oh, I know, Stone! I feel just the same way myself! That poor boy, and his mother a widow with little children to care for, too! It's just too awful, and you were there when it happened! No wonder you're snappish!"

Ballinger stared at her blankly for a moment, wondering what on earth the woman was babbling about. Then he remembered: that Indian boy who'd got himself killed up on Whiteface Mountain. A knack for thinking on his feet had earned Ballinger the respect and fear, if not the love, of many a business magnate in the city, and now an idea formed itself in his mind, a way for him to have a thorough search 'round the woods at the base of the mountain for the white stag.

Putting on a remorseful face, Ballinger said, "You're right, you know, Allie . . . I just can't get poor Natty out of my head, he and his mother and the little ones. And I left Lake Placid without even a visit to her to offer my condolences or give her some money to help her until one of the youngsters is old enough to help! My conscience is nagging me. But how can I make up for what's been left undone?"

Allie blithely stepped right into the trap he had set for her. "Why, you must go back, Stone! Tell her how sorry we are and give her money, a lot of it, so the children don't go hungry this winter! Oh, and I know! Christmas will be here soon! I can speak to the ladies of our acquaintance and ask if they have any clothes or toys their own children don't use anymore to send to the poor little things! It'll be like a mission collection!"

This suggestion pleased Ballinger less. He didn't want to waste time consoling some lumpish Indian matron and her runny-nosed brats, and he would have to if Allison collected Christmas gifts for them, so he could give her a full report of their gratitude. A man was lord in his own castle, Ballinger believed, but living in the castle was much more pleasant if the lord's wife was kept moderately content. So he answered, "That's a capital idea, my dear! I'm sure to feel relieved in my mind if I can do something, no matter how small, to help that poor woman! A widow, too. You get to work on your mission, and I'll arrange matters at the office so that things will run smoothly without me for a month, then off I'll go."

Allie's face fell, and Ballinger cursed himself for letting slip the length of time he planned on being gone. "A month! But Stone, why so long? Surely you can deliver the gifts and the money and be back home in a week or two at the most!"

His ability to think on his feet saved him again. "Why, of course, I mean to be back as soon as I possibly can!" he said, rising from his chair and walking around the table to press a kiss on Allison's rosy cheek. "The less time I'm away from you, the better, my rose! I meant that I'll arrange things so I could be gone for a month *if I must!* I've heard stories of winters in the mountains. The weather's unpredictable, and the trains are often stopped for days by snowstorms. It's also bitterly cold. Even the roads can be snowed under, so not even a horse and sleigh can get through. But that's not always how it is, even in the mountains. Be sure that I'll return as quickly as I can. You don't want the orphans to miss their Christmas gifts, do you?"

Allie mustered a smile. "Well, then, as long as you promise to be back as soon as you possibly can, Stone. We do owe that poor family something, since the boy died while tracking for you. I suppose that I can spare you for two weeks."

"That's my brave one!" Ballinger exclaimed, kissing her again. "Now, as soon as you've finished breakfasting, you call 'round to all your lady friends and collect all their cast-offs for the Indian children. I'll leave for the office now and start fixing things so that they'll tick along smoothly without me for a little while!"

Fifteen minutes later, Ballinger marched out of his front door to where his driver waited for him with his new automobile. He felt a deep, self-satisfied glow, as he always did when he had closed an important deal. Now he could go off to Lake Placid, to the mountain, without any questions from the one person who dared question his activities. Within a week, he told himself, he would be on Whiteface, searching for the great white stag.

Mr. Leahy, the owner and host of the Northwoods Inn, was not happy to see J. Winston Ballinger standing on the steps of the neat frame house next to the inn, where he lived with his family in the off-season. Ballinger stood shivering in his city overcoat, annoyed that Leahy did not immediately take him over to the inn where, Ballinger assumed, his usual rooms were aired, warmed, and waiting for him. It was cold this far north, every bit as cold as Ballinger had warned his wife it would be when he spoke of the delays he might face in getting back to the city.

"Why, Mr. Ballinger, the inn's shut up for the winter," the innkeeper said when he heard Ballinger's demand that he be shown to his rooms and given a hot meal. "After September, why, there's no point in keeping it open. Folks just don't want to come up here hunting when the snow's ten feet deep."

"Well, it's not ten feet deep now, is it?" Ballinger replied, trying to keep a tight rein on his temper.

"Why, no, but I tell you, it's all shut up, and the staff sent away for the winter. There's no profit in keeping it open when no guests want to come."

"I'm here now, man, and I want a room and a meal, if it's not too much to ask," Ballinger snapped. He was tired from the long trip, first by train from the city, then in a buggy he was able to hire, with a driver, from the livery stable in town. Now the driver and buggy were gone, and he was standing on the front stoop of this fool's house, arguing about a room at an inn that clearly had many. It was growing colder, too, and the wind was picking up.

"Why, I can't open it now. You'd be like a dried pea rattling around in a ten-gallon jar. There's no firewood hauled, no linens on the beds, nothing. You'll have to find a place in town."

"I'll stay here in your house, then," Ballinger said briskly. "I'll eat what your family eats." Mrs. Leahy, who had come up behind her husband, gasped in dismay at the proposition.

"We just haven't got room, sir," Leahy explained. "We're happy to feed you supper, and you can sleep in the living room for tonight if you like, but for more than a night, it just isn't possible."

"Nonsense!" Ballinger snapped. "I see children yonder, next to the wood stove. Have them double up, two to a bed, and I'll have their room."

"They're already sleeping three to a bed," Leahy said, getting exasperated with this man who seemed to think he owned Leahy's house. "We haven't got but two bedrooms upstairs, and the two littlest ones sleep on a trundle bed in the Missus' and my room. The six oldest sleep in the other room, three to a bed, like I said."

The result of the discussion was that Ballinger found himself bedded down on a mattress improvised from some bear and deer skins that adorned the floor and walls of the Leahy home, with two thin quilts and his own overcoat as covers. This after a thoroughly unsatisfactory meal of bread, cheese, and the little dab of venison stew left over from the meal enjoyed earlier by the Leahys and their brood.

The next morning, Leahy and Ballinger stood on the porch of the deserted Northwoods Inn. Ballinger had insisted on seeing the hostelry with his own eyes, and it was clear, even to him, that it was shut up tight for the winter. Wooden shutters were fixed firmly over all of the inn's many windows, to keep ice from the roof and random tree branches from smashing the glass panes. No smoke rose from its chimneys, and the front and back yards, which in the summer were alive with the comings and goings of guests, guides, and domestic workers, were desolate and abandoned.

"You see, sir, it's shut up tight as a tick, like I told you last night, and there's no staff to open it back up, nor run it if it was open. You'll just have to find somewhere else to stay while you're here. And if you don't mind my asking, why *are* you here? The North Woods are pleasant enough in the summer, and a good retreat, so I'm told, from the heat of the cities downstate. But once winter starts coming on, the summer folk do well to stay where they came from. Even us who were born here can't do nothing but hunker down and hold on till spring comes again. Winters aren't kind, here in the mountains."

Ballinger was reluctant to reveal the real purpose of his late-season visit to the Northwoods Inn, but he realized that, without the innkeeper's help, he had little chance of finding and killing the great white stag. He decided to start with the decoy mission, the one that was most likely to appeal to Leahy.

"Well, sir, I got thinking about what happened back in July, poor Natty falling down that slope and getting his skull smashed in. I began to feel very sorry for his mother, all those children to feed, and the breadwinner suddenly gone. Mrs. Ballinger, too, she has a soft spot for children. Most women do, you know. She felt badly about the little ones. With their mother scraping to feed them, there'd be no money to spare for Christmas gifts. Mrs. Ballinger collected up a crate of toys and clothes from her friends who have children, things their little ones don't use anymore. That's what's in that box the liveryman left on your front porch. My wife insisted—and I felt I had to, too—that I come back and give the Christmas crate to Natty's mother, along with a sum of money to ensure their comfort, the poor orphans."

Leahy's brow furrowed clear up to his receding hairline at this news. "Why, that's kind of you, Mr. Ballinger, and of your wife. A good-hearted lady she is. But Vangie Johnson and her children aren't in any want. Anton LeFranc gave her a nice sum, after the inquest, that I was given to understand had come from you. And she's got kin who're taking care of her and her children, providing aid and comfort, you know. Vangie's not without friends in these parts."

Ballinger was shocked to learn that LeFranc had actually given the money to the dead man's mother. He had fully expected the guide to keep it for himself, in return for his silence on the matter of questions raised. Again, Ballinger's mental agility came to his aid. "Well, of course, I provided funds for the upkeep of the widow and her brood. It was the only decent thing to do. But then I began thinking, was it enough? I felt very badly that the boy died while tracking for me, you know. My conscience would give me no peace till I came up to see to it myself. And then Mrs. Ballinger's Christmas box . . ."

"I can deliver the money and the presents to Vangie for you, Mr. Ballinger," Leahy replied. "As a matter of fact, I'd best give them to LeFranc to give them to her, him being kin by marriage to her and all. Vangie's shy about talking to anybody who's not kin to her. Most Indian women are. LeFranc's out running his traplines now, in the beaver meadows in the valley, like all the summer guides do this time of year, when the plews are prime; but when he comes in, I'll see to it that he delivers the things to Vangie."

It was time, Ballinger thought, *to introduce the real reason for his journey to the North.* "I wouldn't mind talking to LeFranc myself, now that you mention it. You see, I figured that, as long as I'm up here, I might as well have another try at that monster buck I shot on the day poor Natty. . . . At any rate, I'll need a guide up the mountain and in the woods at its base. He wouldn't have gone too far, not with a wound like the one I gave him. I'm sure that he's out there, and I mean to find him."

This time Leahy's jaw dropped clear to the collar of his bearskin coat. "Why, Mr. Ballinger, you know that my guides looked for him, all around the lake and up the mountain. There was no trace to be seen of your white deer. I can't see that looking now, with the snows likely to set in any day, will turn him up."

"Are you calling me a liar, Leahy? I saw that deer, clear as I see you now. He's out there somewhere." Ballinger took a deep breath to calm his temper, then continued. "I would be most grateful if you could contact LeFranc, or any of your guides, for that matter, and inform them that I need their services."

"Mr. Ballinger, that just ain't possible," Leahy responded. "I told you, they're all out tending to their winter living, trapping beaver and mink all along the waterways hereabouts. There's no telling where LeFranc or any of them might be right now. You'd have to wait till they come in. And even then, I doubt they would consent to guide you. This ain't the time of year for city folks hunting. To be sure, if one of the boys came across a moose or a nice deer, he'd shoot it for his own use, but now's just not the time for sport hunting. I don't doubt that you shot a white buck, not at all, but it would be impossible, and dangerous, for you to try to find him this time of year."

Ballinger's first instinct was to strike the stupid man, but he fought down the impulse. He needed Leahy's help if he was to kill the white stag and put his mind to rest. He drew a deep breath, let it out again, and spoke.

"All the same, I would take it kindly if you would keep your eyes open for one of your guides, or any man who's competent at tracking, and present my proposition to him. Tell him I will pay double the summer rates, triple if we find the white stag and I kill it."

Leahy shook his head doubtfully. "I'll do that Mr. Ballinger, but I'm telling you, it's not likely that you'll find anyone who'll guide you, not this time of year. But come back to the house with me now. The Missus will have dinner almost ready by this time, and there's a nip in the air, no mistaking."

"Thank you, Mr. Leahy," Ballinger replied. "I'll be along presently. I think I'd like to walk around for a bit, breathe in some of your clear mountain air. There's nothing like it, especially when there's a chill to it."

Leahy took his leave, walking down the wooden steps that stretched across the front façade of the inn and off across the yard toward his house. Ballinger stayed on the porch of the Northwoods Inn, staring unseeing at the great mountain before him.

"I'll guide you, Mr. Ballinger," a quiet voice said from the shadow of the now naked and desolate lilac bush that grew beside the porch. "I'll take you to where the white stag lives."

Ballinger gave a jerk of surprise at the sound of the voice. He had thought that he and Leahy were alone, and Leahy hadn't spoken to the person sitting on the bottom step of the porch when he went down. *He must not have seen him either*, Ballinger thought. The figure on the bottom step *was* hard to see, crouched in the shadow of the lilac bush like that. It seemed to Ballinger that there was more shadow clinging to the man than was being cast by the denuded bush, but he pushed that thought from his mind. He thudded down the steps to speak to the man.

"Well, it's good to know that someone in these hills wants to make some extra money. That's good economic sense. I'll hire you on the terms I told Leahy: twice an experienced guide's summer pay, triple if we find the white stag and I kill him."

The man rose to his feet as Ballinger spoke. Something about the way he stood seemed odd to the hunter; instead of facing Ballinger head-on, like most people would when speaking with someone, this fellow stood at an angle to him, with his head turned slightly to the left and his chin tucked down, to look at the white man. It gave him a shifty air, and Ballinger wondered briefly if the man planned on robbing him once they were in the woods alone. He did not care. So great was his lust for the trophy he was after, he was willing to take the chance. Besides, the man was thin and young, an Indian, by the color of his hair, eyes, and skin. Ballinger, who was a full head taller and fifty pounds heavier, was sure he could take him if the woodsman tried anything.

"Sure, Mr. Ballinger, that would be fine. Go down to Mr. Leahy's house and ask him to fit you out with a pack and gear. I'll be waiting for you right here when you're ready."

Ballinger, who thought that all men should be ready at his beck and call, didn't ask how the guide would know when he might be ready to meet him by the lilac bush. "That's capital, my good man, just capital! I'm anxious to get out in the forest, so I'll get behind Leahy, make sure he moves quickly. We have a deal, then!" He thrust out his hand, ready to shake on it, but the other man did not reach out to meet his hand.

Ballinger, not wanting to stand like a fool with his hand stretched out, rejected, changed the gesture to a hearty slap on the arm, only somehow the younger man, seeming almost not to have moved at all, evaded Ballinger's touch.

"Sure, Mr. Ballinger, that's fine," the man repeated. Ballinger, a little nonplussed by the other's rejection of his handshake, began to move off toward Leahy's house, but he stopped and turned back. "How are you called, fellow? In case I have to come looking for you when I'm ready to start, I'd better know your name. You look familiar. I must have seen you around the hotel this summer."

"You can call me Sam," the young man replied with a small smile. "Likely you did see me around. There's lots of us, up here in the woods. And I've heard that we all look alike to you white men."

"Sam, then. You must be related to some of the Indians who staff the place in the summer." Suddenly it dawned on him who the man reminded him of. "You're kin to Natty, aren't you, the Indian guide who died this summer? You look uncommonly like him."

"You might say I'm kin to him, Mr. Ballinger," the man replied.

"I knew you looked familiar. Well, Sam, I'm off. I hope to be ready to leave early in the morning. It might take that long for Leahy to gather up supplies for me."

"All right, Mr. Ballinger. I'll be waiting for you."

Ballinger strode off, leaving the guide standing in the shadow of the lilac bush, staring at the white man's retreating back.

Leahy had been remarkably quick about gathering up the pack and frame Ballinger would need and the items he would need to fill it. He also scrambled up a bearskin coat, boots that still fit Ballinger's feet comfortably when he had on two pairs of woolen socks, and other items of clothing more suitable to the climate than Ballinger's city clothes. He also provided a small hatchet, matches, a knife, and most important of all, food. This was mostly in the form of pemmican and twice-baked trail biscuits. There was also a tarpaulin and a coil of rope to make a shelter, along with a bedroll. Although Ballinger knew the man found his presence to be an infringement on his comfortable winter family life, the man seemed reluctant to let him go.

"Sam, he said his name was?" Leahy asked for the fifth time, questioning Ballinger about the man he had engaged to guide him. "I swear, I never heard of an Indian in these parts that goes by Sam, and I know most of the ones who live near Lake Placid. They come to me for summer work, guiding, housekeeping, or fishing and hunting to keep the inn in fresh foodstuffs. I don't know one named Sam." He frowned. "What did he look like, this Sam you met? And on the steps of my own inn, too."

"Thin, wiry, black hair and eyes, red skin. The way they all look," Ballinger replied. "Youngish, I'd say around twenty or so, not so tall as I am."

"That don't tell me much," Leahy answered. "What say I go with you to meet this Sam, just so I can be sure that he's a respectable Injun and not some renegade?"

Ballinger snorted. "I won't hear of it, I tell you! I can take care of myself, I assure you. I won't have you scaring him off with your questions and suspicions. And I notice you haven't located one of your trusted guides as of yet."

So Ballinger had paid him, handsomely, for the food and gear, with a generous something extra for the nights he had slept in Leahy's house. When he went to the inn's porch, a full two days later than he had told the guide, Sam was waiting, standing where he had been the last time Ballinger saw him, almost as though he hadn't moved from the spot at all. He carried no gun and no gear, only a hunting knife in a sheath on his belt and a possibles bag with the strap slung over his right shoulder so the bag rode under his left arm. Ballinger tried to give him his pack to carry, as he would have given it to one of the inn's guides in the summer, but Sam shook his head.

"No, sir, Mr. Ballinger," he'd said. "I can't carry your pack." He offered no explanation, but when Ballinger tried to insist and hand him the pack anyway, the guide just walked away, off down the road that led to the trail that went to Whiteface Mountain. Something about the set of the man's narrow back made Ballinger reluctant to insist, and so he awkwardly shouldered the pack himself.

Now, five days out, the pack was weighing terribly on him. He considered himself a strong man, but he hadn't had to hike before, carrying his own gear, along with his rifle and ammunition. He longed to discard something, just to lighten the burden, but when he went over the contents of the pack in his mind, he couldn't think of an item that he wouldn't miss later. Not only that, but it had begun to snow, and the snow was sticking. That made hiking with a loaded pack even more exhausting. When they stopped each night, he only had the energy to gnaw a strip of pemmican and a biscuit, then rig up his tarp, spread the bedroll, take off his boots, and crawl, fully clothed, into it. Sam never offered to set up the tarp for him, and the same strange reluctance he'd felt about demanding that he carry the pack caused him to set up his own sleeping space. Sam did build the fire, though, and kept it going all night. When Ballinger retired for the night, the last thing he saw was the guide hunched by the fire, a black figure against the orange flames. And when he woke, too soon, he always felt, in the morning, Sam was still there, and the fire still burned. The guide never asked for a share of Ballinger's food, but just sat silent while he ate; then, once Ballinger had packed up, he stood up, scooped handfuls of dirt over the coals of the fire, and walked off down the trail.

Finally, at long last, they had come to the foot of the mountain. "So you think he's up here on Whiteface, do you?" Ballinger asked.

"I know so, Mr. Ballinger," the guide replied. *He was,* Ballinger thought, *even more reticent than the usual native guides, who were no great talkers themselves.*

"Seen him up there, have you?" Ballinger asked, interested. Despite his exhaustion and cold, the thought of killing the great white stag set his heart to beating fast and warmed him.

Sam didn't answer but turned his head in that odd, sideways manner that let Ballinger see only the left side of his face and gave a half-smile. "He's there. He's waiting for you."

Ballinger took the guide's words as a good sign and eagerly, if slowly, followed Sam up the trail. The higher they went, the colder the wind blew, prodding into every opening of his winter clothes. His cheeks burned and his eyes watered with the wind's bite, but at the same time, he began to sweat under the heavy skin coat. Finally he stopped and called out to the guide. "Sam! Sam, I need to stop now for the night! I'm going to drop where I stand!"

Sam turned, keeping the left side of his face toward Ballinger, as always. He wondered if the boy had some sort of deformity or birthmark on the right side of his face that he was shy about letting other people see. "I know a good place to camp, a little farther along. You can take off your pack and rest a bit, then leave it at the camp. We can go on to a place I know. It'll be daylight for a while longer."

So he had trudged on, following the guide's back in its deerskin jacket. The boy wore no hat or gloves, only the jacket, which seemed too thin to offer much protection against the wind and the cold. *Well,* Ballinger thought, *these lesser races feel the cold and heat less than we white men do.* Sam soon walked off the trail a little ways and stopped in front of a small cave that had been formed when several huge boulders had fallen against and on top of one another during some long-ago rock slide.

"You go in there, take off the pack, and rest awhile. I'll find wood and start a fire." Ballinger gratefully complied, easing the straps off of his sore shoulders, then crawling into the little cave, first removing the rolled tarp and spreading it to cover the relatively smooth floor of the cave so that he would have something between himself and the stone besides his pants. He pulled the pack into the mouth of the cave, standing it on edge in hopes of blocking some of the wind.

The wind didn't come into the small enclosure, though. It was snug enough: somewhat too snug. Out of the wind, but still sweating from the hiking, he began to feel hot, so he took off his coat and used it to further pad the floor and walls of the cave. He was so tired that he soon fell asleep.

"Mr. Ballinger! Wake up, sir! We have to walk now, go to the place where the white stag lives. Now, while it's still light!"

Ballinger startled awake and crawled blearily out of the cave. Sam had somehow found enough wood on the mountainside to make a fire, and Ballinger sat between it and the mouth of the cave and ate a generous piece of pemmican and drank water from the canteen that he had filled at the last water source. Sam didn't sit, but went a little ways off from the fire, where he stood staring up the slope before them. When Ballinger finished eating, he pushed his pack into the cave and followed the guide up the slope.

Shortly, though, Ballinger cursed and stopped in his tracks. "Damn it all! I've left my coat back in the cave! We must go back for it. The wind's just too fierce."

"No, Mr. Ballinger! If you want to see the white stag, you have to keep on! He's up here, I know! We must go to him, now!"

Even now, with the wind numbing his ears and cheeks, his desire for his trophy outweighed his need to get out of the wind.

"So you have seen him up here? While you were out gathering wood?"

"Yes, sir. I know he is here. Not much farther now."

"All right, then. Lead on, Sam. But mind, if I don't get a shot at him today, I'll warm myself by tanning your hide for you with my belt."

"Do not worry, Mr. Ballinger. You will see him soon." The guide turned and continued up the slide, picking his way carefully, and Ballinger, afraid of dislodging the rocks, followed close behind.

They climbed steadily, and the exertion helped Ballinger fight off the encroaching chill wind. At last, Sam stopped.

"Is he near here?" Ballinger whispered hoarsely.

Sam smiled. "Yes, sir, he is here. Can't you hear him?"

Ballinger strained his ears to hear, over the wind's sounds, for the "Whuff! Whuff!" noise that startled deer make. Try as he might, he couldn't hear anything that sounded like a deer. There was only the wind, and under it, a faint rattling sound, like the branches of winter trees knocking together. But there were no trees up here, other than the stunted spruce.

"What's that noise, that rattling sound?" he demanded.

"That's their bones, Mr. Ballinger. All the creatures whose lives you ended, for no reason but your own pleasure. Their flesh fell wasted on the rocks, and the wind dried out their bones. Those are their bones now, rattling in the wind. The white stag brough them here." Sam walked up the slope a few more yards, then turned around and, for the first time, faced the hunter, the mad wolf, full-on. He leaned his back against a boulder that was the size and shape of a large black bear. Ballinger followed him. His teeth began to chatter, only partly from the cold.

He looked up at Sam, only now that he could see the man's whole face, he realized it wasn't Sam at all. It was Natty, who'd died on the mountain in July. The right side of his head, just at the temple, was still misshapen from the blows Ballinger had struck with a stone.

Ballinger knew then that he ought to have gone back for the bear-skin coat. He was losing his mind, becoming delirious with the cold. Natty was dead. He couldn't be up there, leaning on the boulder shaped like a bear. But it wasn't a boulder at all, he now saw, but a real bear, and Ballinger could see that it rested awkwardly on its forelegs, just the stumps of them, pressing on the rocks, for its paws had been cut off. He remembered ordering the guide who had been skinning it to do it, because he wanted to have a child's plaything made of its claws.

He watched, shuddering with the cold, as Natty, or Sam—*it was Sam*, he told himself, *Natty is dead*—reached into the possibles bag he wore at his left side and took out a handful of something. He knelt beside the bear and laid the things—claws, they were, as long as a man's little finger—in front of the truncated forelimbs, four to a leg. The bear made a little moan—but it was the wind, only the wind—and from the claws rose shadowy paws that joined with the forelegs, making them whole. Natty—*Sam!*—rose to his feet and leaned against the bear again, resting his left arm along the creature's back. *My relative. I am sorry.* Ballinger heard a whisper on the wind. *My relative. You are forgiven*, the wind growled back to itself.

Ballinger's shivering grew more violent, and he walked on up the trail. If you're freezing to death, brisk exercise will warm you, he seemed to remember someone telling him. He walked past the man and the stone-bear, but they only watched. *I might as well find what's making that rattling sound*, he thought. *Wind-dried bones, indeed! Natty ought to know better than to tell me such goblin tales.* He walked along, stumbling every now and then, and sure enough, soon he didn't feel cold anymore. *Whoever told me that was right*, he thought with satisfaction.

But soon the rattling sounded less like wood knocking in the wind and more like other things, hooves, perhaps, or stones dislodged by hooves sliding down the mountainside. *It's him!* he thought. *I must catch up to him!* He groped around himself, searching for his rifle, but he had left it back at the cave, with his coat. He soon forgot about it, all things driven from his mind but his desire for the white deer, his driving need to see it once again.

He seemed to have trouble walking; he couldn't feel his feet. *Someone's cut them off,* he thought. He tripped over something he couldn't see and fell to his knees. The day was moving toward sundown, and the tiny part of his mind not taken over by delirium whispered that he should get back to shelter, to his bearskin coat and his gun. He regretted more than ever the absence of the gun, for around him in the lengthening shadows he caught glimpses of animals tracking him. Out of the corner of his eye he was sure he saw a buck with his head raised high, but when he looked directly at the creature, it wasn't there.

He climbed to his feet and stumbled on, ignoring a cat face with huge green eyes, glaring from atop a boulder, and a moose with massive, outspread antlers blocking his path, only to fade just before he staggered into it. *Delirium, it's only delirium,* he told himself. *There are no creatures here on the mountain, except for him. The white stag.*

He fell again, but this time he couldn't rise. He was on his hands and knees, panting, when he heard someone walk up beside him: the scrape of a woodsman's boots on the stone. He turned his head and saw boots and the legs attached to them, clad in the worn woolen pants that the woodsmen wore. He craned his neck to look higher, and recognized the Indian beadwork decorating the hilt of the hunting knife that the man wore at his side. "Natty!" he gasped. "It's good that you're here. Help me up, boy. The white stag . . . he's near, but my legs can't seem to . . ."

Samoset squatted down near his head, in the same posture from which Ballinger himself had examined a body on the mountainside, back in July. "Don't worry, Mr. Ballinger. He's close by. He's coming to you."

All Ballinger could do was crouch with his head bowed, panting. He could see the thick clouds of his breath dissipating in the frigid air as they left his lips. Something ice cold touched his neck, and he screamed and fell on his side; it was the black bear whose paws he'd ordered cut off. It whuffed and drew back to stand beside the Native guide. Both watched him with the same dispassionate gaze.

Then Samoset turned his head to look up the mountainside. A blade of the sunset light slashed across his head, and Ballinger could see even more clearly the damage he had done. The ghost turned back to him and smiled, coldly. "Here he is, sir. Best brace yourself. He's wanting something in payment for his animals that you killed and wasted." The ghosts of man and bear moved back from Ballinger as a rock, then another, slid down the slope to come to rest against his body.

He managed to roll back onto his hands and knees. With a super-human effort, he stood up, knees shaking as though they were made of rotten wood.

The sun had almost fully set now, but the white stag didn't need the sun's light to be seen. He glowed with his own light as he stepped down the mountain toward the trembling man. Only it wasn't his coat that glowed now. He was bones, pure bones, as he walked toward Ballinger, shining white. Only the eyes in the denuded skull were dark, and they were fixed full on Ballinger. Two of the ribs on one side had a hole smashed through them, directly over where the heart would have been. *I knew I hit him true!* Ballinger thought, despite the fear growing in him.

The skeleton deer stopped when it was a yard away from him. The great dark eyes fixed on his for a moment. *It's delirium!* he thought, for it seemed to him that, somehow, the thing was communicating with him, asking a question, though not in words.

Do you regret? it asked, and an image came into his mind, of skinned carcasses lying in heaps behind the Northwoods Inn, where the guides skinned out the animals that their clients killed.

Why should I be sorry? Ballinger thought wildly. *God gave Man dominion over all the creatures of land, sea, and sky. God gave them to me! God gave . . .*

I am God here, the reply came, and the stag, bracing on the bones of his hind legs, drew back, lowered his skull, and drove his antlers into Ballinger's stomach.

Gravity wanted to help him avoid death. He was below the thing on the slope, and as it lunged, Ballinger started falling backward. But then someone pushed him hard, from behind, into the thing's glowing antlers.

Ballinger's scream was faint, and bubbled at the end. The white stag drew back and raised his head with its gore-soaked antlers, and Ballinger was allowed at last to fall. He fell sprawling back down the mountain, landing with his feet higher than his head. He struggled to pull air into his punctured lungs for a little while, but then the bubbling gasps stopped, and only the wind among stones broke the silence.

The great white stag stepped around the body and walked over to the spirits, man and bear, who waited for him among the shadows in the forms of all the creatures most hunted by white men in the mountains. Now the stag was no longer a skeleton. Flesh filled out his shining white coat, and no mark showed where Ballinger's bullet had once struck.

He communicated with the spirits who had gathered to see their vengeance taken on at least one of the men who hunted for pleasure rather than need. *The man is dead*, it told them, *and his spirit will never reach a place of rest, nor will it remain here, on my mountain. Are you satisfied, my relatives?*

In response, most of the spirits scattered, drifting away to meadow, beaver pond, or forest. The last to leave but one was the ghost bear. It rose on its hind legs to meet Samoset face to face and whined once, softly. *Thank you, my relative, for helping me*, the ghost man told it. It dropped to all fours and ambled off down the mountain. Only the spirit stag and the ghost man remained.

I am sorry, my relative, the ghost communicated to the spirit. *I should not have helped him waste our relatives.*

You are forgiven, the stag told him. *We do what we must to feed our young. You paid for your mistake by bringing him here, to my mountain, where I am strong.*

Spirit and ghost touched then, with the ghost man pressing his forehead to the spirit's below where the mighty antlers sprang.

Where will you go, my relative and my friend? the stag asked the ghost.

I would like best to stay here, on your mountain, if you will allow it. I would like to watch over your land and your creatures forever.
So it shall be.

As the sun rose, it colored the rime-iced stones a chilly pink. Misty clouds colored the dawn sky a pale blue. Two spirits walked, a man and a great white stag, side by side up the slide, toward the summit of the mountain. As they walked, the man-shape slowly dissolved and reshaped itself, and a raven flew off to keep vigil on the mountain's peak. The stag watched him go, then sprang up the slide in mighty leaps. If anyone had been watching, they would have sworn that the gleaming stag had disappeared, becoming a part of the rock slide on the flank of Whiteface Mountain.

Fox Hill

Woody Sins

Sweat dripped down Henry's face and soaked his shirt as he rode down the old road on his ATV. The road, now little more than two ruts with a grass strip down the middle, had once led through the wilderness, bringing the hearty settlers from distant lands here to tame it to their will. The land was cleared; homes were built for families with names like Kessler, Bauer, and Staubb.

But it didn't last. The stony glacial ground and the perennially fierce winters drove the families out. A few hardy souls carried on and moved out to the main road. The cleared patches of farmland were consolidated into larger holdings. But, after several generations of battling the rocks and swamps, flies and snow, the descendants of the original settlers moved to the cities and forsook farm and woodlot. The land was returning to the wilderness from which it had been wrenched so long ago.

Forsaken, yes, but not totally abandoned. A few families lingered to pursue other occupations, while continuing to steward field, forest, and fen. Henry was one of these, a descendant of one of the Early Ones whose tombstones now populated the small, ill-kept cemeteries of long forgotten churchyards, whose edifices had tumbled to the ground many years past. He headed down the muddy road in the late afternoon of an especially humid July day, with a mattock across the handlebars of the much-repaired ATV he was driving, and a double barreled, twelve-gauge

Savage shotgun in a gun bag strapped to the equipment rack of the ATV. A small satchel on the back of the machine held a half-full flask of Tennessee sour mash whiskey, a box of buckshot shells, and a bottle of insect repellent.

Henry grew up on the family dairy farm, mending the fences destroyed by the winter's fury, making hay in the hot, humid summers to feed the cows during the dark winters, endless shoveling of manure and snow, and carrying out the ever-present task of milking. These jobs served as shackles to the farm, never allowing the inmates to stray far. It was what also forced the later generations away.

As he moved on, Henry noted in his mind the places of interest, as told to him by his father as together they pursued the ceaseless toil of another life. He passed a small field beyond which bubbled a fresh, cool spring. He stopped to slake a growing thirst but was soon driven back by mosquitoes and blackflies. He traveled on, thankful that the ATV could outrun even the most persistent insects. He passed the overgrown field that revealed, to those who knew precisely where to look, the faint impressions of the foundation where the cabin of his ancestors had been. He passed the location of a small sawmill, now completely lost to time and undergrowth. He passed the gate in a stone fence where his parents met for the first time so many years ago. He passed the foundations of other tiny farms long abandoned.

Soon he came to the goal of his mission. As the land grew more and more forsaken, the native wildlife began to flourish. In particular, the beavers had returned in numbers and were damming up the creek that bisected the land, cutting off all hope of a dry crossing. Henry had set out to eliminate one of these dams and its guardians, if he could. He turned down a trail off the main road that led across the creek at a now flooded fording and gunned the engine to get across without drowning the ATV. As he crossed, the water lapped around the machine, dangerously close to the intake. The engine sputtered. The water reached almost up to the bottom of the seat. Henry lifted his legs as high as he could, but he still got his boots wet in the slow-moving water. Soon he was across. He revved the engine again to make sure any water that had seeped into it was expelled.

Henry drove between clumps of brush that hid the crumbled walls of a barn and a small cellar hole, the location of an impossibly small house. He parked near the cellar hole and took a swig of the flask, and, after a liberal application of bug spray, he grabbed the mattock, walked down to the creek and over to the beaver dam that was blocking the waters. It had been pushed out before, just to be rebuilt immediately afterward by the industrious rodents.

Henry set to work on the dam with the mattock. He knew that the beavers would be out soon after sunset to repair the hole he was about to tear in the dam. When they did, he would be there with the shotgun . . .

Soon his task was done. Water gurgled through a large rent in the dam. Satisfied, Henry went back to the ATV, retrieved the gun and bag of ammo, and found a log to sit behind in clear view of the hole in the dam. He then waited for dusk.

The mosquitoes were beginning to ignore the fly dope Henry had applied. Swatting and cursing, he reached for the spray and reapplied it to his sweat-covered skin. *Fly spray won't work like that*, he thought. He put the spray back in his bag just as the setting sun dipped behind the trees across the receding beaver pond. Suddenly, Henry had an uneasy feeling he was being watched. He turned to meet the gaze of a large bobcat that had come to the creek for a drink. The cat was as startled to see Henry as Henry was to see it. Before Henry could aim his shotgun, the bobcat snarled and dashed into the brush and up the hill behind the creek. Henry stared into the gloom, setting the safety of his shotgun off. The sun set behind the trees as he stood. The daylight was slowly replaced by a gray dusk.

He stared for a time into the increasing shadow. After a while, he remembered that he had come here to dispose of some beavers that were supposed to be rebuilding their dam. He turned silently to the creek. He dropped the shotgun as he gazed in disbelief. The creek in front of him was galloping along unrestricted in its course to the sea. There was no sign of the beaver dam.

The forest around him seemed engulfed by the gray mist, neither cold nor warm. The humid air no longer pressed in around him. The buzzing insects ignored him. Henry stood for a few minutes, trying to rationalize what he was seeing. The gray dusk did not get any deeper. The sounds around him seemed muted, as if coming to him from a distance.

As he stared in wonder at what he thought he saw, he heard voices up the hill, in the direction of his ATV. *Probably some poachers or hunters*, he thought. He started up the hill to confront the interlopers. He took only a few steps before he noticed lights at the top of the small hill, coming from the dark form of a house.

"Too much, JD!" he chuckled to himself. Nonetheless, with no beavers to shoot, he couldn't do much here. He crept up the hill to the house. It was very snug for a house, more like a well-kept shack. There were two windows facing in his direction. As he approached, he nearly stumbled into a hole near the foundation, where steps led to a cellar. He recovered his wits and quietly peered into a window where the yellow light was coming from. Inside, he saw a scene directly out of *Little House on the Prairie*. A candle sputtered in a sconce on a small wooden table. In the corner was a wooden bed, with straw coming out from under the linens. An iron stove sat next to a pile of wood in one corner. The walls were sparsely decorated with the trappings of a very simple life.

Henry stared in disbelief. This sure is a whopper of a dream! He walked around the house. He could see where he left his ATV, hidden now by a large rose bush planted by a small garden. Daffodils were planted in neat rows along the path that led past the house. Henry could see the bulk of a barn on the other side, a feeble light shining through some of the low-set windows. He walked across the path, contemplating the wonder of it all.

He soon heard the soft tinkling of bells; not the sweet music of sleigh bells, nor the grand booming of a church bell. It was the harsh, un-melody of cowbells.

A small herd of cows was making its way up the path from the ford that he'd crossed earlier. Behind was a short, rather plump man chasing behind with a small switch in his hand, with which he prodded the stragglers.

"In die Scheune mit Ihnen!"

The language was unknown to Henry, although he had watched enough *Hogan's Heroes* reruns and war movies to peg it as German. He ducked into the brush near a swamp that lay near the barn. For some reason, he didn't want to be seen. The strange parade soon entered the barn and disappeared. The smell of cow dung came to his nostrils, familiar, yet somehow strange to him. The light within was extinguished. The man he'd seen earlier was making his way up the hill to the house. Suddenly, the man turned around and stared directly at the bushes where Henry had hidden himself. Henry hunkered down even farther into the alders. He heard a door slam.

Henry glanced uneasily around. Up the hill to his right, away from the barn, he saw more lights twinkling. In the farther distance, more lights faintly glimmered through the ghastly grayness. He looked to where the ATV was parked. He could just make it out in the grayness, more of a shadow than an actual object. As quietly as possible, Henry slogged through the swamp and to a freshly plowed field, away from the strange scene. In his youth, this had been one of many hay fields that made up the family farm. It was once owned by a family named Bauer.

He trudged through the field and through a hedge to the next field. His family had always called this plot of land "Kesslers," in memory of the former owners. The crumbling stone and cement ruins of the cattle barn and a small horse barn across the main road was all that was left of that enterprise. As he approached the location of the ruins, he heard more voices, in the same strange language. He hid himself behind a large boulder in a hedge and peered at the scene.

The ruins had been replaced with a barn running parallel to the road. A wooden bridge passed from a large stone ramp built to the side of the barn and another bridge passed through the barn, across the road, and over to the horse barn beyond. Henry could just make out the faint smells and sounds of the animals within.

As he watched, a young woman came to a stone-lined well dug near the side of the barn. She wore a plain dress, tied in the middle. Henry couldn't make out any colors, but the clothes were old fashioned and very utilitarian looking. She had a lantern in one hand and a small wooden bucket in the other. The woman walked to the well, lowered another bucket on a windlass, and drew up some water, with which she filled the bucket that she'd been carrying. She picked up the bucket and walked back under the barn bridge. She hummed a tune as she walked. Soon she disappeared behind the barn. Henry heard a door slam. At one time a house sat on the hill beyond the barn, and Henry knew that, although he couldn't see the house, it was, somehow, there again, like the other buildings he had seen. He walked over to the well and peered into the depths. He knew the well. It was very deep but had been filled in a long time ago, when the farm was abandoned. Now it gaped wide and menacing in the gloom.

Suddenly, the fear that was creeping up in Henry's mind burst forth. He had to get away, get back to where he belonged. His heart raced as he resolved to get his ATV—and get out!

He sprinted to the road. The fastest way back was down that road, across the creek, and back to the ford. He would cross over the beaver dam that was always built between the stone piers of a long-collapsed bridge and avoid the crossing that was used in his youth to get hay across the creek. As he approached, he could see no sign of the crossing, only the alders and shrubs that grew by the water. He approached the bridge, for bridge it was, a smudge against the surrounding flora. He continued with much trepidation, his breath coming in sharp gasps. He carefully set his foot on the small plank bridge. It didn't yield. Screwing up his courage, he dashed across the twelve-foot span and didn't stop until he got well off the bridge and its piers to the opposite shore. He stopped and doubled over from his recent exertions, gasping for breath and nursing a stitch in his side.

Suddenly, a dog barked. In terror, he looked up and noticed the dark bulk of a house to the right of the road. To the left, another house loomed farther off the path. These houses, he realized, were the ones he had seen earlier from his swampy hiding place. They were dark now. Henry prepared himself for another sprint and dashed past the shadow houses and into a cut in a hill the road passed through. As he ran, he heard a strange voice call out. The dog stopped barking.

Henry jogged on, fear gripping him, his side burning, until he came to the spot where he had turned off the road and crossed the flooded creek, such a long time ago it seemed. He raced across the ford, now so dry that the water didn't even go over his ankles. He quietly walked up the path, looking for his ATV and glancing around in terror.

Suddenly, a shadow stood before him. It was the small man who chased the cows up from the creek and back into the barn. Henry stopped abruptly. His heart leaped to his throat. A chill blast of air smote him, swirling the dead leaves that lay around him, in his face, in his hair.

"Kommen Sie mit."

"I don't understand."

The figure gestured for him to follow.

He followed the now silent figure past the house and barn, past the small garden, past the ghost-like ATV. The wind had died down, but the air was still as cold as the grave. The pair walked into a wooded area past the farm buildings and finally up a hill in the woods that Henry knew as the Fox Hill, after a family of foxes that had lived there in his youth. Near the top, the figure stopped and pointed to a spot near his feet. Henry could see a stone, around the size of a softball, half buried in the humus of the forest floor. It was whitish, and it looked like it was made of quartz. It was difficult to tell in the deep gray light.

"What do you want?" Henry said, looking up. He was alone. The figure had vanished. The air returned to the neutral temperature of the unnatural twilight.

Henry woke with the sun beaming at him through the trees. The blackflies were out for breakfast. His whole body ached. He struggled to his feet, swatting flies and rubbing his eyes, which now stung with the residue of the fly repellent. He looked about him. The beavers had done their work, and the dam was repaired. His gun lay where he had dropped it.

Just a dream, he thought. He got to his feet as he cursed his luck in falling asleep so readily and missing the beavers. He had the last swallow of hooch for breakfast, picked up his trappings, and headed up the hill to the cellar hole and his waiting ATV. Although it was still early in the morning, he began to feel the heat of the day. He soon reached the top of the hill. There sat the ATV by the overgrown path, just where he had left it. With a yawn, he glanced around him. As his eyes fell on the cellar hole to his left, the images of the night flooded over him.

How can I dream of people talking in German? he thought. *I don't speak German!*

He ran through the underbrush, through the woods to the top of Fox Hill. There, after a brief search, he found a quartz stone just visible beneath last year's leaves. He grabbed the rock and attempted to turn it over, without success. He trudged back to the ATV, retrieved it, along with the shotgun and mattock, and used the mattock to pry the stone up. The air suddenly became chill again, as it had in his dream. He began to dig.

It wasn't long, a mere minute or so, before Henry's pick hit something. He got to his knees and began to move loose soil out of the small hole. He was sweating, even though the air was still frigid, as if he were standing next to an open freezer. With a loud curse, he suddenly pulled his hand back and tucked it under his arm. His shirt was soon spotted red with blood. He removed his hand and saw blood oozing from a large gash across two of his fingertips, mixing with the dirt and debris on his hands. He went back down the hill and rinsed his hand in the stream, now swollen back to its beaver-impaired level. The hot air pressed in on him, making him sweat even worse. He made a makeshift bandage from a strip of material from his shirt sleeve and, after deciding it was not nearly as bad as he originally supposed, went back up Fox Hill to resume his work.

The air on top of the hill was still cold. Henry picked up a stick and prodded the dirt in the hole. Pieces of glass from an antique Mason jar glinted in the dirt. He had cut himself on one of these shards. He poked around the hole until he found most of the pieces of the jar, which was shattered by the mattock. Henry also dislodged the rusted remains of the jar lid, not in place on the jar, but under it. Henry continued to dig and prod, but he found nothing else, only the broken jar and its lid. If it had contained anything, it was long gone.

Henry shivered in the cold and stood up, thoroughly bewildered. He was meant to find something, but it was no longer there. He picked up his mattock and turned back down the hill. His hand was throbbing, and he supposed he should get back and dress it properly. Suddenly, he looked up and saw the faint form of a short, rather plump man, like a shadow in the perpetual gloom of the forest. The shadow looked at Henry. After a few moments, it seemed to shrug its shoulders, as if to say, "I don't get it either," and slowly dissolved. Henry was left staring at the ferns on the slope, in astonishment. The muggy air soon engulfed him again.

CHAPTER 12

Bang!

Gerhardt Storsberg

Our group was about to embark on a hunting expedition in the heart of the Adirondack Mountains, where the trees stand tall and the rivers flow freely. Our faces were weathered by years spent in the wilderness. I had packed my gear weeks before in exuberant anticipation and was excited to see my friends. We possessed a camaraderie forged through shared experiences and a deep respect for the untamed beauty surrounding us. We also enjoyed eating, so we hunted.

I was less familiar with this area than the other members of my group, but I still had experience as a hunter. Being a skilled woodsman with a keen eye for spotting game takes years to master. Bill was the man who stood out in the group. He had been a guide in his younger years and killed a lot of game throughout his life. I hoped to gain even more experience by hunting with him. We knew Bill, and his presence instilled confidence in all of us. He called my name as we started our journey. "Dave, come here," he said. I walked up to him and knew he wanted to tell me something. "I know your family emigrated from Scotland, but hunting in the Adirondacks is very different; it is not open farmland but filled with dense forest. Bullets can come from any direction, and the landscape is very rugged. Stay aware and cautious." When Bill finished his lecture, he returned to arranging his hunting gear. I knew he was right.

Scotland had forest, but it was nowhere near as thick as this seemingly impenetrable mass of trees, shrubs, rocks, plants, and water we would be traveling through. As young men, we had hunted farmland and open highlands in Scotland. I had hunted in the Adirondacks a few times but wasn't as comfortable as I had been back in my country. I heeded his admonitions and followed our group into the woods. As we ventured into the trees, our senses heightened, attuned to the subtle signs of life around us.

The crisp autumn air always seemed to carry the promise of adventure in my mind. I knew we all relished the challenge ahead. We began our hunt with rifles slung over our shoulders and packs filled with provisions.

The going was tough, and we trudged through the dense undergrowth for hours, following the faint trails left by deer and bears. Bill offered occasional advice, and conversation flowed freely among us. We discussed the fall of society and how the younger generations should have held on to traditions that were important to us. Jokes were told, and punctuated bursts of laughter filled the air. When there was a lull in our talking, you would hear the occasional call of a bird overhead warning of our presence.

As the day wore on, we found ourselves deep in a remote corner of the Adirondacks. This area was remote even for Bill. He had led us far from our familiar paths in the hopes of finding better and bigger game. Undeterred by fatigue, we pressed on, our determination unwavering in the face of uncertainty.

We pressed on like this for another hour, and Bill signaled for us to stop. He had spotted some good tracks and suggested we split up and try to push the deer toward an area called flowed lands. It was a large, swampy area of water. If we could force the deer in that direction, the water would limit its travel direction, thus increasing our chances of killing it. We should go in different directions, he suggested, and the conversations ended. Quiet was the rule, and I was now on my own.

As I walked, I reflected on Bill's words and pushed along a ridge to reach the east end of the water he had told us about. The area was beautiful—large white pines towered above me. Maples, beech, and poplar decorated the landscape with the varied colors of fall, and the wind distributed the smells of fall throughout the forest floor. An old saying states, "The fastest way to the universe is to start your journey in the forest." I finally understood what this meant.

After a while, I was exhausted and rested on a large rock. I reached into my pack for water and put the canteen to my lips. I was overcome by how wonderful simple things like this can be. I sat back and enjoyed my short respite. The woods ahead were dense and thick, and the swamp I sought was nowhere to be seen. Dampness seemed to engulf everything I touched, and sweat poured from my brow; it was wet but not what I was searching for.

I continued to follow the ridge. It was rugged and filled with glacial deposits of ancient rocks and boulders. I was bushwhacking, so there was no trail to make my travel easier. At one point, I couldn't continue; there was a deep gulley that was impossible to navigate. I'd have to drop off the ridge and follow the valley for a way. I knew going down was my only option.

When I finally reached the bottom, the ground area had transitioned to eastern hemlock. Hemlocks like this tend to be on the sides of hills and near wet areas. I could see some tag alders in the distance, indicating water was nearby. I danced from rock to rock, hoping to keep my feet dry, but it was useless. Anyone who has ever been in the Adirondack woods is aware of the constant mud along the paths.

I had found a herd path that the deer had made. This was a promising sign.

The mud was thick and heavy from the prints of the animals' hooves. I could see an opening through the trees and finally saw the water I had been searching for. I reached a feeder creek and pushed toward a large boulder that might afford me a better view of the swamp and lake. I slipped while climbing over some roots to reach the rock outcropping. Suddenly, I heard a loud "Bang!" Where did that shot come from? I couldn't see anything through the thick cover of the trees, and I could see nothing across the swamp. Had someone shot a deer or simply taken a hopeful shot? I couldn't tell. I ducked, unsure where the shot had come from. I was confused. What should I do? I ran toward another open area for a better view. I had panicked and was reckless. Running is one thing you should not do with a gun. In the chaos of pursuing the sound of the "Bang," I was separated from the group and lost. Panic gripped my chest as I realized I was in trouble. I was alone in the vast wilderness, without knowing which direction my companions had gone.

♣♣♣

Desperation set in as I frantically searched for any sign of my fellow hunters. I called out their names, my voice echoing through the trees, but there was no response. I reached to fire a distress signal from my rifle and was shocked to discover I had lost my ammunition. The forest seemed to close in around me. I panicked, and I was suffocating with the oppressive silence of the woods.

Fear began to gnaw at my resolve, but I knew I had to stay calm for any hope of survival. Drawing on my years of experience, I took stock of my surroundings, searching for clues that might lead me back to safety.

The sun began to dip below the horizon, casting long shadows across the forest floor. With each passing minute, the evening chill crept closer, a stark reminder of the harsh reality of life in the wilderness and my situation.

Drawing my rifle closer, I pressed on, determined to return to civilization. Every rustle of leaves and snap of twigs sent shivers down my spine, and I imagined the creatures lurking in the darkness, waiting to pounce on their unsuspecting prey.

♣♣♣

The hours turned into days as I wandered through the forest, my stomach growling with hunger and my body growing weak from exhaustion. I refused to give up hope, believing that help would soon arrive. Just when I thought I could go on no longer, a glimmer of hope appeared on the horizon.

Through the thick canopy of trees, I spotted the shape of a man. He was distant, and the low light made me question my perception. I yelled and pushed my way toward him. He didn't see me. There was no direct route. The terrain was rugged and filled with obstacles. He was gone before I could reach the spot where I thought I saw him. Frustration gripped me, and I yelled in frustration.

I pushed forward; disappointment slowed my pace. I began to think of my family. Despair overwhelmed me, and I sat against a tree, weeping as I fell to the ground.

I eventually lost my sense of time. My thoughts turned increasingly to my family. I imagined my wife's worried expression as she waited for me to return, her gentle touch soothing the children's fears. I pictured Emily and Thomas playing in the yard, their laughter echoing through the house. And with each passing day, the ache in my heart grew more unbearable.

One day, as I continued to trudge through the mud and leaf-covered forest, I stumbled upon a small clearing bathed in golden sunlight. A pine tree stood in the center of the clearing, its branches reaching toward the sky like outstretched arms. And beneath the tree, nestled in a bed of soft moss, I saw something that made my heart leap with joy—a delicate patch of wildflowers, their petals a vibrant splash of color against the backdrop of green.

For a moment, I forgot about my loneliness, my longing for home. I knelt beside the flowers, breathing in their sweet fragrance and marveling at their beauty. And in that moment, I felt a sense of peace wash over me—a sense of connection to the natural world and the beauty surrounding me.

As I gazed up at the towering pine tree, I felt a surge of gratitude for the simple pleasures of life, the beauty of the wilderness, and the love of my family. And in that moment, I silently vowed to cherish every moment and savor every precious memory.

The sun dipped below the horizon, and the stars began to twinkle overhead. Another day had ended. I sat beneath the pine tree, my heart full of love and gratitude. And though I was still far from home, I knew that I was not alone—for in the wilderness, surrounded by the beauty of nature, I had momentary solace, hope, and the strength to carry on.

🌲🌲🌲

The forest loomed dark and foreboding when I arose in the morning. The ancient trees stretched toward the sky like gnarled fingers clawing at the heavens. Among the tangled underbrush, a lone figure, I stumbled, my breath ragged and challenging, my senses dulled by exhaustion and despair. I was making narratives in my brain. I was struggling, and I was acutely aware of it.

It had started as a simple hunting trip—a chance to escape the suffocating confines of city life and reconnect with nature. As I ventured deeper into the wilderness, the familiar landmarks began to fade, and I was swallowed up by the dense foliage surrounding me. I was still confused. When would my suffering end?

I heard a loud "Bang!" again. That's all I recalled. I had fallen asleep and stumbled awake at the sound of the "Bang!" I tried to get my bearings. What happened? Where had the shot come from? Would they help me? Try as I might, I couldn't put it all together. I had been hunting in that area for years. Why was I so confused?

I checked myself over and found nothing.

Rubbing my eyes, I tried to focus. I was hungry and tired. I sat up and looked at my surroundings.

My situation had placed me in a very dense area of the Adirondack Mountains. It was beautiful but intimidating. I had become a city boy in my everyday life, but I yearned to relive my time in the woods during my younger days. Why was something so familiar now so intimidating? I stood and scanned the area again for a way out.

I gazed up at the soaring white pines and reminded myself of my pledge to appreciate life's simple pleasures, the beauty of the wilderness, and the love of my family. Thinking about them would sustain me and give me hope. And in that moment, I felt refreshed.

Another day came and went; the sun dipped below the horizon, and the stars began to twinkle at night. I sat beneath my tree, and I tried to fill my heart full of love and gratitude. I was still lost and far from home, but I knew I was not alone—for in the wilderness, surrounded by the beauty of nature, I would occasionally find solace, hope, and strength.

The next day, I trudged deeper into the forest, and the weather worsened. Dark clouds gathered overhead, casting a pall over the landscape. The air grew colder, and a fine mist settled around me, seeping into my clothes and chilling me to the bone. The ground beneath my feet grew sodden with each step, turning the once-tranquil trail into a quagmire of mud and slush.

The sun came out, and I saw the fog lifting from the swampy area directly before me. The ground was damp, and tag alders surrounded the banks of the murky water near a beaver dam a little way down the bank. It would be challenging travel, but it was my only option, so I began to walk.

My confidence waned with each passing minute, replaced by a creeping sense of unease. I tried to retrace my steps and find my way back to civilization, but the forest seemed to shift and change around me, leading me further astray. Suddenly, I caught a glimpse again of something walking through the woods. It was unclear, and my imagination quickly led me to believe it was another person. I dashed toward the movement, only to be blocked by a large bog. I was cut off again. By the time I navigated the rugged terrain, the silhouette had disappeared. I yelled and waved my hands, but the effort remained unnoticed like before. The frustration of my situation was becoming worse the more I thought about it.

Night fell, and I was again alone in the wilderness, the darkness pressing on all sides. I huddled beneath a makeshift shelter, the cold seeping into my bones as I tried to ward off the chill. But even as I curled up beneath my meager protection, sleep eluded me; it was chased away by the haunting whispers of the night.

Days continued to turn into nights, and still, I pressed onward, my determination unyielding despite the countless obstacles in my path. I relied on my instincts to guide me through the wilderness. I continued to navigate treacherous terrain and weathered fierce storms, each hardship steeling my resolve.

But as the days stretched on, I finally began to lose hope. I had again lost track of time. I felt like a ship adrift on a vast and endless sea, my fate determined by the capricious whims of nature. I longed for the familiar comforts of home—the warmth of a fire, the soft embrace of a loved one—but they seemed like distant memories, fading with each passing day.

I clung to a sliver of hope—a belief that I would one day find my way out of the forest and emerge from this trial stronger and wiser. It was a fragile thread, frayed and worn from the weight of my suffering, but it was enough to keep me going.

Every day continued to be familiar. The forest, even in moments of beauty, was becoming redundant. My moods varied from hopeful to desperate. It was like a never-ending dream that I couldn't escape; I yearned for a way out.

As I trudged through the undergrowth, I caught sight of something in the distance—a glimmer of light, dancing amid the shadows like a beacon of hope. With renewed determination, I forged ahead, my heart pounding in my chest as I drew closer and closer to what I hoped was salvation.

As I looked out at the world beyond the forest, I saw a brilliant beam of light in the distance. It promised a new day—I continued to hope for rescue. In the depths of the wilderness, I, again, was overcome with the strength to survive and the courage to face whatever challenges lay ahead.

The dark clouds seemed to separate as I approached, and the light broke through the clouds. It was almost surreal. As I moved forward, the light beam illuminated the path before me. The ground was soft and sweet with the smell of the earth and pine. I felt as if I was floating.

🌲🌲🌲

A group of hikers was just arriving at Calamity Brook, and they heard a loud "Bang!"

"What the heck was that?" one of the hikers asked.

"It sounded like a gunshot," said another member of the group.

They scanned the area where they thought they had heard the noise and saw no one. They noticed the sun breaking through the clouds as they peered into the swamp. It was a blinding light and illuminated a large area. Mist seemed to rise from around them and float toward the sky.

"Wow," exclaimed one of the hikers, "that mist almost looks like the shape of a human. Do you see that?"

They turned their gaze to look, but the shape disappeared quickly toward the sky. When their eyes drifted back toward the trail, they spotted an unusual shape near the creek. They slowly walked over and saw a headstone. "A headstone?" said one of the hikers. "What is that doing here in the middle of the woods?"

The group leader had been in this area before and knew why it was there. "That's a grave marker," he said.

"For what?" asked the members of his group.

"It's called Calamity Brook in honor of Dave Henderson and his crew. They encountered many hardships here, and there was an accident with a gun. Henderson was an immigrant from Scotland in the mid-nineteenth century and spent time in this area. He died more than a hundred years ago from a gunshot wound he received during a hunting trip. Legend has it that he died somewhere in this location, and they never found his body. Some people say you can sometimes glimpse his ghost as he wanders through the woods looking to be found and rescued. He never was."

As I floated toward the sky, I noticed a group of men standing and staring at something. Were they looking for me? Would I be rescued? I focused my blurring vision on them and smiled. Dave Henderson was inscribed on a stone. That's me. That's my name! I finally understood what had happened and felt relief. I heard a "Bang! Bang! Bang!" I was not afraid; I was dreamily aware now that it was my gun—it had killed me. It had fired when I slipped on the rocks. My own gun delivered the mortal shot!

I wasn't angry as I floated toward the light, and the thunderclap "Bang!" guided me peacefully upward. I would no longer be haunted by the "Bang" of my gun. I had finally found my way home. My ghost would never be seen again.

A Brief History of the Area

Calamity Creek, situated in the Adirondack Mountains of New York State, holds a storied history deeply intertwined with the region's exploration, settlement, and natural disasters.

The creek's name originates from a series of calamitous events in the mid-nineteenth century. During the mid-1800s, the Adirondacks witnessed a surge in logging activity driven by the demand for timber. Calamity Creek became a focal point for logging operations due to its proximity to valuable stands of timber. However, the rugged terrain and unpredictable weather of the Adirondacks made logging here extremely challenging.

In 1845, a catastrophic flood ravaged the region, causing widespread destruction to the logging infrastructure along Calamity Creek. This event, coupled with subsequent floods and landslides, earned the creek its ominous name.

Despite the setbacks, logging continued in the area, and Calamity Creek became a notable landmark for loggers, explorers, and settlers venturing into the Adirondacks. The creek's rugged beauty and surrounding wilderness also attracted outdoor enthusiasts and adventurers, further contributing to its significance in the region.

Chapter 13

Terror at Camp Russell

Daniel Swift

"Mikey, you got everything packed and in the car?" his mother shouted up the stairs.

"Yeah, Mom. I'll be right down," Mikey replied.

The ride up through the Adirondacks to Camp Russell was always serene. Filled with its sweet sappy scent of the thick pines, the fresh mountain air always made Mikey feel more at home.

As they entered Camp Russell, which was nestled along White Lake in the Hamlet of Woodgate, New York, the dried pine needles covering the road crunched beneath their car's tires. "Looks like there is a spot over there by the TeePee," Mikey said enthusiastically.

As Mikey gathered his stuff, the sounds of scouts running around pecked its way into his head like that of a woodpecker. Wasn't that long ago, he was that young scout running around causing mischief. But with his promotion to the position of senior patrol leader of the troop, he wanted to make a strong impression this year.

"Looks like Mr. Mitchell's over there," he stated as he closed the trunk.

Mr. Mitchell was a tall, strong man who preferred to be called "Tigger" because of his bouncing personality. Tigger was a man well versed in the outdoors, and he always made every outing special and fun. A true champion for the whole scouting experience.

"Hey, Tigger!" Mikey yelled as he sat beside his mother's car.

"Oh, good. Mikey, can you get the boys ready for the swim test after they have finished settling into their tents?" Tigger asked in his baritone voice.

"Sure," Mikey replied as his mom helped him carry his stuff up the short trail to campsite Daniel Beard, where Troop 48 always stayed.

The site was set up in an oval shape. Around the border were the canvas tents that could have been plucked right out of an old war movie. Traditional and nostalgic they were, being set up on a wooden platform with two camp cots per tent.

Mikey placed his footlocker at the foot of one of the beds nearest to the path and then took a few moments to cinch up the flaps of his tent with a paracord. This kept the mosquitos and blackflies from getting inside. That was his least favorite part of being in the Adirondacks . . . the bugs.

On the far side of the site, the younger boys were playing tag. "Troop 48! Round up!" Mikey yelled.

"Hey, what's up, Mikey?" asked one of the boys.

"Tigger wants us to get ready for the swim test. So, let's go."

As they got their swim gear on, their parents crowded around Tigger, who was standing between the lean-to and the camp's fire pit.

"Okay, folks, gather 'round," Tigger stated over the many voices. "Troop 48, I said listen up! Welcome to Camp Russell '99! This week should be a great one. Parents, if for any reason you need to be contacted, I will reach out to you." Tigger then paused for a moment. "Lastly, I was able to book the Trappers Cabin for Thursday evening."

Hearing this news, the chatter among the boys grew in eager anticipation. They were filled with excitement at finally staying in the cabin as other troops had done in the past.

"Troop!" Tigger sounded, quieting down the ever-growing chatter. "Let's head down to the waterfront. Say your good-byes and line up over by the headquarters building in fifteen minutes."

Back in the parking lot, the parents said their good-byes. "Okay, Mikey, have a great week, and I will see you at the closing ceremony on Friday," Mikey's mother told him.

"Thanks, Mom. Love you," he replied as he hugged her quickly and then headed over to the headquarters building.

The smell of white pine was abundantly strong as the wind blew through the parade field behind the nursing station. At one end were the flagpoles and on the other stood the mess hall. High overhead, the hand-carved totem poles were visually astounding in the central hub of the entire camp.

As they reached the path to the waterfront, they could see the shimmer of diamonds on a brilliant blue blanket that was the lake. The wind blew, swaying the boats by the dock as the sound of the boys in the water swelled.

"Line up over here and listen to Rick the lifeguard," Tigger said as he guided them along the fence.

As Rick finished up the previous group of boys and made his way over to the gate, the youngest scout whispered in shock, "He is missing an arm!"

Quickly, Mikey nudged the boy and gave him a look that said, "Shut up!"

Rick began in a boisterous tone, "Okay, scouts! Welcome to the waterfront. There will be free swim times during the week and the mile swim on Wednesday. In order for us to know what level swimmer you are, we will be doing a swim test here in a moment. There are three levels . . ."

Mikey, having gone through this over the last couple of years knew the drill by now and slightly tuned out Rick as he continued his speech.

"Okay, so if you are going to go for the advanced swimmer, head on down to the foot of the dock," Rick exclaimed in authoritative enthusiasm. After the troop had finished their swim tests, Mikey and Harry were happy that they passed and could do the mile swim again this year.

Later that evening, as the blanket of stars hung overhead and the fire crackled, the flames danced about the hot coals. The boys were talking about the merit badges they were starting the next morning.

"What badges are you taking this year, Harry?" asked Mikey.

"Oh, I am taking Lifesaving and Environmental Conservation."

"Nice. Me, too. I need to earn those to complete my required merit badges."

Interrupting their conversation, the sound of "Taps" (the military song for the end of day) could be heard in the distance. "All right, boys, time for bed," Tigger stated as he stirred the fire, spreading out the flames to let them die out.

The first few days flew by, and as the Thursday morning glow peeked through the tent flaps and the warm wind blew, Mikey awoke to the sound of the younger scouts chatting in excitement. Between the water games that afternoon and the cabin that evening, the boys were eager to start their day.

The oppressive heat seemed to be abundantly hotter than the other days. There were no clouds in the brilliant blue sky, and the humidity just made everything stickier. There was nothing but sunshine and sweat in the weather forecast.

When that afternoon's classes had been released, the boys gathered their things for the water games and made their way down to the waterfront. A few hours later, the scouts of Troop 48, taking turns hauling a greasy watermelon, marched back to camp to get ready for their evening at the cabin.

Mikey, particularly pleased with himself as his chest glistened from the greasy slime of the Crisco, said to Harry, "Never thought I would have ever participated in the melon chase, let alone get it."

"Watching you all wrestling a Crisco-covered watermelon in the water was hilarious!" Harry said with a chuckle.

Around nightfall, standing in front of the registration building, Tigger signed them into the Trappers Cabin for the night.

"This should be a great night. We get to sleep in the best spot of the loft," Mikey told Harry.

"Wait! You guys are staying in the Trappers Cabin?" Charlie, a boy from the capital district asked in a subtly shocked voice. "Sorry that I overheard but . . . the trappers cabin?!"

"Yeah, why?"

"Well, my brother Johnny told me a story about that cabin."

"Yeah? Well, I met your brother, and I don't know if I would believe him," Mikey said with a laugh.

"Well, Johnny wouldn't have told me unless it was true," Charlie responded with a smug tone. "He told me . . ."

He paused for a moment, then continued in an almost whispering voice. "Some years back, a troop stayed at the cabin, and that night, strange things happened.

"See, it seems that, as the troop settled in, a scout said that he saw some weird lights and heard some strange sounds. But when they went to investigate . . . well . . . they never found anything wrong. In the morning, however, when they went to leave, that boy was acting strange, and by the end of camp, he had vanished . . . like poof . . . gone!

"Apparently, the search for him somehow ended up at that cabin . . . under the trapdoor . . . but all they found were some scratches on the ground and a scout sock.

"Now, some say that he just disappeared. Some say that he simply ran away. But Johnny thinks that what really happened is a Camp Russell mystery. A mystery so dark that even old man Frank the woodcarver won't talk about it."

"Well, that seems like a delusional story to me," Mikey interrupted. "Sounds like Johnny was telling you a story there, Charlie."

"No way! Johnny told me it is true."

"Don't you think that would have been in the news?" Mikey asked, then continued in his best newscaster voice with an extremely mocking tone. "Another scouting mystery from Camp Russell. Investigations into these disturbing reports have yet to be resolved, but authorities are still on the case."

"Yeah, whatever, Mikey. Don't say I didn't warn you," Charlie said as he walked away.

"That Charlie . . . what a nut he is," Harry stated.

"Oh, don't I know it. Yesterday, he told me that old man Frank was really an FBI informant and that he is here because he is in witness protection. 'Cause, I mean, that totally makes sense," replied Mikey in utter amusement.

"Okay, guys! Let's head out," Tigger announced while the red sun sank behind the mountains.

Made out of thick logs, the cabin looked like an Adirondack dream home. Set back deep in the woods, it was something out of an old hunting documentary. With a few touches here and a few touches there, this place could be some city slicker's home away from home. A true escape into the Adirondack landscape.

The front porch was worn and weathered, and the cabin was obviously clear on just how old the place must have been. The hinges to the door were cast iron, and the rope that fed through the door, acting like a doorknob, was heavily frayed.

"All right, older boys have use of the loft, and the younger scouts are down below," Tigger said as he pulled the rope to release the door latch, opening the door.

As darkness took hold and the creatures of the night began to stir, the cabin was aglow from the wood stove. The boys, nestled into their beds for the night, needed some rest, and even Tigger was falling fast asleep.

Around two in the morning, Mikey awoke to a slight chill in the air. The soft warm amber glow of the woodstove flickered as it danced about the room, and Mikey could see that each boy was still asleep as he tended to the fire.

Closing the cast iron door, Mikey thought he heard something behind him. A sudden freeze filled the room, and Mikey could see his breath as he turned the handle, locking the door to the wood stove. Then in his peripheral vision a shadowy figure dashed, giving him even more of a hair-raising sensation.

Subconsciously remembering that story Charlie had told him about the cabin, Mikey slowly looked over toward the trapdoor to find nothing over there. He balled his fists and rubbed his eyes, allowing them to once again refocus in the very dim light.

To his amazement, the trapdoor now looked slightly ajar and had light protruding through the old wooden slats. Each bright beam of light enveloped the cabin in a sheet of brilliance. It seemed, however, like no one else even noticed it, nor awoke to its glow.

As Mikey slowly crept nearer to the trapdoor, he could feel a spider-like tingle walking down his spine. Slowly he reached out his trembling hand to open the hatch, but the light suddenly flickered fast and then went completely out.

Mikey audibly gasped as the sudden darkness of the night took over, and the sound of the trapdoor slamming shut echoed throughout the cabin.

"Mikey . . . what are you doing?" Tigger groggily asked.

"Sorry, Tigger. I swear there was a light coming out from under the old trapdoor."

"That door doesn't work. Hasn't been usable in years. Just go back to bed," Tigger said through a yawn. "Everyone go back to bed," he finished as he rested his head back upon his pillow.

Mikey laid back down overlooking the cabin from the loft. His eyes darted about the room. He focused on this corner and then that corner until his eyes grew heavy, and the light of the stove disappeared behind his heavy, exhausted eyelids.

"Beep, beep, beep, beep" sounded Mikey's watch as he pushed the button frantically, turning off the alarm.

That's weird. I didn't have an alarm set, he thought as he looked to see the time. "Ugh . . . three-thirty," he whispered.

Slipping down again from the loft, he put another log into the wood stove and grabbed his flashlight to go use the bathroom. He walked toward the door and got that tingling feeling again as the hair on the back of his neck stood up. He brushed his neck with his hand and looked around to find nothing there, yet again.

After relieving his rather full bladder, Mikey stepped back onto the porch of the cabin. An owl hooted in the moonlight, startling him. "Damn owl scared me." he said aloud.

Taking the rope handle into his hand, suddenly Mikey was shaking as if he was outdoors in the middle of winter. Trembling in place, his breath billowing from behind his chattering teeth, he could hear strange scratching sounds from beneath the cabin.

"Nope! There is nothing there," he said aloud as he tugged the rope. As soon as the door closed behind him, however, he could feel all the warmth from within disappear. The stove still had a fire burning, but the bunks were empty.

Mikey looked puzzled as he quickly shifted his eyes about the dark, cold cabin. Nothing was as it was supposed to be. In fact, there were now animal furs hanging on the walls and an old oil lantern hung from the loft.

Suddenly, a glow from beneath the trapdoor pulled his attention, and Mikey stumbled, tripping over a large pair of boots. He landed hard on his butt and bounced his head off the log cabin wall.

As he rubbed his head, his eyes refocused. The light from the trapdoor shone like the sun. He placed his hand in front of his eyes as he squinted trying to focus through the blinding light.

A grizzly looking man climbed out of the trapdoor. His shaggy hair and a long beard made it hard to see his face. His clothes were dark and dingy, and the smell of sweat filled the air, making Mikey gag as he held his nose.

The dark figure closed the door behind him. In doing so, he draped the cabin in a heavy blanket of black. Not even the stars or the moon could now be seen through the old dirty windows. There was nothing but darkness.

The sound of a match strike and the momentary smell of sulfur filled the air, and a soft glow flickered until the man lit the oil lantern. He then sat by the trapdoor in his grimy old Adirondack chair.

Whimpering cries of children could be heard from beneath the trapdoor, as he sat there puffing away at his corn cob tobacco pipe. The warm red glow showed on his cheeks. His old eyes, twinkling but beyond eerie, gave a sense of excitement as he smirked at the trapdoor.

Mikey listened intently to the muffled cries from beneath the floor. They were almost too hard to make out, but it sounded like they said, "Please! Please just let us go!"

As the man sat there smiling, Mikey began to inch his way toward the trapdoor. As he held his breath, tears welled up in his eyes. He could feel the growing sickness of worry within his stomach. His heart nearly skipped beats from the unknown horrors that were beneath.

Inches from the door, with his eyes fixed upon the bearded man, Mikey barely touched the cold, damp wood when the stale air shifted. The gaze of the man's eyes flashed to Mikey, and the pleasure in them dissolved. He lunged toward Mikey and screamed a horrifying, blood-curdling sound. The shriek was so bone chilling and deafening that it echoed throughout the cabin.

The fear and terror within Mikey was abundant as he let out an ear-piercing scream. He trembled as the icy heat of the man's grasp sucked the life force and energy from him. It left him in a pure catatonic state of fear.

"Mikey! *Wake up!*" exclaimed Tigger as he shook Mikey in his sleeping bag. "Wake up, Mikey! You're having a nightmare."

Popping up quickly, Mikey swung and hit Tigger square in the jaw as he screamed. "I'm so sorry! I didn't mean to hit you!" Mikey mumbled through sobs as everyone looked startled and confused.

"Mikey, you were having a nightmare. We are in the cabin at Camp Russell. You are safe," Tigger stated as he rubbed his jawline.

"Tigger! There was a man over there. He was smoking, and there were children under the trapdoor! I swear it! Please, look at the door!"

"Mikey, I told you that the door doesn't work. There are no children below the door, and there is no man. I swear. You are safe," Tigger exclaimed. "Okay, there is nothing else to see here. Mikey is fine, and we all need some rest."

Still trembling and silently crying, Mikey laid back down in the loft, his mind wandering in thought. *There is no way that was just a dream. It felt so real.*

When the morning light broke and the songbirds began to sing, the boys began to stir. Mikey, still lying there, was still wondering what happened. Who really was that dark man?

The night gave no relief to the sweltering heat. With sweat dripping from every pore, Mikey still felt on edge. He was still confused and very tired from the lack of sleep, but he needed to get the troop back for morning roll call and breakfast.

As they filed out of the cabin, Mikey hung back for another moment. Taking one last look at the trapdoor, he noticed it was still locked and unusable. "Weird," he said, closing the door behind him.

After the morning roll call, sitting at the table for breakfast, Charlie walked by and jokingly asked, "How was your night at the cabin, Mikey? I heard you had a rough one."

"Screw you, Charlie. Who told you that?" Mikey replied in frustrated anger.

"Oh, it's all over camp. How the great watermelon king was afraid of the cabin. Having nightmares."

"Yeah, okay, Charlie," he said as Charlie patted his shoulder, laughing. Mikey winced in pain, holding his shoulder.

Mikey couldn't shake the weird feeling he had all day. Something was off, and he could feel it. That nightmare was far too real to be just a dream, but how was he the only one to have seen any of it?

While Mikey and the other scouts packed up all their belongings to go home, Harry checked in on Mikey. "You good there, Mikey? You had a rough night and have not been yourself today."

"Yeah. I will be okay. Just that dream was so real," he answered as he took off his shirt to change into a clean one. "Man, I am tired of sweating so much."

"What is that?" Harry asked with a look of concern.

"What is what?"

"That mark on your shoulder," Harry stated as he pointed to a large, purple mark in the shape of a handprint.

"I . . . I don't know. It was not there yesterday," replied Mikey. *That is the place where the man grabbed me*, he thought to himself while continuing to inspect the mark. "No wonder it hurt when Charlie touched me."

"Maybe we should tell Tigger," Harry said as he started to walk out of Mikey's tent.

"No. I will be fine. I am sure I must have hurt it during that nightmare," Mikey replied quickly.

"In the shape of a hand?"

"I don't know, Harry! But we are not telling Tigger!" Mikey stated sternly.

Around dinner, as the parents began to crowd the camp and with the closing bonfire ceremony just hours away, Mikey was sitting on the porch of the headquarters building. As he sat there overlooking camp, he could swear that, just for a moment, the man could be seen over by the trading post—and that, among the noise and confusion, the man had made his way into camp.

Come on, you're seeing things, he reminded himself.

Suddenly, Mikey could hear a slight commotion billowing to the point that tempers were flying. Sitting on the edge of his chair, Mikey listened intently to those inside the building.

"I don't think you get it! Another boy has seen him!" exclaimed one of them. Mikey swore it sounded like old man Frank.

"Now, cut it out. It is just old camp lore. Nothing more," stated the other.

"Don't say I didn't warn you!" he heard as the floorboards just on the other side of the door creaked and the knob began to turn.

Mikey jumped up and dashed around the corner of the building, hiding behind the bushes. His eyes peered through the leaves. It was indeed old man Frank, who stomped off across the courtyard to his woodshop while muttering to himself.

Mikey quickly followed. His mind raced with questions about the camp lore. Before he knew it, he was standing in front of Frank's woodcarving shop. Piles of wood scraps, sawdust, and curly wood shavings blanketed the ground.

Mikey stretched out his hand to knock on the door when it swung open. Standing in the doorway was Frank, looking startled by someone standing at his door. "Oh! What is it? How can I help you?" Frank asked through suppressed frustration.

"I am sorry to bother you. I just wanted to ask you some questions about the man from the trappers cabin," Mikey responded timidly.

"Ah, so it was you who saw him, then?" Frank responded in his elderly raspy voice.

"Yes, sir. I saw him last night. And to be honest, I swear that . . . just for a moment . . . I saw him here in camp, too."

Taking a moment and then exhaling a deep sigh, Frank invited Mikey inside.

Mikey looked behind himself and then stepped into the wood shop. The smell of stain, paint, and wood filled the space and made his nose tingle. Mikey pinched his nose to stop himself from sneezing and then sniffled in deep.

"Please sit down. I will be right back," Frank stated as he shifted his way around the half-carved twenty-foot totem pole he was working on.

The shop was very well lit, and the countless tools of a craftsman littered the place. Scraps of used sandpaper littered the edges of the floor, and small animal carvings and hand-carved signage for local businesses could be seen in every nook and corner.

Frank returned with a small box in his hand. As he wiped his rough hand across the top of the box, his eyes began to well up with tears. With a quick sniffle, Frank began in almost a whisper, "Inside this box are articles from throughout my time here at Camp Russell. Many years ago . . . before Camp Russell purchased the woods across the road . . . an old trapper lived there. He was a nice man. However, as he grew older, so, too, did his mind."

"Do you mean to say that the trapper went insane?" Mikey asked.

"Well, it seems that, as time went on, the trapper was less pleased with the scout camp being here. He blamed his fur trading business failures on the camp and vowed to see the camp shut down. Years went by, and although he tried to bury the camp, he ultimately failed and passed away. His family then sold his lands to us for conservation purposes."

"I see, but how is it that I was able to see him, then?" Mikey asked.

"Ah yes, well that brings me to the box. Here in this box are clippings from all the times a scout reported seeing strange things in the old cabin. Seems like you are the latest in a long line of those who have come across the ghost of the trapper himself."

Frank handed the box over to Mikey and sat down beside him. Hesitating for a moment, Mikey opened the box and peered inside. The contents inside were old news clippings and some old photos. At the bottom of the box was one green scout sock that was stiffened by dried blood that had soaked into the fibers.

"Is this the sock that was found beneath the trapdoor?" Mikey asked.

"Yes. How did you know that?" Frank asked in surprise.

"Someone told me that a boy disappeared and all they found was a sock."

"Well, yes, that is partly true. It is true that this sock was found beneath the cabin in the woods. The boy did not vanish, however. We know where he is. In fact, he never left this camp at all."

"I'm sorry. What do you mean?"

Clearing his throat, Frank then continued, "The spirit of the trapper haunts the woods during the summer months. His blood thirst to destroy the camp has kept his spirit alive. And . . . well . . . when the temperatures get like it has been this week . . . some say that his spirit returns and takes one victim."

"One victim?" Mikey responded with confused shock. "Does this mean that I am this year's victim?"

"Not if we get you out of here before he can finish what he started last night," Frank said as he lifted his hand and placed it upon Mikey's shoulder. "I know he left his mark on you. He has attached himself to you, and he has until the end of the closing campfire to finish taking your soul. If he succeeds, you will be trapped here as well."

"Well, once my mother arrives, I'll just leave. I will tell her that I do not want to stay for the fire and just head home," Mikey replied in a shaking voice.

"If only it was that simple. So long as that mark is on you . . . his spirit is bonded with you. We need to end this tonight, and I think I know how we can do that."

Still worried, Mikey asked, "Okay. What do I need to do?"

As everyone gathered into the closing campfire, the darkness of nightfall blanketed the sky and the nocturnal creatures began to stir. The Order of the Arrow conducted their ceremony, and with a whoosh, a flood of yellow and orange lit up the ceremonial fire pit. The flames danced high above the six-foot-high tinder pile that composed the fire's framework, as the warmth could be felt even in the back row of the benches.

Shortly after, Mikey could feel an eerie sensation running down his spine. His eyes widened and focused upon the flames as the mark on his shoulder began to burn. Wincing from the pain, he gasped as, through the fire and flames, he saw him.

Like the devil emerging from the flames of hell, the trapper lunged forward and grabbed hold of Mikey's shirt as he said, "Your soul is mine," in a cold whisper.

"*Now!*" yelled an elderly voice from behind the last row of seating. It was Frank, and as he marched inward toward Mikey, the spirit of the trapper laughed and then began to breathe in Mikey's spirit, sucking in deep to steal the very life right out of him.

As Mikey's body began to falter, Mikey reached into his pocket and placed a small token upon the evil spirit's hand and said, "With this token, I banish you! I banish you from this place never to return!" he yelled as Frank placed a lantern upon the ground. "Into the flames you must go! Back to hell with you!"

Slowly and in a swirling tornado motion, the trapper's spirit let out a horrifying screech as it fell into the small light of the lantern, yelling, "I shall return again!"

To Mikey's amazement, and with a blink of his eyes, the flames from the fire were brightly dancing about yet again. No one had noticed the events that had just transpired, and they were singing the words to the closing song of "Taps."

Day is done, gone the sun,

From the lake, from the hills, from the sky;

All is well, safely rest, God is nigh . . .

Once everyone had headed home, Frank asked, "Has the mark been lifted from you?"

"Yes. Thank you! Thank you for everything!" exclaimed Mikey as he and his mother drove away.

Frank, now standing in the woodshop holding the lantern, he set it down near that box. As the lantern's light flickered, a shadow drew his eyes up to a photo that was hanging on the wall. In it were two younger men. One of them was obviously a younger version of Frank, and the other . . . well . . . he looked like a beardless version of the trapper.

"Until next year, dear brother. Until next year," Frank whispered with an evil grin.

CHAPTER 14

Chocolate to Die For

Dennis Webster

The spring of 1934 in the Adirondacks was especially harsh as the drawn-out winter kept the snowpack thick and stubborn with flower buds anxious to emerge and face the northern-wind-cracked sunbeams. Mary and Susan McCloud were still in their late teens when they left the comfort of their father's Albany homestead to sally forth on launching their own chocolatier business in the midst of the park that was emerging from a nineteenth-century logging and lodge destination into one that lured worldwide tourists with its rugged pine trees, rubble mountain charm, and fresh, crisp, chilled air. The twins had purchased with their hard-earned savings a humble home in North Creek that was close to the shadow from the peaks of Gore Mountain. Susan was the business brains of their operation as the beauty queen used her icy ID and talent with money to crunch numbers and plan all aspects of the chocolate business. The sisters had sold some chocolates out of their father's mercantile business and were able to squirrel away funds to launch Heavenly Chocolates. Mary was always in the shadow of her sister Susan's stunning looks and outgoing personality. She had been called "pitiful" by some for the polio she had as a child that left her with a limp and required the nineteen-year-old to walk with a cane. She didn't have Susan's height, Aphrodite bodily form, striking blue eyes, or wavy sable hair, but she did have her father's tender, sweet, and quiet personality. Her hair and eyes were the exact color as her father's as the twins were obviously not identical.

Many whispered that the good Lord pulled an ace of diamonds out of his human design deck for Susan while Mary's draw had been the two of hearts. The one thing Mary had that Susan could never acquire was a talented touch in regard to chocolate preparatory and enhanced cocoa flavor profiles that delighted the tongues of those who paid pennies for otherworldly sweets.

The sisters had yet to marry and shared the upstairs of the humble home in North Creek with the downstairs living quarters turned into the storefront of their business and the kitchen in the back housing all manner of chocolate-making accoutrements. Within the first year, they had made enough to stay solvent with their business as the tourists skiing Gore Mountain in the winter and outdoor hikers and nature enthusiasts in the other seasons discovered the quaint little abode of chocolate that housed what some said was the queen regent of beauty and chocolate in the Adirondacks in Susan McCloud. Her beauty and charm made her the face and voice of the growing business. There was hardly a mention of the quiet little chef in the back who was the engineer of the successful cocoa-based sweets that marveled the tastebuds of all who partook. Susan had erected a curtain in the doorway to the kitchen so shoppers could not see the person who was behind making the chocolates. All assumed it was Susan who made all the magic happen, not knowing the little lady with the limp was the chocolate wizard behind the curtain that made the successful spells of Heavenly Chocolates. Mary's mysterious cocoa bean supplier was a man named Carlos in Albany who had relocated from Ecuador. She went solo and met the man who barely spoke English, yet Mary's ability to speak fluent Spanish garnered her a valuable bean prize.

When the business first began, Susan had been kind and patient with Mary. One newly introduced recipe, however, would launch the business into worldwide fame but would then propel Susan into such a state of jealousy and arrogance that her dark triad personality could not escape with anything other than her twin sister's annihilation. Susan may have been jealous of her sister, but that didn't stop her from basking in the success by buying many fancy dresses with the excuse she had to represent the business. Heavenly Chocolates had also caught the fancy of the young bachelor of the richest family in the Adirondacks, Richard Horn, whose father owned a majority of the sawmills that supplied sturdy ancient pines to a bulging American northeastern population. The Horns also had built the largest cabins and hotels along the shores of Mirror Lake, Lake George, and Saranac Lake that hosted the world's richest and Hollywood's silent film stars who were looking for a New Babylon east. The chocolates from the twin sisters sold very well outside of the gift shops and front lobbies. Susan reveled in the success and attention garnered from the rich and famous clientele. She thought less and less of business and more of the fandom that was rising including praise from Charlie Chaplin, whom she had met on a supply run to the large Horn cabin on the shore of Mirror Lake in Lake Placid.

One day Mary awoke from her sleep with a smile and immediately went to wake Susan. She grabbed her cane, limped along, and went into her sister's room. She gently shook the leg of her twin.

"Sister, awake."

Susan rolled over and said, "What is it?" She was agitated as she hated her beauty sleep to be interrupted.

"I had a ghost appear to me last night, or it was a dream. She was lovely. She didn't tell me her name but she gave me a new recipe. I was able to procure the best black gold from Carlos on my most recent trip to Albany that will make this a reality."

"Why are you telling me this, Mary?"

"I was excited, sister, as the recipe came to me. I believe it's a gift from an angel."

"Don't be silly," said Susan as she pulled her hair up and pinned it into a messy morning bun. "Ghosts do not exist, and angels have better things to do than hand out chocolate recipes."

"You'll see, sister," replied Mary with a big smile. "I will make you proud."

Susan was looking at her fingernails, and without looking up, indifferently stated, "You always make me proud."

▲▲▲

Mary named the new recipe "Angel Delight" as she felt it had been divinely delivered by her ghost. The product lived up to the name as it quickly took off and outsold all the other Heavenly Chocolates combined. Chocolatiers worldwide soon raved about the dark chocolate whose flavor profile they could not replicate. The success soon brought in a surge of cash that shocked the sisters but also created a fashionista and socialite monster out of Susan. Her arrogance and elite airs grew faster than the sales of Angel Delight—so much so that Susan relegated Mary to the back kitchen and mandated she stay back there when visitors arrived.

This soon built up in the frail twin sister regret that her sister was not including her in the success or giving her any credit for the burgeoning business. Even when their beloved father paid a visit to toast their success, he spent the majority of the evening having to entertain Susan and heap demanded praise upon her brilliance. Their father did get a quick minute to bolt behind the curtain and praise Mary when he held her hand and said, "I'm very proud of you, my talented daughter." These few words boosted Mary's confidence where she had decided enough was enough and she would ask her sister for a greater role in the business side of Heavenly Chocolates.

That night Mary was awake in her bed, which was unusual as she normally slept soundly as long days cooking chocolate drained her energy although she loved making her sweet delights. She sat awake and had a premonition that Susan's ego had grown to God-like proportions and disaster to her was imminent. She rolled over and looked at her sister's bed that was empty. Susan had been absent more and more as her travels to Lake George and Lake Placid had her more gone than at the business.

Mary was sad because she missed how close they had been as little girls, but she felt she needed to protect the recipe for Angel Delight. She got up, put on her robe, lit a candle, and walked with her candlestick down the stairs, through the curtain, and back to the area where she had all her recipes jotted on scraps of paper. She took a small mason jar from the pantry, placed the recipe inside, and screwed the lid shut as tight as her little hands would allow. She looked around then knew where she could hide it. If something happened to her, or if Susan decided to jettison her from Heavenly Chocolates, the divine-delivered chocolate recipe would be safe. Little did Mary know she would not live another twenty-four hours after hiding the beloved and successful recipe.

Mary's body lay in the small coffin in the living room as only her father and a few distant relatives made the trek to North Creek to say good-bye. No patrons to Heavenly Chocolates paid their respects as none knew of the sweet little chocolatier hidden behind the curtain. Susan was on display even though the audience was small; she still had to make her appearance and look distraught. She sat in her fine new black funeral outfit and wept for her dead twin sister, although behind her act was an evil woman who had used cyanide to poison Mary to death. Nobody suspected foul play as Mary had been sickly most of her life. Mary had made the fatal mistake of pushing her sister for more recognition. Susan made the mistake of her ego thinking that making chocolates was easy and she had all her sister's talent.

The onset of the Great Depression that taxed people's purse strings, along with the declination of the quality of the chocolates, caused the erosion of the business of Heavenly Chocolates; the business ultimately closed. Susan had desperately tried to replicate the recipes and couldn't even duplicate the tastes of the recipes she found in the kitchen let alone Angel Delight. Susan scoured every inch of the house and could not find the recipe. Even though she could not replicate it, the world's best chocolatiers had messaged and visited her with a large buyout offer. She realized she murdered her sister before being properly prepared.

Susan spent the last years of her life praying for forgiveness and asking her sister to come to her and let her know she is fine in the afterlife. And, if it's not too much trouble, tell her the recipe for Angel Delight. Neither ever happened, and Susan's decline in her beauty fell in line with the decline of her wealth and popularity.

Little did anybody suspect that Mary's ghost would lurk among the shadows, watching, and biding her time to find the right person among the living to whom she'd reveal herself and award her secret chocolate recipe. She had decided in her phantasmagorical plane that eternal patience would pay off once the right person came along. The little two-story house in North Creek returned to being private residence and hosted many families for a hundred years before chocolate resurrection came in the form of a lady who had dreamed of starting her own business in the bosom of the Adirondacks.

Kim Williams was a student of Adirondack history and an aspiring chef. She had read about the past chocolate business that had been run out of the humble abode in North Creek. She heard there was a chocolate recipe named Angel Delight that had been hailed around the world and celebrated as the best chocolate on earth, yet the recipe of the McCloud sisters had been lost and decades of replication attempts had failed.

Kim knew it was destiny when she discovered the original location of Heavenly Chocolates was up for sale. Her purchase offer was accepted, and she decided to use her chef desire to become a chocolatier. She named the new business Barkeater Chocolates after the English translation of the Mohican word *Adirondack*. Kim moved in along with her ten-year-old daughter, Tina, and her mischievous black-and-white cat, Broomhilda.

Kim's beloved husband, Glenn, had died a year earlier from a snowmobile accident but had left her enough of an estate that she could start a new life and launch her venture. She wished Glenn could be there to see it, but she spoke to his spirit every night before going to sleep. She was a believer in the afterlife and ghosts. She knew he was listening and approving her going for her dream.

She had the desire and the drive to make Barkeater Chocolates a success, but her only doubt was her chocolate-making ability. She was trained in French cuisine, but making crepes was not the same as making sweet treats. She was optimistic, she was happy, and she was ready for success.

Worn. That is the only word that Kim could think of after eighteen months of launching Barkeater Chocolates, building the brand, and throwing all her positive lifeforce into the business only to see sales trickle and her beloved dead husband's funds depleted. She had received a lot of compliments on her flavorful chocolates, the logo, the packaging, her stellar customer service attitude, and gratitude to customers. She had checked all the success boxes yet was worn. Worn and tired. She expanded her stress to two words.

She was deep-down grateful she was living the dream, but a few more sparkles, rainbows, and unicorns immersed in her dream would be wonderful. She tried her best yet the skiers from Gore Mountain, the Adirondack enthusiasts, and the locals were just not buying enough chocolates to cover her monthly mortgage, let alone the ingredient expenses. She had to take a chance and go with no health insurance for herself, which didn't scare her, but not having any coverage for her beloved Tina did bother her immensely. She knew the legend of Mary and Susan. The legend of the lost recipe. She hoped she would have a eureka moment within the bosom of the same kitchen that had birthed Angel Delight.

Kim did like living in the house where Barkeaters was operating as she and Tina occupied the two bedrooms upstairs. The August evening was cool enough that she had the windows open to allow the crisp Adirondack Mountain air to permeate and enhance her home. She had tucked Tina into her bed, kissed her on the forehead, and wished her sweet dreams. Kim spent a few moments in her office looking over bills, planning purchases, and posting promotions of upcoming chocolate events on her social media pages. She had learned that hosting chocolate-making sessions and other events boosted sales.

Kim finally surrendered and took off her reading glasses and set them on the mounds of paperwork, shut off her laptop, and strolled downstairs to decompress. She stumbled upon Broomhilda who had decided not to go out stalking the woods adjacent to the house. She gave her black kitty a treat and went to her fridge and took out a bottle of white wine that had been a gift from a grateful customer. It had been sitting for months, as Kim was not a drinker, but she decided to indulge with a single glass. She sat in her chair in the room between the first-floor kitchen and the store area that hosted the shelves of product. Soon she drifted asleep with a blanket across her lap and Broomhilda nestled in the nook between her body and the inside edge of the comfy, cushiony chair.

Awake. Kim woke up but still had her eyes shut; she had a feeling something or someone was watching. She knew it was not Tina. She didn't know how she knew but she just did. She opened her eyes, and the room was dark except for a faint light in the corner. She sat up unable to move or speak but she saw it. It was a person standing at the edge of the darkness and the moonbeam that was emanating through the window. Broomhilda was sitting on the floor staring at whatever this was so Kim knew she was not dreaming. It took a step toward her, and she saw clearly that this was a spirit as she could see through her. It was a ghost, and she couldn't believe it yet there it was: a full body entity. It was a small woman with her hair pulled back. When she took another step, she had a slight limp. The ghost had a kind face, and it was at that point that Kim knew who it was. "Mary?" she asked. The ghost of Mary McCloud smiled, looked down to Broomhilda, and pointed. She then dissipated.

Kim stood there for a minute stunned and wondering to herself, *Did I really just see the ghost of Mary?* She heard a meow and looked over to Broomhilda who was staring at the basement door. Kim walked over and opened the door, and her sweet black kitty ran down the steps. She felt that was odd as her cat never wanted to go down there. Kim followed but turned on the light so she wouldn't trip on the uneven wooden steps. When she got to the basement landing, she heard Broomhilda meowing from the back corner where the light barely landed; it was an area Kim avoided as the dirt floor made her hesitant. She walked over to the cat. "What is it, sweetie?" she asked. Her cat looked up with her jade eyes striking out from her sable coat.

"Meow." The cat stood up, looked down at the dirt, and scratched her paw upon it. Kim knelt down, and Broomhilda bolted to the side, sat, and watched.

"What is under there?" Kim said aloud as she pulled away loose dirt until she saw the metal top of a mason jar. She dug the rest of it out and could see there was a piece of paper sealed inside. "Weird," she muttered to herself as she went back to the basement stairs where her kitty had already bolted ahead of her and up. Kim went into the kitchen and set the jar on the counter. She was tired as it was still the witching hour and she needed her rest as she had a busy schedule. She was planning on starting to teach Tina to cook and assist on some of the recipes.

Kim woke up with Tina standing next to her bed holding Broomhilda. "Good morning, Mom. You getting up? We're hungry," she said with a big smile.

Kim sat up and rubbed the sleep from her eyes. "I'm up."

She followed her loved ones down into the kitchen thinking what had happened last night was real. She entered the kitchen and saw the dusty old mason jar sitting there and knew it had happened. Tina had set Broomhilda down who was meowing over her empty dish, so Kim placed a spackle of the dry tuna-flavored cat food the kitty loved. She then made breakfast for herself and Tina.

"Are you going to teach me the recipes today, Mom?" asked Tina as she was bouncing around the kitchen with an apron in her hand.

"Please hand me that jar," said Kim as she was curious to see why the ghost had wanted her to have it.

"This thing is dirty," said Tina as she handed the jar to her mother and sat in the chair next to her. Kim turned the screwed-on lid, and it came off easier than she had thought. She looked inside, and there was a folded piece of paper nestled at the bottom. She took out the paper, unfolded it, and was shocked by what she had in her hands.

"What is it, Mom?"

"Angel Delight," replied Kim in a stunned fashion. She couldn't believe it. It was the spirit of Mary handing down her long-lost chocolate recipe. Her ghost had handed over to her perhaps the greatest chocolate recipe the world had known. She stared at it and knew right then that Barkeater Chocolates would survive and thrive. She would be honored to pass on Mary's legacy to consumers' sweet palates.

"Are we going to make that today?" asked Tina as she placed her chin on her mother's shoulder and looked at the handwritten Angel Delight recipe.

"We will learn this recipe together, sweetie."

CHAPTER 15

The Unknown Soul

Larry Weill

As the girls looked out on the slope, they observed a pale blue orb of light hovering above the ground, accompanied by a mournful moaning sound that infiltrated their very souls. It was a haunting sound they could never forget.

LATE 1890S

The Calhoun family house was a dilapidated structure on an unpaved hillside road outside of Gloversville, New York. The dirt road, which no longer exists, ran through a tract of land bordering the Mountain Lake Electric Railroad on Bleecker Mountain. The house was old and "out-of-square," with a sloping front porch and dirty, cracked white paint that barely covered the decaying wood frame beneath. A lattice of vines covered portions of the front and side walls of the residence, and there were no attempts to address the lawn in any way. It had gone completely wild.

There was only one other house on the lane, and it was in worse shape than the Calhouns'. Located about a quarter mile away, it had been abandoned the previous year when the tenants had moved out and deserted the property. It was in such a state of disrepair that finding a buyer would have been impossible.

Family life inside the Calhoun house was as grim as the exterior appearance of the dwelling. The father, James Calhoun, was an extreme alcoholic who was aggressively abusive to his wife and children. He was often absent from the residence for weeks at a time, during which the family was left to fend for themselves. He referred to himself as a hunting and fishing guide, although his negative reputation and belligerent personality ensured his services were seldom requested in the area.

James's wife was Elizabeth Calhoun. She was four years younger than James, and often found herself on the wrong end of his violent temper. His consumption of whiskey was a daily event, which resulted in him being either drunk or hungover most of the time. It was during these intervals that his uncontrolled rage hit its peak, and Elizabeth often herded their three children into a locked bedroom to ride out the storm.

The Calhouns had three children, a son and two daughters. The oldest of the three was Clyde, their only son, who was sixteen. Next was Carrie, the older daughter, who was thirteen, while the younger daughter, Catherine, was eleven. Within the family, the mother loved all three of their children, and they lived in relative peace when their father was out of the house. Since James drank the majority of the revenue from his guide service, Elizabeth was left to produce whatever she could from taking in sewing and cleaning work from members of their local church. It was a rough life, and her minimal income barely covered the costs of putting food on the table. At times, Clyde appeared with a satchel full of potatoes, onions, and corn, which Elizabeth knew had been "acquired without payment" from some of the local farms. However, the family was so desperate for food and other bare necessities that she didn't ask. She couldn't afford to.

The three children were all quite different from one another. Carrie acted older than her years and often tried to help her mother in holding things together, taking care of the household while her mother worked on her sewing business. Carrie was quiet and caring, and was sometimes able to soothe the temper of her abusive father when he happened to be at home.

Clyde was much more outspoken, even when he knew that his remarks would result in belt whippings from his father. Even though he was intelligent and inquisitive, he had dropped out of school when he was fifteen because he knew that no one in his household cared. He could pick up odd jobs out in town and augment that with his midnight visits to farmers' fields. He was a strapping young lad who could fend for himself in a fistfight, and he often became involved in questionable activities in town. Clyde regularly appeared with bruises on his face and body from his father's beatings, which he accepted because there were no alternatives. Living in the Calhoun residence was not an easy way of life.

Catherine, the younger sibling, was a quiet and withdrawn girl who lived in continuous fear of her father. Elizabeth tried to free her of her terror by reading and singing with her and helping her with her schoolwork. But Catherine could never hide the fear she felt living within the same walls as the man who beat his mother on a weekly basis. She often cried herself to sleep, dreaming of the day she would leave the household and take her place in another setting. Any other setting.

Clyde also spent much of his time thinking about moving away from home, freeing himself from the daily horrors of his alcoholic father. He didn't relish the thought of leaving behind the rest of his family, who would bear the brunt of James's rage. But what could he do about that? He sometimes prayed for his father's death, which made him feel even worse. Clyde had left home on a couple occasions when he was fourteen and fifteen, only to return within a day or two because he could find no one to take him in and provide a place to sleep for the night. However, he remained optimistic that he could finally escape and start a new life for himself somewhere else. Anywhere else.

JULY 3, 1902

It was a Thursday afternoon in July when Clyde made up his mind to leave home. It was a clear day, hot and sunny without a chance of rain in the area. From the front of their house, Clyde could see the electric train cars climbing the tracks on Bleecker Mountain en route to the lake and hotel on top of the hill. The following day would be July 4, with even more visitors and holiday revelers looking to join the party outside the hotel.

Clyde felt truly blessed that his friend, Michael, had offered him a place to stay inside the Mountain Lake Hotel. Michael had been a schoolmate who was hired to work on the grounds around the building. He had promised to smuggle Clyde into a storage room in the basement of the hotel, where he could stay for as long as possible until he was discovered. Clyde was extremely grateful for this assistance even though he knew it was a temporary shelter at best.

The following day was July 4, and the morning sky showed the promise of another fine day. Clyde left the house early and walked back into the old shed that was located behind the residence. It hadn't been used in many years and was in worse condition than the house. The windows on the sides of the structure were broken, and the door did not close completely. The entire interior of the shack smelled of rotting vegetation and decaying wood. But Clyde had used the shed to store and accumulate a "runaway sack" with an extra set of clothes, a loaf of bread, and a small bag of salted beef jerky. He knew it wouldn't be enough to last him more than two days, but it was all he could gather in his plan to get away. The only items of value he carried in his pockets were two silver dollars and a gold pocket watch he had inherited when his uncle passed away. The pocket watch had an engraving on the inside of the front cover: "EC, 1868," commemorating the year his uncle had retired from work. As an afterthought, he added an extra pair of socks to the sack before returning to the main house. He was about ready to make his escape.

James had been absent from the household for several days, so it was just Elizabeth and the three children sitting around the dining table that evening. Dinner was sparse: potatoes with a small bit of roasted chicken that Elizabeth had been given by a fellow church parishioner as payment for mending some undergarments. But the presence of any meat on the table elevated the meal to the "extravagant" level in the Calhoun household, which they consumed in celebration of the July 4 holiday.

It was almost 8:00 p.m. when Clyde slipped out the back door of the house and returned to the storage shed. He paused for a few minutes to ensure that he was not being observed from the kitchen window, and then gathered the sack and threw the strap over his shoulder. His initial path took him straight back from the shed, away from the house and the road. He did not want to be seen walking directly up the hill as that would have attracted attention from family members.

Once out of sight behind a small earthen berm, he turned left and began his ascent uphill. He followed this path for about three hundred yards before turning left once again, doubling back toward the dirt road. By this time, the sun had dropped below the mountain, and darkness was approaching rapidly. Clyde wanted to get to the top of the mountain before it was pitch black, but it appeared as though he would not come close to achieving this goal.

After crossing the road, Clyde walked over another two hundred yards of dirt and grass before sighting the tracks of the Mountain Lake Electric Railroad. This was a welcome sight as he knew he could follow the track bed up the mountain, which would lead him to the hotel and safety.

The darkness was almost complete as Clyde commenced his trek up the steep incline. He could feel the crunch of the crushed stone beneath his feet, although he could not see the railway tracks themselves. It was simply too dark, and his eyes were not yet completely adjusted to provide sufficient night vision.

Suddenly, in the distance, he heard a loud *bang* as a violent collision took place between two large, heavy objects. He heard the approach of a train car on the tracks, although it did not resemble anything he had heard before. (Since the Calhoun house was located near the Mountain Lake railroad tracks, he was familiar with the normal sounds of the train cars.) But this sounded louder and higher pitched than anything he had experienced in the past. Something else set off the "WARNING" flashers in Clyde's mind: the car was approaching much faster than he expected, and he could hear loud shrieks of passengers screaming in the darkness.

Clyde began to panic as the rail car approached with frightening speed. Even worse was the fact that he didn't know where he stood on the track bed. He quickly leaped over a yard of stones, hoping to get clear of the tracks and gain safety in the grass beyond. But he was mistaken about his position; he was actually on the other side of the rails from where he imagined. He tripped and fell over the first rail, which caused his knee to come smashing to the ground on a wooden track tie. With no time to spare, he sprang to his feet and tried to dive head-first across the remaining track. He almost made it.

The "car" was a combination of two electric train cars, numbers 1 and 5, which had collided and were hurtling down the steep grade at an excessive sixty miles per hour. The front right corner of car number 1 struck Clyde's body straight-on, sending him flying a full fifty feet through the air, perpendicular to the direction of the tracks. He never had a chance as the impact killed him instantly. His body came to rest in a deep, narrow depression, covered with a layer of dirt and vegetation. The force of the collision between the two train cars and the improper shifting of gears by the conductor served to blow the circuit breakers and threw both cars into total darkness. As a result, Clyde's death was completely unobserved by those on the train.

The two cars continued their perilously rapid descent down the mountain, approaching a tight left-hand curve that could never accommodate the speed of the runaway railcars. The two cars jumped the rails and flew off the tracks, creating a dreadful, catastrophic disaster scene. The first car (car number 1) flipped onto its side, landing on top of many passengers who had flown through the open sides of the car. Many of those unfortunate individuals were crushed beneath the weight of the vehicle. The other car (car number 5) fared slightly better, remaining upright, but still held a great many injured passengers.

In total, fourteen passengers lost their lives that night, with another sixty injured and in dire need of immediate aid. Anyone within earshot range of the accident scene responded to assist the wounded. Within two hours, power was restored, and help arrived from the hospital in Gloversville. Emergency workers and officials from the Electric Train Company accounted for all the passengers and train conductors, even those who were dead and wounded. The total tally came to about 130 individuals, all of whom were located. The scene of the accident took weeks to clear, but it was finally accomplished to the best of expectations. All the injured had been rescued, and all the bodies of the deceased had been recovered.

Or so they thought.

Two hundred yards up the hill, in a naturally built concealment, lay the body of Clyde Calhoun. The runaway who wasn't there. Who shouldn't have been there. Who was never missed except by his own family, who could never have guessed his fate.

JULY 4, 1905

It was three years after Clyde's disappearance, and the family pondered his whereabouts. They surmised that he had run away, but they always expected him to return home at some point. It was also a full year since James had been killed in a barroom brawl in the city, stabbed to death by another drunken bully who had accused him of stealing his money clip. Elizabeth attended the funeral along with Carrie and Catherine, although there were no tears shed for the patriarch. It was a family that had been emotionally bankrupt for many years, and there was no residual sorrow felt for the departed. They only wondered where Clyde had gone and whether he knew of the death of his father.

On that steamy, hot night in the summer of 1905, Carrie sat on the crooked porch on the front of their home, talking quietly with her younger sister Catherine. It was late, just past 10:20 p.m., and the train cars of the new railroad (called the Adirondack Lakes Traction Company) had ceased operations for the evening. It was quiet, without so much as a rustle of wind in the air.

Suddenly, from out of nowhere, an eerie sound pierced the night air from the grassy expanse of ground in front of the house. It was an unearthly groan, as if someone was in pain and calling for help. Carrie and Catherine both bolted upright in their seats, ears straining to locate the source. They were both mesmerized by a combination of curiosity and fear. The sound seemed to be human in nature, yet there was no one on the mountainside at that time of night. Just a detached moan that echoed across the slope.

The girls told their mother about their experience the following day, and she immediately discounted their story as originating from local animals, perhaps fighting on the edge of the woods.

"Could be anything," she explained patiently. "Could be raccoons, or deer, or even someone's cats getting themselves in a tussle over a mouse," she reasoned.

To prove her point to her daughters, Elizabeth kept them company on the porch the following evening, sitting on a wicker chair while her children conversed. Carrie was now sixteen and was looking forward to graduating from high school and getting a real job to help Elizabeth with the family's finances. The nighttime air was quiet, and the sky was pitch black.

"Well, I don't hear anything out there," said Elizabeth, gazing out from the property. "Must be like I said, just a couple animals barking at each other. I'm going back inside."

The rest of the night remained quiet, and the anguished moans heard in the night were quickly forgotten in the coming weeks. Whatever its cause seemed to have vanished completely, and the girls never gave it another thought.

JULY 4, 1906

Another Fourth of July celebration, and Elizabeth, Carrie, and Catherine once again sat on chairs in front of their dilapidated house. With each successive year, the structure looked more and more worn, with little remaining paint still covering the tired wooden shingles. Elizabeth worried about the future of her two daughters and prayed fervently that they would find spouses who would care for them and look after them in their grown years. Elizabeth herself was getting older and feeling less capable of providing for her family by herself. It was not a good life.

As the three sat on the porch, quietly discussing events of the day, Catherine leaned forward while gazing into the distance.

"Momma, what is that light I'm seeing across the way?" she asked. "It looks like one of the fireworks, but it's real close to the ground."

Elizabeth and Carrie followed Catherine's stare into the distance, their faces registering a combination of curiosity and fear.

"I don't know, honey," said Elizabeth in a halting tone. "I don't recognize that as anything I've ever seen."

The next thing they heard was a low, groaning tone that froze their blood. It sounded most definitely human in origin, although they could not make out any specific words. It was eerie beyond eerie, and appeared to be aligned with the orb of blue light, which slowly moved in a pattern that was not quite circular. None of the women had seen such a sight, and they sat transfixed by the sounds in the night.

"Someone might be hurt out there, Mother," cried Carrie. "I think we should light the lantern and take a walk to see if anyone's out there."

"We're not going out there tonight," replied Elizabeth, still staring into the darkness. "We'll have plenty of time to investigate it tomorrow morning, when we can see where we're going. But for now, I think we should all just head inside. There will be plenty of time to search in the morning."

The three women headed inside the house, and Elizabeth quickly sent Catherine to bed. After getting her settled in for the night, Elizabeth quietly signaled Carrie to rejoin her on the front porch. She spoke in hushed tones while still keeping an ear cocked toward the side of the hill. The blue orb was still visible in the distance.

"Honey, there is something very strange going on here," she whispered, her hands resting on Carrie's shoulders.

"What's that, Momma?" asked Carrie.

"Last year, you and your sister told me about a moaning sound coming from out across that same place, near the railroad tracks. I didn't believe you then, but does this sound like the same thing?"

Carrie's eyes grew wide, and she caught her breath in recognition of the similarities.

"Yes, Momma! That's exactly what it sounded like! Just like that."

"That's even more odd, because of one thing that I can't explain," said Elizabeth, her voice quavering as she spoke.

"What's that, Momma?" asked Carrie.

"Because the last time you heard this moaning sound was exactly one year ago, on the Fourth of July. And now again tonight, also on the Fourth. Isn't that odd?"

"It is, Momma," replied Carrie. "But why did you want to get Catherine to sleep before telling me about this?"

"She has nightmares enough as it is," replied Elizabeth. "She doesn't need to be hearing about scary sounds in the night any more than she has already."

The two women pondered on the significance of the Fourth of July coincidence for a few minutes before agreeing to investigate the area the following morning. They had already experienced enough mystery for the night.

The following morning, Elizabeth and her two daughters set off on foot across the grassy expanse leading to the railroad tracks. It was a warm morning with the direct sunlight beating down in full force from the east. The trio had no clue what they might find, but they kept their eyes glued to the ground as they approached the steel rails leading up the hill.

Elizabeth had never considered the possibility of encountering a ghostly presence; it was not something she remotely contemplated. All the victims of the train wreck of 1902 had been accounted for, with not a soul missing. Somehow there had to be another explanation.

But what?

After two hours of walking the hillside tracks, heads bent toward the ground searching for any clue, the family gave up and returned home. Unfortunately, they had only ventured ten feet across the tracks and had not come within ten yards of the shallow pit that still contained Clyde's skeletal remains. So close but yet so far. Their beloved brother and son would remain undiscovered.

August 17, 1906

Parson James Parson was the clergyman presiding over the local Protestant church on the outskirts of town. Many folks in his congregation had fun calling him "Parson Parson," although he was commonly known as "Parson Jim" to his friends. No matter. He tolerated all the kidding with his good-natured personality. He had become accustomed to the jokes since his arrival a decade earlier. He was a superb orator and spiritual leader, and he had gained the full faith and trust of his parishioners.

The parson had a number of side interests, one of which was the collection and interpretation of stories involving the supernatural. He was often called upon to counsel those who suffered from nightmares and delusions, often effecting impressive "cures." He was well versed in beliefs involving ghosts and apparitions, and he had a comforting way of explaining these phenomena to those who had encountered them.

On this Friday morning, the parson answered the knock on his office door to find Elizabeth Calhoun, a favorite member of his congregation, standing alone in the hallway. Attired in a blue dress and matching blue bonnet, she attempted a smile through a face creased with concern. The parson recognized her discomfort and immediately invited her into his office.

"Elizabeth, Elizabeth, it is so wonderful to see you," he cried. "But you look so worried; I can see it in your face. Please tell me what is bothering you, or what I can do for you."

"I'm so sorry, Parson, I didn't mean to worry you so. I was trying to look happy. I guess it didn't work."

"No, Elizabeth, it didn't work," he replied. "Please tell me it isn't one of your children." (The parson was well aware that Clyde had been missing for a full four years.)

"No, both the girls are okay, and we're getting by pretty well right now, thank you."

"Have you heard any news about your son?" the minister asked, gently probing to discover the problem.

"No, it isn't anything like that," stammered Elizabeth, not knowing how to approach the problem. "It's something we've seen and heard from our house that we can't explain. It's noises and lights, and . . . and . . . it's scaring the heck out of my younger daughter. And to tell you the truth, Carrie and I are both pretty scared, too."

"Really?" said the parson, leaning forward in interest. "Please tell me about it. What you saw, what you heard, when, and where; anything you can remember."

"Well, it's been two years in a row that we've been hearing strange sounds outside our house," Elizabeth began. "It's been an eerie, moaning sound, almost human-like, coming from the direction of the train tracks. The first time, on the Fourth of July of last year, the two girls heard it without me. But this year, also on the Fourth of July, I heard it, too, with my own ears."

The parson listened intently, his face a mask of total interest and concentration. "And both times this happened on the Fourth of July?" he asked.

"Yes, both times on the same day. But this year, along with the sounds we saw a bright blue light, like an orb, slowly moving around in the same direction as the moaning. It was mighty strange, and not like anything I'd ever seen before."

"Did you try moving toward the light to find out if anything was out there?" asked the parson.

"No, not until the next morning," admitted Elizabeth, her eyes cast downward. "To tell you the truth, I was a bit scared to walk out there with the children. It was awfully dark, and it just didn't seem like a good idea. We spent a couple hours the next morning looking around but didn't see anything."

"I don't know about the sounds you've been hearing, but there have been many stories of similar balls of light that have been linked to spirits in different locations," said the parson. "There is a Civil War battlefield in Pennsylvania where people see these lights almost every night."

"Do you think that's what we've got on the side of the mountain?" asked Elizabeth.

"Tough to say," ventured the minister, clearly intrigued by the story. "But I'd like to stop by your home sometime soon and have a look for myself. I'm not sure what I'd expect to find, but I'd like to see if I can come up with an explanation of some kind."

Elizabeth agreed that the parson could come up to the house the following week and spend the evening while planting himself on the front porch. Even though it wasn't the Fourth of July, they agreed that the light and sounds had appeared in the past and just might do so again.

Unfortunately, they didn't. On the appointed evening, Parson Jim, Elizabeth, and her two daughters sat out front looking, quietly conversing while keeping their senses honed on the field across the road. The only surprise encountered by the clergyman was the dreadful appearance of the house, which appeared to be rotting from its foundation. He made a mental note to address the matter with his church council members to see if help was available. After spending a night sleeping on a couch in the living room, he returned to the town the following morning. The mystery remained unsolved.

JULY 1, 1907

It had been almost a full year since Elizabeth had discussed the haunting events with the church parson. It was hard to believe that her son had been gone for five years without a single word of any kind. She was beginning to believe that he had either perished, or had perhaps moved somewhere very far away. None of it made sense, and it hurt her entire family as though something had snuffed out Clyde's life and his memory forever.

On this particular morning, three days before the Fourth of July celebration, Elizabeth paid yet another call to the church minister looking for his assistance one more time.

Parson Jim was in the church's library room refilling a stack of reference books when he recognized Elizabeth's form entering the room.

"And a fine good morning to you," he intoned, smiling at his visitor. "And to what do I owe the pleasure of your presence this morning?"

"Good morning, Parson," Elizabeth replied. "I'm really here to pick up some sewing work from Debbie Swift, but as long as I'm here I wanted to ask you if you'd mind visiting our place one more time on Thursday evening."

The parson thought for a moment before quickly recognizing the significance of the date. "Thursday evening; the Fourth of July, right?"

"Yes, Parson, the Fourth of July. All of us want to find out what is going on out there, and we believe that whatever we've seen these past two years will appear again." She looked at him with a desperate expression, her eyes searching for an answer.

The clergyman shifted his feet awkwardly and returned her look with a consoling smile.

"Elizabeth, just to let you know, I've researched your story and the phenomena of the blue orbs, and I've read that they are often linked to spirits from the past; lost souls and other similar forms of spirit energy. But that makes no sense if we try to connect that to the catastrophe of the mountain railroad crash, because everyone on the train was accounted for, even those who perished that night."

Elizabeth took the parson's arm in her hand and gazed at him with intense appeal.

"Please come by the house on Thursday evening before sundown," she pleaded. "Just this one last time. If we don't see anything, I will never make mention of this again. You have my word as a Christian lady."

Even though the parson had previously arranged plans for the evening, he agreed to be present at the Calhouns' house on the night of the Fourth. There were some obligations that he felt bound to fulfill as the religious head of his church, and this was one of them. He would keep his word.

July 4, 1907

True to his word, the parson made his way on horseback to the Calhouns' rickety house by 7:00 p.m. that evening. The family had finished their evening meal, which consisted of some biscuits, a plate of donated root vegetables, and a trout that Catherine had caught in the lake at the bottom of the hill.

The parson was a man who was attuned to the feelings of his parishioners, and he quickly recognized the nervous mindset of Elizabeth and her daughters as he approached the three on the sagging porch. They were seated on the platform, each eying him with silent glances but without making a sound. It was as though they were expecting to see an apparition appear from the shrubbery beside the doorway; their nervous energy was almost palpable. He decided it would be best to try to put the women at ease as quickly as possible.

"Well, it looks like we're set to have ourselves a party!" exclaimed the parson. "See, I even brought along the refreshment," he continued as he extracted a small parcel of peppermint candies from his front pocket.

Catherine and Carrie's eyes lit up as they caught sight of the mints. They barely had money to purchase flour for their bread, so having a treat like candy was a rare experience.

As the girls shared the confectionery candies, Parson Jim turned to Elizabeth and asked, "So what time do you expect to see or hear from this spot across the road, if it appears?"

"It's been about an hour after dark these past two years," Elizabeth replied, looking toward Carrie for confirmation.

"That's right, Mother," nodded Carrie. "But we didn't see the light the first year. We only heard the sounds. The blue light appeared last year and only last year."

Elizabeth looked back at the parson, nodding in agreement.

"And if this appears in the same place as last year, you'll see it across the road and slightly up the mountain. Right about there," she said, pointing to a gap between some trees.

"Okay then, I guess we just wait," said the parson as he stepped back off the porch to tether his horse to a small maple tree. "It's a nice enough night, so we can just pass the time chatting while we sit here."

The next few hours flew by rapidly, and the parson kept the family entertained with stories from the history of the church. He was a cheerful individual with a contagious sense of humor, and he quickly put the three women at ease with tales from around the congregation. As the minutes ticked by, the group hardly noticed that the sun had dropped over the hillside and the sky was growing darker. But still, the mood was light and airy, all compliments of the storytelling minister. No one appeared concerned in the least.

The parson's horse heard it first.

The parson and the women were all giggling over a story about a raccoon that had found its way into the church during a sermon. Suddenly, the horse whinnied and pricked its ears, then stomped a foot into the earth. It was obviously focused on something coming from across the field in front of the house, and the entire family quickly snapped to attention.

"What's that I hear?" whispered Carrie, who stood up and peered through the trees toward the railway tracks. "I think I heard that same noise . . . it's out there!"

"I heard it, too! Just listen," cried Elizabeth as she turned her gaze toward the clergyman. "Do you hear that?"

The parson didn't reply. He held up a hand, signaling for silence as he strained his ears toward the source of the noise. It was as Elizabeth had described: a low, mournful call that indeed did sound human. It was a cross between a call and a cry, but without recognizable words. The parson closed his eyes as he listened, concentrating on the tones within vocal notes. Every fiber in his body was tuned in to the call, as though he could communicate with whatever the source of the sound.

"Mother, look," whispered Carrie, tapping her mother's arm while pointing through the tree. "It's out there again!"

Elizabeth and the parson followed Carrie's stare. Once again, the blue orb of light appeared across the field, moving slowly in a rotation close to the ground. It was an unworldly, glowing sphere that didn't appear connected to anything. It rose and fell without a pattern, although it did appear to be linked to the source of the moaning calls. The parson and the three women stood transfixed, as though hypnotized by its presence. Whatever it was, it had no earthly reason for being there. But it was there nonetheless.

"Elizabeth, is that the same place you saw the light last year?" asked the parson. Can you remember if it's in the same spot?"

"Yes, I do remember," said Elizabeth. "That is the same location, right at the same place on that hill. Exactly the same as last Fourth of July. Exactly!"

The parson stood next to one of the porch posts and placed the left side of his face on the wooden beam. He then picked a location between two sapling trees along the roadside where he could see the blue light, making a mental note about the alignment of the sighting.

"What are you doing, Parson?" asked Carrie.

"I'm creating a line of bearing from the porch to the light," explained the clergyman. "For us to get to the bottom of this we'll have to search along the line I'm observing. I don't know if we'll find anything, but Kenneth Morrow is one of our church members who is also a surveyor. If anyone can pinpoint the source of this light, it will be him. I'm going to get him up here sometime next week. This has me intrigued the same as you."

Despite the late hour, Parson Jim departed on horseback rather than stay the night. He thanked Elizabeth for asking him to come over that night to observe the annual apparition. It was more than he had anticipated encountering, and he was determined to get to the bottom of the mystery.

JULY 18, 1907

It had been two weeks since the parson's visit to the Calhoun residence. It was a cloudless Friday morning, and the sun was already heating up the summer air. On the dirt road, a pair of chestnut horses pulled an old wooden carriage with a pair of men and a large box of instruments. One of the men was Parson Jim, and the other was a short man with sandy brown hair and a lengthy brown beard. Elizabeth recognized him as Ken Morrow, another dedicated parishioner she'd come to know over the years. A man of few words, he was a professional surveyor who had gained a superb reputation in the community.

Elizabeth emerged on the front porch as she heard the approach of the horse and carriage, which pulled off the lane and onto the grassy verge in front of the residence.

"Morning to you!" cried the clergyman to the woman. "I brought along someone who I think you know."

Elizabeth approached the wagon and shifted her gaze to the other visitor.

"Good morning, Ken, thank you for coming," she said in greeting. "I hadn't expected to see you so soon . . . I hope the parson explained what this is all about."

"Yes, ma'am," the surveyor replied. "I've got to admit that I've never been asked to perform my services for such a reason, but I've also got to say that I'm kind of excited to help. I don't know whether my survey equipment is capable of helping you find lost spirits, but it will be an adventure giving it a shot."

The parson helped Ken to unload his instrument box from the wagon, and they removed several lengths of Gunter's chain and a compass from the chest.

"What are those?" asked Carrie, who had joined her mother on the porch.

"The Gunter's chain is a very old tool used for setting out straight lines to mark property edges and other linear borders," the surveyor explained. "Except today we're going to use it to lay down a straight line between your porch and the railroad tracks across the field where you saw the lights. Then we're going to search along that line of bearing to see if anything is worth investigating further."

Ken started the process by aligning his Gunter surveying compass to mark the line between the front porch post and the narrow gap between the two saplings that the parson had noted during his previous visit. After the parson paced his steps to the opening in the trees, Ken staked one end of the chain into the ground at the porch post and then extended the rest of the links to reach the spot marked by the clergyman. He then pulled the chain tight to ensure they had a straight and true line of bearing on the sighting.

"There we go," said Ken as he viewed the line of chain links through the top of his compass. "If what you described is correct, all we need to do is extend this line until we reach the train tracks, maybe even a bit farther, and we'll be ready to start searching. Are you okay with that?" he asked Elizabeth and the parson.

"Sounds logical," said the parson, while Elizabeth nodded in agreement.

While Ken remained near the starting point on the porch, monitoring the placement of chains through the compass, the parson and Elizabeth carried additional lengths of chain across the property and into the expanse of grass across the lane. Each length of the twelve survey chains was about sixty-six feet long, so they had the capability of extending the line almost eight hundred feet.

The work went slowly, and the day got even hotter as the morning gave way to afternoon. Each time that the parson or Elizabeth staked down another length of chain, the surveyor returned to his compass to ensure the line remained perfectly straight. All the while, the two kept their eyes to the ground, looking for the unknown clue that might present itself at any step.

At almost seven hundred feet, Parson Jim pulled the chain up to the edge of the railroad tracks and staked it into the ground.

"We'll start the last length on the other side of the tracks," he said to Elizabeth, who was close behind. "The last thing we want to do is leave chain strung across the tracks and cause another train to derail."

"Good thinking," she replied, feeling foolish that she hadn't thought of that herself.

"I'll stake the first link on this final chain length into the ground using just an eyeball," Parson Jim said to Elizabeth. "Then you pull it in as straight a line as you can by looking back over the first eleven lengths. Since it's the last section of chain we've got, you can't help but be fairly on-target. Then maybe we'll take a break and start the real search by mid-afternoon."

"I'll be ready for that!" said Elizabeth. "I never knew that chain links so thin could weigh so much. My arms are aching."

While the minister was hammering the first link into the cinder-laced soil, Elizabeth was unraveling the last length of chain. She was walking backwards to visually maintain the alignment of the last chain with those leading back to the front porch. Without watching her step, she retreated over the edge of a concealed pit in the ground, which caused her to fall over backwards. Thankfully, there were no rocks lining the edge of the small crevice, and her fall was cushioned by soft soil and a layer of tall grass and weeds. Her tumble caused a loud thump, which was heard by Parson Jim about forty feet away.

"Ouch, ugh!" cried Elizabeth as she rolled onto her side, trying to extract herself from her entangled position.

"Are you all right?" asked the parson, no longer able to see his parishioner.

"Why, yes, I'm fine," replied Elizabeth. "I was just clumsy and didn't watch where I was going. I backed myself into a . . ."

Elizabeth's voice had suddenly gone mute in mid-sentence.

"Elizabeth?" called the parson.

"Aah . . . aaaahhh . . . aaaaaaiiieeee." The woman's voice screamed out in terror, unrecognizable to the clergyman who stood just a few feet away.

Parson Jim vaulted over the short patch of grass separating himself from the sound of her screams. Meanwhile, Elizabeth rapidly crawled on all fours to escape the small pit in the field. Her expression was that of pure terror, eyes bulging and her complexion deathly white.

"Elizabeth, Elizabeth, my dear, what has happened?"

Elizabeth did not answer. Once she was able to gain her footing, she rapidly sprinted past the parson and shot down the hillside, her screams still piercing the summer air.

Parson Jim was a mentally strong individual who was not easily frightened. He believed that his faith would protect him from all evils, both manmade and supernatural. So without a moment's pause, he approached the pit in the ground and lifted the concealing vegetation out of the way. He instantly saw the cause of Elizabeth's terror. There, in the bottom of the depression, lay a human skeleton.

The state of decay of the body was such that almost no clothing remained, although he could detect some rotting leather material from the deceased's shoes. But the parson could detect a metallic glint from beneath the midsection of the skeleton. He bent down low and reached through to extract a gold pocket watch, which he slipped into his front pocket. Once he lifted the gold timepiece, he also detected another reflection, which turned out to be caused by a pair of large silver coins. He placed these two in his pocket along with the watch, and he then turned to retrace his footsteps back down the incline.

There was no need to conduct a further search of the property. The parson was fairly certain they had located the object of their search.

By the time Parson Jim reached the house, Elizabeth was already inside sitting on a couch. Carrie was attempting to calm her down with a glass of water and waving a hand fan by her forehead. She was obviously still distraught.

"Elizabeth, I'm sorry this had to happen to you. It must have been very frightening," said the parson. "But I think you accidently discovered the source of your spirit energy. That had to be it."

Elizabeth did not speak but nodded her concurrence.

"I don't know who the deceased might be," continued the parson, "but I did find some possible clues next to the remains. But finding the owner of these might be impossible."

The clergyman opened his hand and showed the coins and the pocket watch to Elizabeth, who instantly froze, staring at the objects. Slowly, she extended her trembling hand and lifted the pocket watch from the parson's hand. She opened the front cover and immediately saw the engraving: "EC, 1868."

Elizabeth and Carrie instantly recognized the timepiece and its significance. Both broke down in tears as they realized the ultimate meaning of the find. Catherine quickly joined them as well, a family finally able to comprehend the fate of their missing son and brother. The parson did all he could to comfort the three, speaking consolingly of their dear departed and promising to make all necessary arrangements for interment. But it did little to calm the distraught family, who was still in tears when Parson Jim departed with the surveyor. Time would be the only full healing element for the Calhoun family.

EPILOGUE

The years following the discovery of Clyde's remains only heaped additional sorrow onto the Calhoun clan. What was left of Clyde's body had been extracted from the hillside and buried in a fitting grave outside the church. Meanwhile Elizabeth fell ill with cancer and passed away in the winter of 1909. Carrie and Catherine were now young adults, although an aunt living in the city of Utica offered to take them in and provide a place to live until they gained their own footing in the world. It seemed quite cruel that they were the only two survivors from their nuclear family at such a young age.

The following year, on the night of July 4, 1910, Carrie made a final return visit to their childhood home. For some unknown reason, she wanted to see it one last time. She also wanted to answer a final question that had bothered her since the day they'd found Clyde's body.

She arrived at the homestead late in the afternoon, having taken a stagecoach to Gloversville and then walked on foot the rest of the day. As the family's old home came into view she caught her breath, stunned by the sight. The now abandoned building had partially collapsed, with the downed porch roof reduced to a pile of rotten timbers blocking the front entrance. A portion of the roof on the left side of the house had fallen into the upper floor of the structure, rendering it unsafe to enter.

Carrie stood transfixed, staring at the wreck while sorting through her many childhood memories. For a full hour, she remained rooted in place, unable to process the events that had led up to this point in her life.

Unable to view the remains of the family home any longer, she turned to face the grassy expanse of field on the other side of the road. It was the Fourth of July, and she had to see for herself whether anything remained of the sights and sounds that had terrorized their family until a few short years ago.

Within the next hour it became totally dark. A few stars made their appearance in the night sky, and a faint wind rustled through the trees overhead.

Carrie watched and waited for anything: sights or sounds from across the way. Instead, all she encountered was a peaceful quiet that promised to extend throughout the coming night. Her face gradually relaxed into a serene smile, and her soul was filled with a sense of warm contentment.

"Goodnight, Clyde," she murmured quietly into the cool night air. She then turned toward the road and began her walk home.

Acknowledgments

We wish to thank our families, friends, and fans who encourage us to continue to scribe stories that we lovingly give to the world. We also wish to thank North Country Books for giving our stories a home and our eagle-eyed editorial friend at North Country Books—Jake Bonar.

About the Editor and Contributors

Holly Aust is a high school student with a creative mind. Aust constantly thinks of ideas for movies and books, and she is an aspiring entrepreneur with many goals in the entertainment industry.

Cheryl Costa is a published and produced playwright, mystery writer, novelist, short story author, and well-known UFO columnist and published UFO statistics researcher. Costa is a story contributor to all four volumes of the Adirondack Mysteries series.

D. M. Delgado is a writer who brings the cultural flavor of her Colombian life to the United States. Delgado is a paranormal investigator with the Ghost Seekers of Central New York, where she uses her skills as a medium to connect with the spirits of the otherworldly realm.

Marie Hannan-Mandel is a professor of English at SUNY Corning Community College, and she lives in Elmira Heights, New York. Hannan-Mandel has been published in four anthologies, including the Adirondack Mysteries series, and she was shortlisted for the Crime Writers' Association (UK) Debut Dagger award.

G. Miki Hayden has a deep body of work that includes many pieces of short fiction published in small magazines, national magazines, and anthologies (including volumes 2, 3, and 4 of the Adirondack Mysteries series and three Mystery Writers of America anthologies). She has published several novels, including one alternate history lauded by *The New York Times*. Hayden, who has taught at the Writer's Digest Online

University since the early 2000s, also has two writing instructions in print. She has had an Edgar short story win.

Marianna Heusler is an Edgar-nominated writer of thirteen published novels and hundreds of short stories. Her cozy mystery series was bought by Harlequin and included in their book club. Heusler lives in New York City with her husband, her son, and her rescue dog, Triscuit.

P. J. McAvoy is a writer who has spent time working in graveyards, libraries, and classrooms, and behind the keyboard. He lives outside of Albany, New York, and spends as much time as possible in the Adirondack Park each summer with his family. McAvoy's latest trip to Wells was much less eventful than the story printed here, and the people of Wells are far more welcoming and less creepy than the ones populating his tale. His day job is in nonprofit communications, and McAvoy is a member of Mystery Writers of America.

Margaret Mendel lives, writes, and draws in New York City. She is an award-winning author with short stories and articles appearing online and in print publications. Mendel has published two mystery novels and a collection of short stories. She is also a self-taught artist and began focusing on drawing portraits at the onset of the COVID-19 pandemic. She is a contributing writer and photographer at a California-based online magazine. Mendel's photographs and drawings have appeared in several New York City exhibitions.

W. K. Pomeroy is a third-generation writer with more than seventy-five published short stories, poems, and articles. He is currently marketing a fantasy novel and a science fiction novel to literary agents, and he has a collection of "Not-for-Children" Christmas stories he is pitching to publishers. Pomeroy served six terms as president of the Utica Writers Club and continues to support creative writers as a member of this group.

Lorena A. Sins was raised on a dairy farm not far from the blue line of the Adirondack Park. She has a PhD in English literature from the

University of Georgia. Sins has taught English, composition, and literature at Dalton State College since 2005. She lives with her husband in Dalton, Georgia, where the adjacent mountains remind her of the Adirondacks.

Woody Sins grew up near the North Country crossroads of West Leyden. Now living in New Hartford, he is a digital engineer working on radar systems. Sins is a story contributor to the Adirondack Mysteries series.

Gerhardt Storsberg is a self-described tall, white, educated, conservative, heterosexual, married father of three. He considers himself a deist who enjoys a good hug. In his free time, Storsberg enjoys listening to audio books on mimes, collecting antique intangibles, and riding his all-wheel-drive unicycle. He lives in Trenton, New York, with his wife of forty-two years (in a row!).

Daniel Swift has climbed all forty-six High Peaks and canoed more than two hundred miles between the lakes. He spent every summer of his youth at Camp Russell on White Lake in the town of Woodgate, New York. After he gained the rank of Eagle Scout in the Boy Scouts of America, Swift continued to explore the Adirondacks and has loved finding different ways to enjoy the majestic views. With that knowledge and understanding of the Adirondacks, he brings some unique realism to his short stories.

Dennis Webster is a paranormal investigator with the Ghost Seekers of Central New York and a published author on haunted locations, true crime, and asylums. When he's not communicating with the dead, Webster is at work creating his next story. He's the editor and story compiler of the Adirondack Mysteries series. He can be reached at denniswbstr@gmail.com.

Larry Weill got his start in the Adirondacks as a wilderness park ranger in the late 1970s and early 1980s. He has worked in both finance and Xerox Corporation's supply chain for thirty years. A retired U.S. Navy captain, Weill attained the rank of rear admiral as commanding officer of the New York Naval Militia. He enjoys writing fiction and memoirs about the Adirondacks, and Weill has numerous books published in multiple genres of Adirondack literature, including titles with North Country Books. He resides in Walworth, New York, just east of Rochester.